BRITTANY GESWEIN

Try to Fix You

First edition

ISBN: 9798986231709

This book was professionally typeset on Reedsy.
Find out more at reedsy.com

For Nick. You're the reason I believe in true love.

Acknowledgments

Everyone loves a good love story, but no one more than me. I have spent most of my life thinking to myself that I could write a book. Last year, I decided to listen to that voice. When my husband bought me a "How to Self-Publish a Novel" instructional guide for Christmas in 2020 (he found it in our Amazon cart), I started work on a life goal.

Trying to write 70,000 words when you have a full-time job teaching middle school (during Covid) and a full-time career as a wife and mother of three has been a balancing act. Try to Fix You is the result of whatever brain power and creative energy I had left after teaching and taking care of my family.

I want to thank Nick, who has spent the last 18 months pestering me relentlessly to "come to bed already." You have been incredibly patient with me as I have pursued writing and I loved having you as a beta reader, even if you were on "Team Paul."

I want to thank anyone in my life who listened to me talk about my book and showed the least bit of interest or excitement. It motivated me to stay focused more than you know, and this book is only a reality because I kept saying it out loud. Geswein gals, girls' trip friends, teachers, students, and Alicia—thanks for listening.

My best friend, Courtney Cooper, is simply a gem. Eighty-five percent of the books I've read in my life have been at her request. She just gets me. She is the reason I love reading. Thank you for being an anchor. Our friendship was a huge inspiration for this creative endeavor.

I want to thank my Mother, Debbie Tevis, and my late grandfather, Spence McCabe, for always having a book (or two or three) nearby and instilling in me a love of literature. My mom graciously agreed to help edit this book and I had to smile when I saw all of the errors marked on my manuscript as it reminded me of when she would revise my high school English papers. You are simply the best. Thanks Mom.

To my dad and sister Chelsea, thank you for always "talking up" my every endeavor. You have always supported me and it has made all the difference.

To Christy Nash, my sister-in-law and beta reader, for taking the time to get excited about this story with me. You have impeccable taste and enthusiasm for days. Thank you for investing in my characters and cheering me on.

To Brandon, for all the moments. I love you.

To Noah, Julian, and Hallie—you are my ultimate love story.

Brigid

We've all had them. The moments when everything in your life is falling apart at the seams. You know what I mean. Everything is going wrong, and you're feeling more hopeless by the minute. And then, in the exact moment you need them most, someone new steps in and makes you stronger. It's the pivotal moment that completely alters the course of your life. They just swoop in and fix everything.

This is not that moment.

Don't get me wrong—my life is a complete disaster right now. But as I scream "screw you" a little louder than necessary to my boyfriend (if you want to call him that), I realize that Paul is not the type to swoop.

Anger is not a good look on me. And it isn't the best weapon to use against him. The more emotional I get, the calmer he becomes, which makes me look and feel like a giant idiot. Yes, I'm emotional. But not in a crazy way. In a passionate way. I feel things. I mean, I *really* feel them. My aunt told me once that she was an empath. I had no idea what that meant. But after Googling it, I have to say—it kind of sounds like me. I literally feel the emotions of the people around me. And maybe that's why a day of exploring downtown Asheville with Paul feels more like an anxiety-ridden roller coaster. This trip was supposed to be a break from work—and from the episode that threatened my entire career and reputation. *Totally not my fault, by the way.* I have a month of vacation. Okay. Let's call it what it is. A sabbatical. Okay, let's be even more honest. I'm being required to take unpaid leave while things get "sorted out".

1

And so of course, when Paul suggests we get away for a few days, I'm all in. After all, I'm not sure how much longer I can stand being alone in my rental house, replaying the "incident" over and over in my mind. Why the hell didn't I "feel" that coming?

The thing is, I probably should have already broken things off with Paul. He's a nice enough guy, but he's kind of panicky. He cares way too much about what people think of him. Like today, we walked into the Asheville Emporium, and I made some friendly comments to the man working behind the counter about all of the unique items on display. Paul gives me *the look*. The one that says, "You're embarrassing me." I can't help it. It's who I am—outgoing, charming, positive. He's more of a wall flower and thinks that inserting yourself into any situation is impolite.

His negative energy is through the roof today. He has complained about the parking situation, the wait at the restaurant where we stopped for lunch, and then the cost of the food. And all of his complaints come out passive-aggressively. He didn't even appreciate the kiss I tried to plant on his cheek to thank him for the delicious meal. "PDA is unnecessary." And it was in that moment that I decided our relationship (if you can even call it that) was never going to work.

I was quiet on the way back to the hotel. Quiet, for me, means something is wrong—which even Paul is able to pick up on. Which brings me to this moment in our hotel room, when he has the audacity to ask—in a pissy voice—why I'm trying to sabotage this trip?

"Screw you."

Yeah. So I lost it. And the thing is, I'm not even sorry about it. Paul was not a long-term solution for my love life. For one, his first reaction when I told him about Jeff McAdams was to ask, "And you're sure you didn't do anything to lead him on?" *How could he even?* Secondly, even though Paul is two years younger than me, he acts like he's ten years older—serious in every situation—which makes me feel like I'm not good enough for him. He's a cute guy and well-mannered (I met him thru a friend), but his temperament never matched mine. Like tonight—I'm shouting expletives at him in the hotel room, and he's dead quiet, just watching me like he feels sorry for me.

2

After my ten-minute rant, where I lay out all of his sins from the day, he says, "You don't have to be so dramatic. I can see we aren't going to move past this. One piece of advice—maybe you should rethink your approach with men."

I'm not sure who breaks up in a hotel during a couple's getaway, but yep—my love life.

So I'm in the lobby on the phone with my best friend, telling her that under no circumstances can I stand the four-and-a-half hour drive back to Nashville with him, when she has a crazy idea.

"You know what? Let me call you right back." Click. She hangs up on me. That's how it is with us. Comfortable.

Piper has been my best friend since third grade, and luckily (although I didn't see it quite like that at the time) she fell in love with my goofy older brother, Dave. They dated in college and got married seven years ago.

Three minutes later, she calls me back with a detailed plan. *Have I told you how much I love her?* Apparently, Dave's boss owns a timeshare at a really nice resort in Panama City, and it's available this week. He'd offered it to Dave a few weeks ago, but Piper had been swamped at work, and they couldn't get away.

Dave's boss, Larry Butters, is a character. He owns Butter's Better Buys—a car dealership with those annoying and somewhat embarrassing commercials. Who would've thought he owned a timeshare? Actually, come to think of it, he's exactly the kind of guy who would own a timeshare.

"Okay, the resort isn't oceanfront, but it has a five-star rating, tons of great reviews, and every amenity—pool, bar, access to the sound."

"I can't do that," dismissing the idea, even though it sounds amazing.

"Why not? It's totally what you need right now."

"Yeah, but I'd feel weird getting a free vacation from Dave's boss. It's kind of random."

"Okay, wow! Are you kidding me? This man has literally been sucked into buying, like, three timeshares. Every time a salesman meets their quarterly goals, he gives them a guest certificate. Think of it as Dave's. You should definitely go."

3

"Alone?"

"You should go, Brigid!" I hear Dave say through the speakerphone in his *I know better than you* older brother's voice.

"Didn't realize I was on speakerphone. What are you guys doing right now? Wait, let me guess. In your pajamas. Kids are asleep. Watching that show on Netflix in your adjustable geriatric bed with your knees propped up?"

"You don't know me," Dave says.

"She totally knows us," Piper admits. "But our life is not yours. You are young (31), unmarried (alone), and hip (how she's referred to me since I moved into a great rental house in the 12 South neighborhood of Nashville). You should be out there having an adventure and putting all of this work crap behind you. Just do it."

"I can't!"

"Why not?"

"Because I'm trapped in Asheville with Paul."

"Well, just put up with him for one more night. Tomorrow morning, you can Uber to the airport and catch a flight out."

There goes the Biltmore. "Guys, I appreciate the help, but I can't."

"It's already booked," Dave says. "Southwest flight number A352, leaving at 6:30 a.m. tomorrow morning. I'll email you the guest certificate to show at the resort."

"Guys, I can't afford this right now."

"It's already paid for. Think of it as an early Christmas present," says Dave. *Christmas is three months away.*

Ten hours later, I'm walking into the airport, and I have to say—I'm not really good at this kind of stuff. Surprising, I know—especially because I'm such a confident, independent woman. Traveling just kicks up my nerves. It's not like I'm scared to fly. I'm mainly just freaked out about security putting me on some sort of terrorist watchlist because I don't have the right-size plastic container for my eye makeup remover.

4

So, with a purse swung across my midsection and a carry-on rolling behind me down the gateway, I catch a glimpse of myself in a mirrored column. *Rough.* Sure, I'm alone and will be doing nothing for a week but sitting on my ass, drinking pina coladas, and listening to "Down by the Boardwalk" while reading the latest book, but still! I secretly wish I could be the kind of young woman that has it all together—instead of the one who looks like the TLC show *What Not to Wear* is secretly filming and planning to ambush. The thing is, I used to be pretty confident. I felt good in my skin and typically had the attitude that the world was watching me and loving what it saw. I was the leading lady—the star of my own life. A little melodramatic. (Maybe Paul wasn't completely wrong.) But ever since this whole situation at work, I've felt completely off-balance. I'm second-guessing everything I do. Every natural instinct to be outgoing and personable suddenly seems awkward and wrong. My appearance definitely reflects my mood as of late—deflated.

It's early, so there isn't much of a line at the security checkpoint, but at the rate the TSA attendants are rushing everyone through that robotic-looking phone booth, you'd think we were on the Titanic. I'm watching the people in front of me carefully, mentally preparing to copy their every movement. *Why is my heart beating out of my chest right now?* I take a deep breath. My shoes come off as quickly as possible and get tossed into the bin. *Great.* I'm wearing mismatched socks. *Figures.* I glance at the woman standing across the roller conveyor from me in her silk blouse, pencil skirt, and pantyhose, as she calmly steps out of her heels and begins placing large bangle bracelets and gorgeous earrings in her bin. We're probably around the same age, and I want to complain that she's making me look bad, but honestly, I'm doing that all by myself.

"Ma'am. Ma'am, empty your pockets. Please place all personal electronic devices larger than a cell phone in a separate bin with nothing placed on or under for x-ray screening." The directive coming from the plump, middle-aged woman sounds harsh, even though I'm sure it plays on repeat all day long. *Shit.* My laptop is in the front pocket of my carry-on. I stop, bend down, and unzip it. The zipper is stuck. A couple of hard yanks and it pops open, ripping the pocket and sending the contents of my baggage cascading to the floor. I'm on my knees, grabbing my sketchpad, book, and chapstick—which goes rolling away. Stuffing these items back into the ripped pocket is useless, so they get added to the bin.

"Ma'am, please place the device in a separate bin."

Right. Crap. I'm tangled in my crossbody purse, which is currently a noose. I wiggle out of it and grab a second bin for my laptop. I look down. Purse. Phone. Wallet. Keys. Sketchpad. Book. Chapstick. Tennis shoes. Laptop. What is left of my carry-on bag gets flopped beside the bins.

"Ma'am. Your sunglasses," the TSA lady says. She's losing her patience with me.

"Sorry." I grab my sunglasses from the top of my head and drop them in the bin. I'm a lunatic.

"Please step forward, ma'am, and place your feet on the marked spots below. Arms up. Palms open." The machine scans me 360 degrees and suddenly screeches to a stop, letting off the most awful high-pitched tone. *Busted.* I don't know why I'm surprised. I watch as the X-ray image of my body lights up near the crotch area.

The TSA lady wearing blue medical gloves informs me that she is going to need to feel inside my waistband and pat me down.

I exhale and try to control my racing heart. A second TSA officer approaches with a detection dog, who begins sniffing my jeans.

"Ma'am, can you untuck your shirt?"

"Sure." I try to remind myself that I've done nothing wrong and they won't find anything. By the way I'm sweating, they probably think I have six ounces of cocaine shoved up my ass.

After a few moments, she steps back and says, "Sometimes this machine will detect lotion and beep. You're free to go. Don't forget to clear your bins."

I scramble to get back into my shoes and gather up all of my items as I watch the woman beside me slip back into her heels, pick up her Burberry tote, and continue on her way. She has it all together. *And I do not.*

"So this place is actually pretty incredible," I say to Piper on the phone as my cab from the airport pulls up to the resort. I had my doubts when we headed in the opposite direction of the Gulf, but it seems this resort bought up some prime real estate sound side and worked their magic. We stopped at the main gatehouse, and I gave the remarkably hospitable woman inside the window my last name. I wait as she types my name into the computer, feeling like a kid trying to sneak into an R-rated movie. I don't legally belong, but I really want to be here. I really need to be here. I make a silent plea and just like that, the bar lifts, and my driver follows her instructions and heads down the brick drive, surrounded by a wall of tall palm trees and lush landscape with bright flowers on either side, to a large stucco building with a giant fountain in front.

"I could definitely get used to this. I can't thank you enough. The airfare. Everything. It's too much."

"Just relax and enjoy. You deserve this," Piper says, and I don't disagree. After a quick panic moment in the cab when I couldn't find my cash to pay the driver, I'm here. I walk into the large, bright lobby with a concierge counter to the left and the reservation desk to the right. Straight ahead is a wall of windows with a view to die for. A large diamond-shaped infinity pool spills into a smaller pool, and then an even smaller pool, before spilling into the bay. Large palm trees surround the oasis, and a giant pavilion with a thatched roof offers libations.

So here I am, in line once again, with the guest certificate pulled up on my phone and my driver's license out—the two requirements—and waiting for them to say that I am not Larry Butters and have no business being here, when I notice an older gentleman in front of me wearing a Vietnam War veteran ball cap. He is listening to the receptionist, who is reviewing the map of the resort, pointing out Wi-Fi passwords, and writing down entrance gate codes.

When he turns around, I smile and say my traditional, "Thank you for your service to our country, sir. It is much appreciated."

I offer him a sturdy handshake, which he accepts wholeheartedly before smiling and saying, "I was proud to serve." *I told you I am personable.* I have never been afraid to talk to strangers and I never pass up an opportunity to recognize an American hero. The man walks outside, and my nerves kick in as the lady behind the desk takes my information and types a few things into her computer.

"Hmmm. Looks like your condo isn't quite ready yet. Can I check your bags and recommend that you head out to our fabulous poolside bar for a refreshment on the house?"

"Absolutely. Thank you." I hand over my luggage. My phone dings, and I look to see a digital drink ticket sent to me by the resort. *Maybe this is going to work out okay after all.*

Outside, I take a moment to breathe in a sigh of relief. Hidden speakers are playing "Toes" by the Zac Brown Band, and the smell of sunscreen fills the air. I am here, and this place is unbelievably nice. Finally, something is going my way, and I'm thinking I may actually be able to settle my brain for the first time in weeks. I head to the bar and sit down beside the older gentleman from before.

"Is this seat taken?" I ask.

"Not at all. Help yourself, my dear."

"Thank you." A young man in a Hawaiian shirt walks up, and I show him my phone.

"What can I get for you?"

"Pina colada?"

"You got it," he responds, and then turns away to begin fixing me a little bit of paradise in a glass.

"Your room isn't ready yet either?" I ask the man.

"Oh, it is. I'm just waiting for someone."

"Taking your wife on a lovely vacation?"

"Actually, I am here to meet up with the boys." The way he says this makes me smile. *Old people are cute.*

"My name's Bo. Bo Gibson."

"Brigid Taylor. Nice to meet you."

"The American Legion is having their big annual Southeastern conference here this weekend. I hope you don't mind a bunch of old vets hanging around. I am the service officer at the Camp Hill post. Ever been to North Carolina?"

"Camped on the Outer Banks once as a kid. It's beautiful."

8

He nods in agreement.

"Service officer, huh? What does that entail?" I ask as the bartender hands me my drink. *Now we're talking.*

"Thanks, Tyler." He does a double take, clearly wondering how I know him, before he realizes he is wearing a resort name tag. He flashes me a smile.

"I assist veterans and their families with VA benefits, employment, and help them find any resources they need."

"Such a worthy thing to do."

"Don't be too impressed. I think I got the job because I was spending too much time hanging around the Legion. So, what do you do for a living, besides carrying around the sunshine?"

Did I mention that I love old people?

"I am a school psychologist, actually. I work for MNPS."

"PMS?"

I chuckle as I suck down another big gulp of my drink.

"MNPS—Metro Nashville Public Schools."

"Oooh. Sounds like a tough job," he says.

"It can be." *Huge understatement.* I'm downing this drink so fast, I'm getting a brain freeze. I nonchalantly touch my forehead. *Ouch.*

"Probably pretty tough to juggle your career with being a wife and mother."

"Hmm? Oh. No. I'm not married."

"Are you here alone?"

Alone. One word pretty much summed it all up. *YEP!*

"Yeah, actually, I am. I'm on a leave of absence from work for a while and thought a little sea air would do me some good," I say out loud while reminding my face not to look pitiful.

"Wow. That sounds nice."

"Actually, it's unpaid leave."

"Oh. Sounds like there's more to the story."

My face says it all. *Yes! There is more. So much more. I am alone. Weak. Humiliated.*

He doesn't question me further.

"Say, do you think you might be able to give me some advice since you're a psychiatrist and all?"

"Well, I'm a psychologist, not a psychiatrist—so technically I'm not a doctor."

"Okay, gotcha."

"But as a psychologist, I am great with advice. Shoot."

"Here's the thing. I'm worried about a buddy of mine. Really worried." Bo gets quiet and stares at his aluminum bottle for a moment before continuing. "I've talked him into joining me and the guys at the conference. I was hoping to use this weekend as an intervention of sorts. He's a hell of a soldier. He's gifted, you know, with numbers. Very analytical. He just got back from his latest tour in the sand—Afghanistan."

"What makes you worried?"

"He hasn't been himself. No one heard from him at all during the last month of his deployment—completely iced us all out. And since he came home, he has been drinking nonstop. He isn't sleeping. He looks like hell." He looks like he wants to say more.

"Go ahead," I say encouragingly.

"I think he has PTSD. I've been around enough vets to know it when I see it. It's an ugly thing. Hell, some of the men I served with have been struggling for the last 40 years. It can be chronic, you know. I've seen guys fall into addiction—lose their marriage, their jobs, their life."

"That is terrible. I've seen it before myself, sadly, in children who were victims of sexual abuse."

"Did something specific happen on his last tour?"

"He won't tell me anything."

"Don't you have connections at the base? Can't you make a few calls and try to see what you can find out?"

"Already have."

"Well, what did they say?"

"That the mission is classified." Bo took off his sunglasses and I could see hurt in his eyes. "He's become like a son to me. Ironic. The one soldier I care about the most is the one I can't seem to help."

Just then the lady from the registration desk walks over and stood facing Bo and me.

"Miss, I am so sorry to interrupt. I wanted to let you know that there has been a mix-up with your guest certificate." *Of course there is.*

"What is it?" I ask.

"Well, it seems Larry Butters has already passed out a guest certificate for this week. The condo has been double-booked," she says nervously.

Bo perks up beside me. "Larry Butters? You know Larry Butters?"

I turn around, surprised by Bo. I should have known other people would recognize the name. He has like dozens of dealerships all over the South and those annoying commercials get embedded into your brain. "My brother sells cars for Larry," I explain.

I turn back to the receptionist. "You have got to be kidding me. I literally just got here, and I really need this vacation," I say with pleading eyes.

Bo speaks up again. "This is a crazy coincidence. Larry Butters is my brother-in-law."

"What? No way. What a small world. So are you the one using the other guest certificate?" I ask. *What are the odds?*

His face is in disbelief. Wait. No. Not disbelief. It's a lightbulb. I am watching as a lightbulb goes off. (You've heard about the lightbulb, right? The one that is so famous in schools. I've seen it like 1,000 times.)

The receptionist and I are both staring at Bo. It's obvious he has something to say. It takes him a moment, and then finally he says, "Ms. Taylor, I have a business proposition for you."

I snicker. *This guy is so cute.* "Oh yeah, what's that, Bo? Are you thinking we should rent a second condo for the week and split the price? That way we both can stay and still save at least a little money."

Before he can answer, the receptionist speaks up, "Actually, we are at 100% capacity for the next two nights. We are hosting an American Legion conference this weekend, and every unit is accounted for. We should have some units opening back up on Monday."

Bo looks at me and then back at her. "It is a two-bedroom unit, correct?"

"Yes. Two bedrooms. Two baths. Full kitchen, dining, and living area.

There is a gorgeous screened balcony overlooking the bay."

"Can you give us a moment to discuss this?" he asks the receptionist.

"Certainly. Meanwhile, I will see if any of our neighboring properties have availability." She walks back inside. Bo turns to look at me.

"Technically, I checked in first. I think it's only fair if my guest certificate is the one honored."

"That's your proposition? That's ridiculous. I was literally right behind you in line."

"Okay, fine. You're right." His eyes peer off into the distance, and I can tell he's trying to come to terms with something. "This is going to sound crazy, but just hear me out." Bo sits his beer down and swivels to face me.

I really don't know what he is thinking right now. I take a deep breath. The coconut fragrance dancing through the air reminds me how much I need to be here. "Go on."

"The truth is, I am not the one using Larry's guest certificate this week."

"But you said…"

He interrupts, "I'm bunking up with three buddies of mine. We are only staying the weekend, so we rented one of the hotel units. Booked the room months ago." I'm suddenly imagining four eighty-year-old men trying to fit into two queen beds. *Yikes!*

"Well then, who is using the certificate?"

"Sgt. Balzly, my friend that I mentioned earlier. He's had a rough go of it lately, and frankly, I was afraid to leave him alone this weekend. I thought he could use a change in scenery. He agreed to come at the last minute so I was grateful that Larry let me use his timeshare."

Oh great. I definitely can't steal a free week in the sun from a man just returning from a war zone.

"This is a God moment. Fate."

"Excuse me?"

"I have been praying all week asking God to show me how to help Balzly. You are the answer to my prayers, young lady."

"How so?" I am so confused.

"Balzly is never going to open up to me. He's never going to let his guard down around the guys. He's too tough. And I highly doubt he'll go to anyone else for help, no matter how much his mom thinks he should. You and Balzly could share the condo for the weekend. Maybe you could talk to him. Get to know him a little. See if you could help."

"Without him knowing, you mean?" *Balzly. What kind of name is that?* I look at him like he's a complete lunatic. I just don't see where I play into this. "I don't see what I could…"

"You're a psychologist. You listen to people for a living. You must be good at getting to the bottom of problems. Offering solutions. Offering support."

"I'm a psychologist, yes, but I'm on vacation." I flash my sweetest "hate to break it to you" face so he knows there is no way I could possibly agree.

"Unpaid leave," he reminds me.

"Regardless, I wasn't planning on working this week. I've actually had some stuff going on." *To say the least.* "I really need a break."

"What if it weren't an unpaid leave of absence? Spend the next three days helping Balzly, and I will make it worth your while. Look around. This resort is beautiful."

I look around. He's not lying. This place is incredible. "I'm not asking you to lead a 24-hour therapy session. Just spend some time with him and get to know him a little. See if you can get to the bottom of anything."

"I can't take your money." *This is ridiculous.*

"If you could help me get the slightest glimpse into what's going on in that boy's head, it would be more than worth it."

"You are something else, Mr. Gibson."

"Would you consider it? Just for the long weekend? I barely got him to agree to come to the conference. If he knows there is a problem with the room, he will bow out."

Perfect. Then I'll be alone in paradise.

"But he needs this." Bo looks around. "At least say you'll think it over." He holds his breath.

I take a deep breath. "I'll think about it."

He smiles at me. "Are you hungry?"

"I could eat." *I am ravished.*

"I'll go wrestle us up some lunch. Sandwich okay?"

"Sure." My head is spinning right now. I knew a free vacation was too good to be true. Why did he have to tell me I was an answer to his prayers? *Ugh. Now I'll never be able to say no.* But let's be perfectly clear, I need to say no. It would be completely crazy, not to mention unsafe, to be pushed together with a complete stranger. He could be an axe murderer for all I know. Bo could be a decoy. There could be other conspirators. This whole thing could be a setup aimed at getting me alone. Okay, maybe I'm going a little *Unsolved Mysteries* here, but still, I have to think this one through. I've made it a habit lately, getting myself stuck in bad situations.

Not to mention that my goal for this week was to work on myself: to figure out what it is about my behavior that makes men like Jeff McAdams think they have an open invitation. Paul's words from two weeks ago echo through my head. "I'm not saying it's your fault. I just think you need to be more aware of how you act around men." Okay, so maybe I could be a little more mindful of how others may perceive me. That can be done. Starting now. And I make a silent resolution to myself.

Somewhere, the universe is laughing because the second my silent resolution is complete, I see him stepping out from the wall of glass and into this oasis.

The dream guy. You know what I'm talking about. The guy you picture in your head when someone says good-looking. He's literally tall, dark, and handsome. Emphasis on tall. There is something rugged about him. I've never seen a man this beautiful in real life before. He steps out, takes a few long glances around the pool and bar area as if he's looking for someone (probably his hot wife), and then heads back in. *This is going to be harder than I thought.*

Two pina coladas later, Bo returns and sits a roasted BLT sandwich in an Arby's wrapper down in front of me, along with an envelope with a bank receipt sticking out.

"Did you just walk to the Arby's across the street?"

"Yep. And the bank too. Do we have a deal?"

"How do I know that I can trust this Sgt. Balzly? He's a perfect stranger."

Bo stands up straight, and his voice takes on a lecturing tone. "He's a highly decorated Marine sergeant who has served his country honorably for six years. He has three advanced degrees and a spotless record of service, which also makes him the perfect gentleman."

He pulls out his phone and scrolls down for a moment before showing me a photo. I am looking at a young man in full battle dress uniform. He is down on one knee on a mountaintop in some distant desert. He has a cigar in his mouth, and an American flag displayed proudly in his hands. He is wearing sunglasses. He looks noble and trustworthy and familiar somehow.

Bo slides the envelope closer to me and nods for me to look inside. The bank receipt says $3,000 and there is a big wad of hundred-dollar bills.

"You just want my honest evaluation, nothing more?"

"That's it."

I think about the current balance in my checking account. Then I take another look at the picture.

"You have a deal."

Balzly

I rarely make mistakes. Some would say I am a perfectionist. Certainly, that is a term I've heard a time or two throughout the years. But they would be wrong. A perfectionist will not allow anyone to see them fail. They would avoid any task if they weren't confident they could achieve perfection. That is not me at all. I will try anything without fear of failure. And why? There is a 99.9% chance that I will not only succeed, but do so exceptionally.

Please do not mistake my honesty for pride. I didn't wish this on myself. In fact, my biggest wish has always been to be normal.

But I am not normal. I am extraordinary.

My phone has been ringing endlessly all evening. Another call from my mother goes to voicemail. I have to cut her some slack. Currently, she is spending way too much time worrying about my life. I'm sure it's hard to turn something like that off. For years she has dedicated herself to each of my whims. My adolescence was made up of a series of passions that I would focus on intensely. My first love was numbers. Then came a fascination with chess, followed by soccer, WWII, the guitar, and learning Latin. Well, you get the point. Every few months, I would pivot into my next big obsession.

My mother made sure that I didn't waste my gifts. Fortunately, my parents could afford to send me to the best schools, hire private tutors, and shuttle me to and from practices and lessons, all thanks to my grandpa.

I graduated first in my class from Auburn and later Vanderbilt. Ironically, it wasn't until the United States Marine Corps got a hold of me that I learned the most important lessons to date: courage, honor, and commitment.

So why am I sitting alone in an empty American Legion Hall in Swansboro, North Carolina, at 2:00 a.m., completely obliterated? I made a mistake. And now I have to live with it.

The sun acts as my alarm, glaring through the old windows of the Legion Hall, badly in need of repairs. My indulgences last night did little to help me escape the images flashing through my mind or the sound of the explosion. Instead, it provided me with an incredible headache. I wipe down the bar, put the small batch of Elijah Craig back on the shelf, and hire an Uber to drive me the 20 miles back to base. *What the hell did I do?* It's not that I don't remember the last 24 hours; it's just that I don't want to. If it weren't for Bo, I'd probably be lying dead somewhere. *Not a completely unappealing idea.*

My barracks at Camp Lejeune are nothing more than a small room with cement block walls painted the color of sand. I have an extra-long twin bed, a desk where my television sits, a mini-fridge with a microwave on top, and a closet filled with issued gear. Not too impressive. It has served me well enough during my active duty.

I think about the apartment in Mountain Brook and the smile on Caroline's face as we christened every room. *How am I going to get this shit out of my head?*

I open the fridge and crack open a beer, taking a long pull. A couple of buddies in my platoon have stopped by to check on me, but there is nothing to say. Honestly, I'm going to be fine. Sure, my confidence has been shaken a little, but what man hasn't gone through something like this? I'm a Marine. And before my hand starts shaking and the consequences of my mistake flood my senses again, I remind myself that I am a Sergeant in the Marine Corps, tough enough to handle anything.

I spun out for the last time three months ago. When I left, my life made sense. A plan for the next step was in place. I had it all. My final deployment as a full-time Marine went according to plan—until it didn't.

As soon as my boots hit the ground on American soil, my Gunnery Sergeant practically demanded that I take leave. According to everyone in my life, I'm not using my time wisely. But I'm a grown man, and if I want to sit in this small and damp room and wallow for a bit, I will. If I want a drink (or two or three), I'll have one.

The truth is, I don't really mind being alone. I've always been that way and it still worries my mother. Little has changed in that department.

When my phone rings later in the day and it is Bo calling to insist I head south for a long weekend away with the old-timers from the Camp Hill post, I can't say no, especially after he talked me off the ledge last night. It doesn't go unnoticed that this "weekend away" involves attending the annual American Legion conference. Bo is all about the Legion. He's big-time at Camp Hill—knows everyone.

I respect the hell out of all those guys, especially Bo. He had the same military occupational specialty as me, which means he understands signal intelligence. Even though cybersecurity during his time in Vietnam looked a lot different, having the same MOS means he gets me. I met him a couple of years ago when some buddies from Camp Lejeune and I were at the Legion Hall for a poker tournament. We got to talking and he invited me back the next week. Before I knew it, I was behind the bar serving Busch Lite and sharing war stories with men who walked the Ho Chi Minh Trail. A guy could do worse.

Bo said something on the phone that stuck with me. *"You need a distraction."*

It's true. I have been so preoccupied with Caroline. Actually, no, not Caroline. I've been completely fixated on every decision that I have made involving Caroline over the last eighteen months.

One of my superpowers has become my greatest burden. I have an eidetic memory. I can study something for thirty seconds or so and recall almost everything about it down to the smallest detail. I use the term "superpower" because that is what Mrs. Lillian called it. She was one of the private math tutors my mother hired to work with me the year I was convinced I wanted to become a global economist. That was the same year I grew four inches.

So here I am, alone in my barracks, remembering every detail—*her blond hair and the way it whipped across her back as she was thrown down. Her screams.*

The way the afternoon sun was pouring through the window.

Technically it isn't a good look to drink on base. And I need a drink. A weekend throwing them back with the old-timers poolside would be a hell of a lot better than getting trashed at the Brass Pelican. Don't get me wrong, that hole in the wall bar is beloved by everyone on base, but I don't need my men seeing me lose my shit. *I've got to get out of this place.*

"Siri, start my playlist."

Listening to music is a total brain workout. I learned early on that it has the biggest impact on my emotional well-being.

My duffel bag is still on the floor by the door, unpacked. I dump it out and toss most of it into the dirty laundry hamper. Coldplay starts playing "The Scientist" over my wireless speaker. I text Bo.

"I'm in. What should I pack?"

"Great! You won't regret it. Pack for hot weather, trucks, and one sweat."

"Trucks? One sweat???"

"Swim trunks. A suit."

"Why do I need a suit?"

"Formal dinner Sunday night."

"K."

"I'm emailing you the information you'll need. See you tomorrow. You sure you don't want to fry down with us? I could have Nancy try to fine you a fight."

"Nah. Driving will be good for me. Time to think. I'll see you around two."

"I'll meet u by the pool."

"K. Thx."

Bo's texting could use some work. Poor guy.

I'm standing in front of my closet, trying to find a piece of clothing not tied to a Caroline memory, when the lyrics from the band I've loved since high school wash over me. *Oh, how I wish I could go back to the start.*

So, 24 hours later, I'm walking into the lobby of a five-star resort, holding my military-issued duffel bag with enough clothes for the weekend. I have to admit, I thought this would be pretty lame, but apparently I misjudged the American Legion planning committee.

They picked one hell of a spot. The resort is perfect—a brand-new facility, meticulously manicured landscape, every amenity. I can't help but contrast it to my living arrangements for the past three months at Camp Leatherneck. It was my second tour in the Helmand Province of Afghanistan, and even though the Marine home base is fairly modern, it doesn't even compare.

I watch as families walk through the main lobby rolling their luggage behind them. It's a grand room, two stories high, with a long registration desk, a concierge counter, and a ramp that heads down into an open area with pub tables and a long bar. Fancy artwork hangs on the walls and unique light fixtures dangle from above.

Two women at the bar are drinking wine and laughing until one of the ladies looks up and makes eye contact with me from across the room. Then, it begins. The flirty glances. The smiles. This isn't unfamiliar to me. It started when I turned 17 and suddenly looked like I was 22. It lasted through college and grad school. At the time, I had little interest in anything other than academics and soccer. I was actually pretty shy around girls. But when I became a Marine, an entirely different world was opened up to me. Suddenly, I was spending most of my time with a bunch of macho guys who were focused on working out and getting laid. I never had much to offer during these male bonding moments and the guys always gave me shit about it. It was easy enough to ignore.

That all changed when I met Caroline. Suddenly I was the one with the crazy stories to share. The one every guy was jealous of.

I'm not sure why the attention from these women at the bar is annoying me. I mean, I did come here for a distraction after all—a female diversion could work. I guarantee I could convince one of these women to join me in my room. I smile at them from across the lobby bar and nod my head. *Maybe later*, I tell myself as I go in search of the pool.

As I look around for Bo, I can't help but notice how relaxed and happy everyone is. This is always hard after a deployment. It's crazy. You join the military to defend the Constitution and keep Americans safe, but when you return from a war zone and see a bunch of safe Americans without a care in the world, you just get sort of pissed off. Especially when you have sacrificed the best years of your life and have nothing and no one to show for it. *I need some fresh air.*

I follow what looks like a newly married couple and step outside the back doors of the main building into what the sign is calling Island Oasis and start doing what I do best—analyzing. The people. Their interactions. The amenities. The grounds. I am trained to notice what no one else notices.

And that's when I see her. *The distraction.* I think the sun would forget to rise staring at this girl. And in a single instant I know everything about her. Her full lips and their half smile. The rate at which her hazel eyes blink. Her dirty blonde hair. The length of her legs.

The small birthmark on her right shoulder blade. The freedom on her left ring finger. Her unspoken confidence.

And at the same time, I know nothing at all.

She turns to look in my direction. We quickly lock eyes. Seconds go by. Just when I think she's going to look away, she doesn't. I smile at her, but instead of returning the favor she exhales, apparently annoyed at the sight of me, and turns back to her drink. *Interesting.* My sunglasses disguise my admiration. *Who is this woman?* I head back inside the crowded lobby to collect intelligence, jumping into the registration line nearest the back wall of glass, my eyes glued to her through the window. Something about her is magnetic. *Do I know her from somewhere?* The lines between her eyebrows show as she scans the pool area, looking for someone. They disappear when the barkeep delivers an icy drink in a fun glass garnished with fruit. She tosses the cherry aside. *Huh.*

I text Bo.

"I'm here."

No response. Great. Ten minutes go by, and I'm considering continuing my search for Bo when suddenly the line starts moving. Finally, I take a few steps up and pull the guest certificate up on my phone when, out of the corner of my eye, I sense movement. An older man, somewhat short in stature, suddenly approaches the woman at the pool bar who has captured my attention. *Her dad maybe?* He hands her something. She looks at it and speaks. I can't read her lips from this angle. The man quickly gets defensive. *This could be trouble.* I'm preparing myself to intervene if necessary.

After a few moments she stands up and throws one arm over his shoulder. *Maybe not.* The man turns, and his identity is revealed. *Unbelievable.* The conference hasn't even started yet and Bo Gibson is already cozied up at the poolside bar with the most incredibly attractive woman I have ever seen. That old man is a smooth talker. I'd threaten to tell Nancy, but she'd just laugh. I hope this is someone he actually knows and that he's not bothering a random woman who is simply trying to enjoy her vacation.

The line moves forward again, and I take a step closer to check-in when I nearly trip over a couple of kids. They are short and cute and reach their hands up to shake mine and to thank me for my service before running back to their parents on the other side of the lobby. *Awkward.* It's not that I don't appreciate patriotic kids with good manners. It's that I can't stand the hero worship I see on their faces. They have no idea how undeserving of it I am.

I wonder how they even knew I was a soldier. Then it hits me. It's the hat—the ball cap with the official United States Marine Corps logo clipped to my duffel strap. I can feel the lump rising in my throat. I pull my luggage around to the other side of my body and search for something else to focus on. Anything to keep me from going back to that night.

The registration clerk will do. She's probably nearing fifty. Her hair is pulled back in a tight bun, and she is wearing a coral-colored, three-quarter-length-sleeve button-up shirt with the resort logo embroidered on the lapel. Her face seems to be hiding behind a pair of thick-rimmed geometric glasses. She looks like one of those women who get home from work and become a totally different person. I can see her now, glasses off, hair let down, slipping out of her heels.

"Sir." The lyrics to "Stacy's Mom" are playing in my head.

"Sir. Sir?"

"Hmm? Oh. Sorry. Hi."

"Welcome to the Sunset Harbour Resort in Panama City. How may I help you today?"

"I'm Sgt. Balzly. I'm checking in for the weekend." I fumble with my phone and slide it across the counter along with my military ID, the two things Bo said I would need. Apparently his brother-in-law has the hookup with timeshares and owns like three at this resort. "I believe it's under Larry Butters."

"Oh," she says with a worried expression on her face. "I must apologize on behalf of the resort. I am afraid there has been a mix-up with your room. You're here with Bo Gibson?" *He's already made a name for himself.* "Apparently another guest certificate has been given out for this same week by Mr. Butters to a Brigid Taylor?" The statement comes out as a question.

"I don't know who that is." I reply.

"Why don't you step into our meeting room and give me a moment to let Mr. Gibson and Ms. Taylor know that you have arrived. We will get this whole thing sorted out."

She ushers me and my bag around the registration desk and through the short hallway to one of the open doors. "Have a seat. This will only take a moment. They're out by the pool."

Ahh. The adorable creature Bo is talking to at the pool is Ms. Taylor who has a guest certificate to the same condo as me. Only one of us can stay. I think back to the face she made the moment she saw me. It was different from the other women at the bar. It was different from Caroline. Come to think of it, it was different than any other woman has ever looked at me before. She looked disinterested—like she had no time to worry herself with me.

A few minutes later the door opens and the receptionist ushers in Bo and the woman. I was right. She doesn't even acknowledge that I am in the room.

What's her story? How does she know Larry Butters? Was she here with someone? Did her lips feel as soft as they looked?

"Hey, guy. Glad you could make it. Sorry about the mix-up with the room," Bo says as he shakes my hand and gives me a stiff pat on the shoulder. *Everyone knows men can't hug unless there's a handshake in between.*

"Don't even worry about it. We'll figure it out."

A man in a suit follows and takes a seat behind the large desk. He explains the situation with the reservations as he slides our driver's licenses across the table to us.

"Seriously? Double-booked?" Ms. Taylor cries out, exasperated. "You have got to be kidding me."

"We are so sorry, ma'am."

"Can't you just find one of us another condo?" she asked, without so much as glancing in my direction.

"If I had anything available I would be escorting you there now. Unfortunately, with the conference this week we are at full capacity."

"What are our options?" she asks.

I liked the way this woman took charge of the situation. She was making this manager sweat. I also liked the way her shirt sleeve kept slightly slipping down one shoulder, revealing her turquoise bra strap. It was making me sweat. Or maybe it's just really hot in here. *I need a drink.*

"We are fully prepared to reimburse one of you for the cost of the room or transfer you to one of our neighboring hotels."

"I knew this was too good to be true," she said as she sat back in her chair. "Timeshares! Ugh!"

There was something in this woman's eyes and tone of voice that was telling me she really needed this. I should know. A big part of my job over the last six years involved analyzing people. I looked at Bo. He was glaring at me and nodding toward the girl. His eyebrows said *make this right.*

Marine Corps leadership principle number eight—make sound and timely decisions.

"Can we both stay and just share the condo? I'm only going to be here three nights—heading out Monday morning. I'd hate for the young lady to miss out."

For the first time since entering the room, Ms. Taylor looked at me. She seemed amused at my suggestion. *Stupid.* Of course she finds this suggestion amusing. What woman would feel comfortable sharing private space with a stranger?

"Of course you would suggest that," she says. She pulls her shirt sleeve back up over her shoulder. The two lines in the middle of her forehead are showing again. *Did she just roll her eyes at me?* What have I done to upset her?

"What is that supposed to mean?" I ask, feeling myself getting heated. Bo intervenes before she can speak again.

"Now, that might not be a bad idea." He turns to face Brigid. "You and I have gotten to know each other a little at the pool this afternoon. I can vouch for Sergeant Balzly. He likes to fly under the radar. He will be spending most of his time with me at the conference anyway. You'll hardly even notice he's there. What do you say?"

I don't like that Bo is having to negotiate on my behalf. I am just trying to be nice. I don't care about the room or where I sleep. *Not that I've even been sleeping much lately anyway.*

"Well?" Bo gives her some sort of look I don't recognize.

"Fine," she says as she throws her hands in the air.

She didn't say much as the concierge drove us to our condo on the other side of the resort in a golf cart. Or when we rode up the elevator alone with our luggage. Or when I couldn't get the key card to work on the first three tries. But just when I finally get the door to open—"Wait!"

She presses it closed again.

"What?" I say, annoyed that now I have to mess with this key card again.

"Are you a mass murderer?" she says this with a serious face.

"What kind of question is that?" I look down at her. The top of her head barely reaches my shoulders. Her eyes are chameleons—an amber starburst at the center and emerald green around the edges.

"Hopefully one that's easy to answer."

I laugh.

I can see regret all over her face. She is definitely having second thoughts about this arrangement. *Time to lay on the charm.* I smile at her and reach out to grab the carry-on bag that hangs from one shoulder, preparing to say something to put her at ease, when suddenly my hand is slapped away, hard.

"What the hell?" I frown.

"Sorry. Reflex."

"I was just trying to help you with your bag."

"I don't need help with it. I think we need to set some boundaries here."

"What? Your husband doesn't like other guys offering to help you carry something heavy?"

"No. I mean, I don't have a husband."

"In a serious relationship?"

"No. It's just been an incredibly long day, and I'm exhausted, and I don't need any complications this weekend." She's being honest.

I take a step back and draw an imaginary line between us with my toe. "Don't worry. I won't make the mistake of touching you again." I may or may not have just sounded like a complete asshole.

She grabs the key card out of my hand and opens the door on the first try, then turns back to scoff at me.

"Showoff," I say under my breath.

We both walk in and do our own quick walk-through of the condo. If she was impressed, she didn't say.

The place is stunning. A great view of the sound, for sure. A big grill out on the balcony. A flat-screen television hangs opposite the couch, and a table set for four separates the living and kitchen space.

"Why don't you take the master suite?" I say, backing across the living room toward the other room with my duffel. "It's got a big soaking tub."

"What are you suggesting?" she says defensively. The lines on her forehead are back.

"That you need to relax."

She lets out an annoyed sigh, goes into her room, and slams the door. I hear the lock turn. I open the refrigerator out of habit. Empty. *That won't do.* I unpack the items in my duffel and head back to the pool.

"Hey, guy! Did you get settled in?" Bo asks as I take a seat next to him at the poolside bar. He looks like a Parrothead in his Jimmy Buffett shirt and khaki shorts.

"You can say that," I say. I order a Woodford Old Fashioned and spend the next five minutes listening to Bo talk on and on about Brigid Taylor. He could practically start her fan club.

"You should spend some time getting to know that girl this weekend."

"Hey. I'm here for the conference."

"Bullshit. Besides, you owe me a favor."

I laugh out loud. "I thought driving my ass all the way down here was the favor."

"What else do you have to do with your time?"

"Speaking of time," I say, "how long have you been drinking?" I can tell he is already feeling pretty good.

Bo reaches out for his fresh bottle as he looks down at his watch. "About 58 years."

Brigid

eriously, universe? I am here trying to avoid men, relax, find myself again, and I end up sharing a condo with the most attractive man I have ever seen in real life. No telling what he thinks of me after the complete fool I just made of myself. Do you want friendly, personable, warm, and loving? Brigid's your girl. Apparently, my attempts to dial it down turn me into a complete lunatic. So, my first impression wasn't the best. But Balzly was also a bit of an ass.

I definitely caught him staring at my chest. One minute he is undressing me with his eyes, and the next he is promising never to touch me again. And hello, you don't reach out to grab someone who is in the middle of asking if you are a murderer. *I can't believe I said that.* But still, I don't need anyone to carry my bag for me. I work out. *Well, I own a gym membership.* Okay, I had to cancel it when I sort of went broke, but the point is, Balzly is exactly the kind of man who will end up getting me in trouble. Here I am being all nice, agreeing to psychoanalyze him while he is trying to seduce me with his eyes. And the way he looked down at me before we walked into the condo. Pretty self-absorbed. The guy is probably more swagger than substance. I'm not falling for it.

So I am sitting on the bathroom counter in this immaculate master suite with freshly shaven legs, painting my toenails and trying to figure out how I am supposed to get him to take his guard down while I keep mine up, when my phone suddenly blasts out the *Golden Girls* theme song. I grab it and quickly wobble on my heels over to the closet and sit down inside, whispering, "Hey."

"Hey." It's Piper. "Why are you whispering?"

"Well, not sure you're going to believe it."

"What now? Did everything work out with the room?"

"Uh huh. Sure. If by 'work out' you mean the condo got double-booked and now I am sharing the space with a complete stranger. I am that desperate for time away."

I don't dare mention the deal. I'm too ashamed.

"Oh no. How did this happen? Dave, get in here!" she screams.

"Don't worry. Everything is fine. It is so beautiful here that I probably won't be spending much time in the condo anyway. And besides, there are two bedrooms, and my room locks."

"That doesn't make me feel better. Dave!"

"Actually, the stranger is a Marine, Sgt. Balzly, or something like that. The American Legion is having a conference here this weekend for veterans, and he is here for that."

"So you're stuck sharing the condo with an old man?"

"That would be much easier, trust me."

"What do you mean? Does he look like a creeper?"

"No, he looks beautiful actually. Remember Meredith from high school?"

"Meredith B or Meredith M?" Dave asks. I'm on speakerphone again.

"Shut up, Dave. You know I'm talking about Meredith B. Anyways, this guy looks a lot like her older brother."

"Hotwheel?" Piper remembers.

"Yeah." Meredith's brother Will was eye candy. Every girl had a crush. But only Piper and I were clever enough to come up with a cool code name for our heartthrob.

"Oooooh! I loved Hotwheel!" I can hear it. I can picture her now—smiling from ear to ear as she claps excitedly and as quickly as humanly possible.

"Everyone loved Hotwheel."

"Yeah. You are screwed." She really emphasizes that last part. She knows me so well.

"Do not say that." I'm in denial. "It's like you have no confidence in me," I complain, even as my brain admits that I also have no confidence in myself.

I step back out of the closet and start picking up the dirty laundry I kicked off before I jumped into the shower. "Paul was right. I need to make some changes."

"This thing with Jeff is not your fault," Piper claims.

"The thing is, though, it feels like my fault. I am the one suffering the consequences. My career is on hold. I'm sure the speculation and gossip is flooding the entire admin building. My savings is drained."

"Paul was wrong. Jeff is literally a terrible human being, and he will get what he has coming to him. Besides, we are just messing with you. We have complete confidence that you can keep yourself from flirting with Hotwheel."

"Uh huh."

"You just enjoy yourself this week and make the best of the situation with this Sgt. Balzly."

"I can do anything for three days," I say, trying to sound convincing. "Love you."

"Love you too," Dave interjects.

"Bye, guys."

Jeff. Ugh! I am nauseous just hearing that name. No! Block it out. Time for some fresh air. I throw on my bathing suit cover-up, a pair of flip-flops, and my sunglasses, and I head back out into the sunshine, feeling a hundred times better than I did pre-shave.

I'm strolling down the sidewalk that weaves in between each stucco building, with lush sabal palms canopying my every step. A young family rides past on their rented bikes, and I step out of the way. Studying the map of the resort makes me more excited. This place has everything: three heated pools, a fine dining restaurant, a spa, a private beach on the bay, a marina, a poolside bar, and every type of water recreation you could imagine. I decide to start with a lazy afternoon at the "Blue Lagoon" pool, a hidden little sanctuary on this side of the resort. Three hours. Three hours of peace. I got some aerobic exercise in. *Swam three laps before feeling the onset of an asthma attack.* Dove into some deep reading. *Finished the prologue of my new Sparks novel and then burst into tears.* Listened to an entirely appropriate Pandora station. *Is one the loneliest number that you'll ever do?* Yes! Three hours spent entirely alone. See. I can do this. I don't need human interaction. This week is all about me.

Piper and Dave were idiots to pass up a week in this amazing place. The girls would have loved it. Who am I kidding? I wish they were here. I basically wish anyone I knew was here. The bad thing about being someplace amazing all by yourself is that it doesn't seem quite as great as it would if you had someone to share it with. I ponder this as I leisurely stroll past the pickleball court and back to the condo. Maybe that is why I have never gone more than a couple of months without a boyfriend. Ugh! What is wrong with me? The condo is quiet when I return. I put my phone on charge in the kitchen. No texts. No emails. I peek inside Sgt. Balzly's room. His closet door is open, and I can see from my spot perched in the doorway that his few clothes are already hung and organized. *Control freak.*

A knock at the door catches me off guard. Would Sgt. Balzly be knocking? And why am I checking my lip gloss in the mirror near the entryway? (It looks perfect, by the way.)

"Hello." I don't recognize the voice. I look through the peephole. Okay, not Sgt. Balzly.

"How can I help you?"

"I'm with Instacart."

Good for you.

"I have your groceries. Would you like for me to leave them on the cart or carry them in?"

"I'm sorry. I didn't order any groceries." This is a setup. I saw something like this on Facebook. This is how they trick young women into opening their hotel rooms before kidnapping them and selling them to human traffickers. "You must have the wrong room."

"Room 3068?"

"Yes, but I didn't order any groceries."

The young man holds up the receipt and looks annoyed. "Call the concierge desk. All orders go through them." He looks down at his watch and seems frustrated that I'm keeping him locked outside.

I call the concierge desk.

"Let me just check on that for you. One moment, please, Ms. Taylor." The people here are so professional. And apparently busy, too, because I am on hold for like five minutes when suddenly the guy starts trying to force his way inside. The doorknob turns frantically. The keycard error noise repeats several times. I hear someone's shoulder hit the door, and then it flies open. Someone screams bloody murder as the vase next to the phone hits the floor and shatters on the tile.

My heart is beating as a wild-eyed Sgt. Balzly pushes through the door, screaming, "What the hell?"

"What?" I am scared to death.

"Why are you screaming?"

I take half a breath. "You scared the shit out of me. Some guy was trying to con his way in here. I thought you were him."

Balzly makes an annoyed look and then turns around to head back outside. I look down and realize what has happened. When the door burst open, I dropped the phone, and it knocked over the decorative vase with the fresh flowers. Shit. There is glass everywhere.

"Sorry about that. My friend has had a long day," I hear Sgt. Balzly explaining to the delivery boy as they both begin carrying groceries into the kitchen and setting them on the counter.

I pick up the phone and place it back on the table and hold the receiver to my ear. Someone is talking through the other line. "Ma'am? Ma'am?"

"I'm here. Sorry."

"That's okay. Sorry about your wait. Your room guest, Sgt. Balzly, ordered and paid for the groceries."

"Thank you." I hang up the phone, feeling completely humiliated. Sgt. Balzly walks the guy to the door and slips him a twenty-dollar bill. "Sorry about that, man." They exchange a knowing look, and then he leaves. I find a broom in the pantry and begin sweeping up the glass.

"Oh no you don't." Sgt. Balzly grabs the broom out of my hand.

"I'm perfectly capable of sweeping up a mess," I protest.

He looks down at my feet. "Do you also know how to pull shards of glass out of bare feet?" Smug!

So I stand on the living room carpet and watch as Sgt. Balzly sweeps up the tile area near the door and picks up the flowers.

"You could have told me you were expecting a delivery." Why am I sounding like such a bitch?

He fires right back at me. "If I had known you were going to launch a complete offensive, I would have met the guy downstairs." He's not smiling. He seems pissed. He dumps the dustpan full of glass into the trash can and then pulls down a glass from the top shelf of a cabinet and puts the flowers into it. The glass is too small.

"Here. I can fix this." I begin work to trim the flowers and arrange them properly while he begins putting the groceries away.

Something about us both being in this small space, working on domestic tasks, seems too intimate. What is it about this man? His eyes. Dark brown. Inscrutable.

"You like to cook?" I ask nonchalantly, trying to break the ice after my freak-out.

"I like to eat." Just when I think he isn't going to say anything else, he adds, "Would you like to have a drink with me?" I turn to see him pulling a couple of cold drinks from the fridge.

I would like to have babies with you. NO! Control yourself Brigid! The last thing I need is to get involved with a forbearing brute in need of psychiatric care.

"No thanks. I was just heading out on the balcony to read for a while." I grab a book from the top of my dresser and head back through the living room and out the sliding door. *What is wrong with me?*

So I sit alone on the screened balcony with my back to the condo trying not to turn around and see what he is doing to cause all the ruckus I hear coming from the kitchen. I am silently congratulating myself on how strong I am. *Yes, I hear how pathetic that sounds.* My biggest accomplishment of the day is restraining myself from flirting with this man.

Suddenly the sliding door opens behind me.

"Good book?"

I shut the book immediately as my stomach growls. "Yep." He keeps catching me off guard.

"Nice evening." He sets a couple of drinks down on the table in front of me and walks a tray of prepped food over to the grill then stops to admire the view.

I remind myself that if I don't start showing a little interest I won't be able to hold up my part of the bargain with Bo. I pick up the Liberty Bell IPA sitting in front of me and use the edge of the table to pop open the cap. Party trick.

He turns when he hears the sound and makes a face I can't decipher. I'm pretty sure he thinks I'm a crazed lunatic.

"I want to apologize if I seemed a little on edge earlier." There. That's a good start.

"In the registration office?" he asks. "Or when you accused me of being a murderer? Or when you destroyed a Waterford Crystal vase because the Instacart delivery boy scared you?"

"You don't have to be so, so..."

"Honest."

Ugh! I pick my book back up and continue reading—well, scanning.

I have always thought men with dark hair on their legs are sexy. How tall is Sgt. Balzly? I am silently measuring him, imagining a ruler from the ground stretching to his calf muscle. It hits again above his kneecap and then his upper hamstring. My eyes keep wandering up. The way his shirt fits him doesn't go unnoticed. How could it? He's standing ten feet away from me, this perfect, statuesque man. My ruler makes its way to his collarbone—one of my favorite places. His long neck, chiseled jaw, those dark, piercing eyes. Good Lord, I am so screwed.

"How do you like your meat?"

"Excuse me?" I can feel the heat on my cheeks.

"Medium? Rare?" he clarifies, holding up a steak with metal tongs.

"Oh. No, thank you. I'm not eating with you." Why did that come out sounding so mean?

"Are you always this...? Never mind."

"What?" I press.

"Uptight?"

I let out a little laugh because I'm pretty sure no one has ever accused me of being uptight. I don't even know how to answer him.

"Are you always this…" Handsome? Charming? Sexy? "…irritating?"

He shoots me a look that I can't read. I think I hurt his feelings. This entire situation is my fault, and I know it. I am so off balance. This isn't fair to him. I hit the reset button.

"Sorry." I set my beer down and try a bit of honesty. "I usually make for better company. I'm at the end of my rope, and it has nothing to do with you or this condo situation. I'm not myself."

He presses his lips into a thin line and then turns back to the grill. "I've actually been doing a dead hang from the end of my rope for the past few weeks as well," he admits, still facing away.

"Work stuff?" I ask.

"Ughhh. Kind of. An occupational hazard, I guess you could say. It's left everyone in my orbit feeling sorry for me."

I think about the information Bo shared with me. I am getting the sense that being pitied is the worse part. This is the moment I need to pivot this entire charade so I can fulfill my obligation to Bo. I need this guy to open up to me. I resign from the pretense of reading and set my book aside, curling my feet up in the seat underneath me. Luckily, censoring what I say pretty much goes out the window after I chug half a beer. "A good-looking Marine sergeant who knows how to cook and has excellent taste in beer. Look at this view. It's hard to feel too sorry for you," I say with a wink and a facetious smile.

"Good looking, huh?" Sgt. Balzly teases as he flips the steaks and moves the veggies around.

"So, Sgt. Balzly, what is life like as a Marine?" I am genuinely interested.

"It's just Balzly." He turns around and motions with his hand. "Life as a Marine is interesting. There are 42 men in my platoon. I am the guy everyone comes to for guidance and support."

"Have you spent a lot of time overseas?"

"Almost the entire time. Japan. Kosovo. Afghanistan. Syria. Iraq. Afghanistan again."

"What's your MOS?"

He turns around and shoots me a quick look—surprise, maybe?

"I'm in signals intelligence, a cryptanalyst."

The wrinkles in my nose appear. "Okay, so I have heard of a cryptographer. What is a cryptanalyst?"

"Cryptographers are expert code writers, and I am an expert code breaker. Could you grab some plates? We're almost done here."

"Sure." I get up and scurry back to the kitchen, suddenly feeling domesticated. I return a moment later with the plates, napkins, and utensils. Before I know it, he is carrying my plate to the grill and filling it with steak, asparagus, and cabbage. He sets it back down in front of me, and something about this small, kind gesture seems incredible.

"What kind of codes do you break?" I ask as we begin to eat.

"All kinds. My team works to intercept enemy communication, decipher the code, and use the intelligence to make decisions on the ground."

"That's amazing. How did you become interested in something like that? Oh wow, this steak is delicious, by the way." Balzly looks pleased with himself and wipes the corner of his mouth with a napkin before answering.

"WWII. I've always loved history. I grew up fascinated with the code talkers in the Pacific. Plus, I've always had a knack for finding what is hidden."

He looks me in the eyes and slowly lifts his bottle to his parted lips. It rests there for a second before he takes a swig, never taking his eyes off of mine.

"Is that so?"

"Sure. The military has invested time and money training me to pick up on clues, see patterns, make sense of what no one else even recognizes."

"So you find codes in numbers?"

"Numbers. Symbols. Languages. People."

"People?"

"Sure. I'm trained to notice everything about everyone." He takes another bite.

"Okay, I'll play along. You met me earlier today. What have you noticed?"

"You sure? This usually doesn't go well," he smiled hesitantly.

I finished the last sip of my IPA.

"Take your best shot."

He looked at me for a long moment, his eyes piercing into me, slightly smug.

"Brigid Taylor. Thirty-one years old. Single. Living in Nashville. A career in education. Trying to hide from me your extroverted personality." He smiles as if this last bit amuses him in some way.

I begin to open my mouth and then close it, but the shocked facial expression remains. *This guy will see right through my plan with Bo.*

"Your driver's license says you turned thirty-one last February 9th. Your accent tells me you are from the South. The tag on your luggage with your address says Nashville. You got hit in the face with a water rocket earlier today and responded the way someone does when they are used to dealing with kids."

"You saw that?" I covered my eyes, feigning embarrassment.

"You chose an IPA over a Bud Light—you're adventurous. You don't hold back. You toss the garnish out of your drink because you don't have time for bullshit. You didn't shave your legs or paint your toenails until you got here, which means that you are so preoccupied with life you aren't making time for yourself. You're trying to read a Nicholas Sparks novel, which tells me you believe in true love, but the fact that you're still on page two after thirty minutes makes me believe that you are too distracted with your current string of bad luck to be swept away. You are clearly grappling with whether or not you want to reveal to me your very charming and outgoing personality."

Then, silence. He looks down at his plate apologetically, as if he has walked in on me undressed. And it sort of felt like he had. This man was intriguing. As a psychologist, I am pretty good at relating to people, figuring out how they think and behave. The tables have just been turned. He was looking at me with a slight wince on his face, just waiting for me to say something like, "How dare you! You don't know me." But instead, I am genuinely impressed.

"Wow. You are good," I say simply. "And you can do this with anyone?"

"Technically, yes, but breaking some codes is more rewarding than others." He stands up and reaches out for my hand with a sultry smile.

And here we go again! I literally just met this guy, and he thinks that he can play his military Jedi mind tricks on me and that I will just swoon into his arms. No!

"Does this usually work?" I ask as the mood on the balcony takes a turn when he recognizes the tone of my voice has changed.

"Pardon." His hand is still reaching out, hanging in midair.

"You think that because you've read me like a book, I'm going to swoon and let you lead me into your bedroom. Ugh! Men!" I sit up straighter, disgusted, posturing for a fight. Why is he smiling? Why is he blushing?

"I'm sorry. I was just reaching for your plate. These dishes aren't going to wash themselves."

Truly, he had seen beneath the surface.

Balzly

Know yourself and seek self-improvement—the first Marine Corps leadership principle and the entire reason why I am sitting in a large conference hall at 9:00 a.m. with Bo and the guys, listening to Dr. Daniel Jenkins give the keynote address on seeking self-improvement. Something has to change. I've been a stranger in my own body since Caroline—since Mike.

The first few weeks after my mistake were the worst. It was all I could do to make it through my day without freaking out on someone. It didn't help that everyone knew what had happened and had seen it with their own eyes. You can only imagine the comments from a bunch of Marines about something like that. I quit eating meals with the guys, bailed as soon as my shift was up, and didn't put in my extra workout at the gym. The calls home stopped. My platoon whispered quietly and tiptoed around me for the rest of the deployment.

I'd never been happier for my boots to hit American soil. I had three weeks of leave saved up—time I had planned on spending with Caroline. Instead, I sat alone for three days, shooting straight whiskey at the Rusty Pelican before being called back in by my gunnery staff sergeant.

"Close the door and sit down," he ordered. He had poured himself a drink but didn't offer me one. "Balzly, you're one hell of a Marine." He lifted his glass to his lips and took a long gulp, turning his chair to face the window, staring out at nothing important. "Your loyalty to Mike—to all your brothers—has been unshakable." He turned back towards me. "This job requires sacrifice. And Mike made the ultimate one. You will not find

39

atonement in the bottom of a glass." He finished his drink and set the glass back down on his desk. "I should know." After a long moment of silence, he asked, "Do you know what Mike would say if he were here to see you like this?" I did know, but I didn't answer. I couldn't. Just hearing someone say his name knocked the air out of my lungs.

He stood, and I did as well. He walked around his desk and stood directly in front of me—his face inches from mine. "He'd call SITFU. So suck it the fuck up, Marine." He reached down and shook my hand. "Dismissed."

Good talk.

I know I can't go on like this. And I don't want to. But I can't get the images out of my head. While the others are hanging on to every word our speaker says, all I can do is picture her long blond hair whipping across her bare back. Once this starts, it always ends badly. Sweat is beading up on the back of my neck, and there is a pounding in my head. Just then, every vet in the room rises and begins clapping and cheering, but my vision is blurry, and all I can hear is the sound of the explosion—of mass chaos everywhere. I want to leave, but I can't move. My head is swimming—no, drowning.

Bo looks down at me and offers a hand. I push his arm away and stumble out of the room. *Set the example*—leadership principle number five. Totally freaking blew it. I've got to clear my head, so I run. I run so far and so fast that eventually I have outrun the thoughts of Caroline that threaten to seep back in.

An hour later, I end up back at the condo, shirtless, chugging a glass of water in front of the open refrigerator, still feeling like a piece of shit, when I hear it. There is music coming from the balcony, and I listen closely, trying to make out what she is playing. Blink-182. That's a welcome surprise. Everything about this girl is a welcome surprise. Last night was the first time in months that I felt like a human being capable of relaxing. Brigid Taylor was a breath of fresh air. She let me cook for her. She let me decode her. She is feisty. Something about her seems a little guarded. Luckily, I was able to act like a human being and not completely scare her off. And by the end of the night, I think she was genuinely enjoying my company.

And then later, while in the shower, it happened again. I'm thinking about how good Brigid's thin and toned frame would feel in my arms. I'm 6'3" and thinking she's probably 5'7"—the perfect height. I'm imagining her head resting on my chest and my lips kissing the top of it. Her hair is blond with streaks of honey. She wears it down and loose, a little wavy, like it's relaxed. I want to sink my hands into it. Her eyes are rounded like almonds, their lids naked, hiding behind thick lashes. One minute I'm thinking about this natural beauty, and the next second I've got the image of Caroline pounding in my head, and I am the Hulk, ready to destroy anything in sight.

I've googled things. I've seen this with other Marines. I know this is a stress reaction to trauma. And I hate it because it makes me feel so weak. I want to get over it, but I don't see how I ever will.

And then her singing interrupts my thoughts.

I'm perched in my bedroom doorway, watching her dance through the condo as she sings along. She has no idea I'm here. She is wearing a red bikini top, knee shorts, and red flip-flops. Her hair is piled up on top of her head, and her sunglasses are tangled atop the heap. She has paint on her hands and cheek and is leaning over the kitchen counter to rinse some paint from her brush. What is she doing out there? I turn to see that she has a small paint easel set up on the table and a watercolor painting in the works. And then she spots me and lets out a quick scream.

"Shit! Sorry. Oh my gosh, you scared me. I didn't know you were here," she says as her hands fall across her chest to elbows, self-consciously.

"Don't apologize. You sing beautifully. And you paint."

"A hobby. It's relaxing," she shrugs as she walks backward. "How was the keynote address?" She points to the conference brochure that I left sitting out on the counter.

"Fine," I lied.

She nods and turns to head into her room. I glance up to see her bare back. Damn. She reappears a moment later with a tank top covering her midsection and picks up her brush from the counter.

"Have a great day," she says noncommittally and heads back toward the balcony.

"Hey. Um. I was wondering." I have no clue what I'm going to say next.

Anything to hold onto this moment with her.

She turns, and her eyes are on me now. That smile.

"Do you have plans later?" Where am I going with this?

"Nope. This trip is one of complete spontaneity," she says proudly.

"Would you be interested in a drive to the beachside? Some buddies have been talking about Pier Park. I'd like to check it out. Maybe grab a bite."

Her teeth are biting her lower lip again, and the line between her eyebrows appears. "Sure, so long as I'm not intruding," she says, watching me to weigh my response.

"Nah. Not at all. Meet you in the lobby at 4:30 p.m.?" Am I coming across as cool as I hope? Probably not.

"Sounds good." And there's that smile. She turns to head back to her painting, and I turn to go find Bo and the guys. I need to apologize.

I'm not exactly sure why, but pretty much from the moment that Brigid said she'd go with me to Pier Park, the weight on my chest lifted. I met the guys for lunch poolside and apologized to Bo. He just shook my hand and gave me a look, but since I had spent the last week shutting down his every effort to help me, he simply said, "See you at the 1:00 p.m. breakout session."

So we spent the afternoon listening to how we could create a win/win for our post, district, and chapter if we started a Legion Riders program at Camp Hill. By the end of the session, Bo's excitement was contagious.

"Do you think we could get the program up and running before the POW/MIA rally next year?" Bo asks as we head back through the main lobby.

"Not sure. I don't even own a bike."

"Oh. Wait a second. There's Brigid," Bo says, willing to table talks on his new startup project.

I turn to look and spot her standing at the bar in the lobby, wearing a sundress and talking with her hands to the lady seated on the stool. Just chatting it up. Not a care in the world. Her smile is out in full force. The lady giggles. Brigid is cracking this woman up. A quick, impromptu hug follows, and Brigid turns around. We make eye contact. She smiles at me, and I wonder at this moment what is different about her smile. Yesterday, two beautiful young women perched at the lobby bar were smiling at me from across the room, and it was meaningless. I couldn't escape quickly enough. Making eye contact with Brigid feels like I've just been punched in the gut. I have difficulty breathing. The feeling takes me by surprise. I don't like surprises, but I decide to make an exception as she walks across the lobby to where we are standing.

"Ms. Taylor." Bo smiles as he reaches out and touches her elbow the way older people do when they don't want you to escape.

"Hello again."

"Hey, Bo. How's your day going?"

"Oh, pretty good. Balzly tells me you're quite the artist."

"Ha! I don't know about all of that." Her eyebrows rise, and the single line appears again between them. "Are we waiting on anyone else?"

"Excuse me?" Bo asks.

"For Pier Park. Sgt. Balzly was kind enough to invite me to tag along with you guys for dinner," she explains.

Bo shoots me a curious look.

Shit. She thinks this is supposed to be a group outing.

My weight shifts from one side to the other as my hands make a vague gesture towards the door. I manage to mumble, "Actually, none of the guys could make it work."

She looks at Bo as he gives an apologetic shoulder shrug. I love that man.

"Oh." The quickest look of disappointment dances across her face. "No worries. Maybe some other time."

"Wait."

Her green eyes meet mine.

"You and I could still go."

I breathe in, hold the air, and breathe out, all the while she bites her lower lip.

"Yes, feed this guy. He's had a rough day putting up with me and my crazy ideas." Bo breaks the spell, and her charming smile returns. "Have you ever ridden a motorcycle?" he asks her.

She glances at me curiously.

"Don't ask. Come with me before he has you on the back of a Harley."

"Okay." She takes a step towards me. "Nice seeing you again, Bo." I think I see him wink at her.

Brigid is quiet as we walk to the parking lot. "This one is mine." I open the passenger-side door of my black Jeep Wrangler.

"Thank you."

"Of course." She steps past me and slides her sun-kissed legs into my Jeep. God, she smells good. Something about her is different today. She has loosened up.

"So, what did you do today?" I ask, trying to keep the conversation light as we head away from the resort, trying to hold onto this version of Brigid as long as I can.

"Well, I spent a few hours this morning painting, which you know, and then I went down to the dock and checked out the situation with the boat rentals."

"What types of boats did they have down there?"

"Pontoons, speed boats, and sailboats. I picked up a brochure." She pulls it out of her purse and browses through it.

Several minutes of silence pass.

"Are you always this intense when you drive?"

Shit. I forgot about this.

"Sorry." She caught me. "I, ugh, I sort of become hyper-focused during certain tasks—driving is one."

"Interesting. Have you had any really sad or scary vehicle-related experiences?"

This question catches me off guard for a second. I look over at her and then back to the road. She seems genuinely interested.

"No. Nothing like that. I just have this habit of remembering the makes, models, and license plate numbers of the vehicles I pass on the road."

"I see. And what does that do for you?"

Her voice takes on a new tone. A serious tone. A calming tone.

"I just like to have all of the information about who's on the road with me."

"How does having that information make you feel?"

Her voice is doing it again.

"Like I'm prepared."

"Prepared for?"

"Anything. An Amber Alert."

"There were only two Amber Alerts in the state of Florida last year."

Could that be all?

"How often do you do this?"

"Always."

I sound completely mad, and I know it. But you can't tell by the sound of her voice.

"What have we passed so far?"

"Do you really want to know? Because it might freak you out."

"Try me."

I glance in the rearview mirror and then at her. She is already turned around, seatbelt off, kneeling up in my front seat, squinting to make out the cars behind us as I rattle off information.

"2017 white Hyundai Sonata, plate number 8UG56BL. 2007 red Chevy Beretta, plate number YOU842. 2020 black Nissan Murano, plate number X8LGS31. 2019 white Chrysler Pacifica, plate number 42BHI7M."

"I don't see any of those vehicles."

"Those were the ones we passed at the resort."

She breathes out a grunted nasal sound.

"Okay then, tell me the last vehicle we passed."

"2018 Peterbilt semi, plate number BIGRIG22. To report bad driving, call 802-944-2214. Weird?"

"More like amazing," she smiles as she settles back in her seat. A few minutes pass in silence.

"How do you know where we're going if you've never been to Pier Park? Do you want me to pull it up on my phone?"

"Oh. I, ugh, looked at the map before we left. We're about two klicks out."

She just smiles. A few more minutes pass in silence.

"It must be hard," she says thoughtfully.

45

"What's that?"

"Living in your head."

I think about how to respond and decide to go with honesty. "It can be."

Brigid

ll I can think about as I stroll down the promenade beneath the most beautiful sky and dodge groups of smiling people is that Paul would hate this. He'd be complaining about the crowds or the wait at the restaurant. Instead, I'm with Sgt. Balzly who is of a different mindset completely. He is smiling, relaxed, willing to pop in and out of any shop that looks interesting. He isn't bothered in the least when the hostess at The Backporch Seafood and Oyster House said there is a 90 minute wait. He is genuinely pleasant company. We have plenty of time on our hands before dinner so we decide to head across the street and check out the pier.

So we're near the end of the pier with our arms resting on the rail looking out over the water and I'm praying that he doesn't catch me glancing at him, which is apparently something I am unable to stop doing. He's just so good-looking. Dark hair, dark eyebrows, chiseled jawline with a five o'clock shadow (my weakness) and a smile that makes me want to bite his lip off. *Stop! You barely know this guy.* From everything Bo said, he is already struggling with something. Plus, he's a Marine, which means a relationship could never work. As my brain is working hard to convince every other inch of my body to hold out, I hear it—a high-pitch scream from behind me. Someone yells, "Oh shit!" A splash. More screams. Something drops at my feet. And then a second splash.

It all happens so fast. I look down to see the inhabitants of a pocket lying on the dock near my feet. One minute I am daydreaming about Sgt. Balzly and the next minute he jumped overboard. I know what you're thinking. *This is the sort of stuff that only happens in movies.* But thirty-five minutes later a seventeen-year-old girl is leaving in an ambulance with a concussion and some broken ribs and a very wet Sgt. Balzly is giving his statement to the police.

Jumping off a pier to save someone is like the last thing Paul would ever do. After all, he never liked to interfere in anyone else's business.

For Sgt. Balzly, this seems like just another day at the office. He ducks into Coastal Casuals and comes back out a few minutes later wearing dry clothes and flip-flops, smiling and asking if I'm still hungry.

So I walk beside him to the restaurant as he carries a plastic shopping bag filled with his wet stuff. A couple of people are looking at him and pointing. One man pats him on the back.

"Inside or out?" the hostess asks the Sergeant with flirty eyes. She nods her head and smiles while gently biting on the end of her pen cap. Did I mention that she is wearing cut-off blue jean shorts with her ass hanging out and a scoop-neck tank top that is advertising three inches of cleavage? She is gorgeous and knows it and is completely hitting on the Sergeant right in front of me. For all she knows I could be his girlfriend. Oh dear. Is this what I look like? Am I unable to see that my outgoing and charming personality actually comes across desperate and needy? *God, I hope not.*

He seems to be both aware and frustrated with this seduction act. He just looks at me and asks, "What would make you happy?"

No one has asked me that question in so long. I don't know if anyone has ever asked me that question.

I smile. "Outside," I say. He is still looking at me, and it's unnerving, but I love it.

We are led out to the front porch, which is oceanside. The liveliness of the crowd seated at the white tables with colorful umbrellas is contagious. The Beach Boys are playing over the speakers and colorful drinks in big glasses are being enjoyed by all.

"What are you thinking?" Sgt. Balzly asks as he peers at me over his menu.

I smile looking down at my own. "A couple of things."

"First?" he asks.

"How did you respond so quickly on the pier? I blinked and you were gone."

He glances around and then back at me.

"I had seen that girl when we walked onto the pier. She was sitting on the railing and talking to that guy that she was with. I kind of thought that might happen."

"What?" I sound skeptical.

"Well, he was standing in front of her in agony. He wanted to wrap his arms around her waist. Then, she started teasing him, leaning back and acting like she was going to fall, trying to get him to grab her. Poor guy. He couldn't take it much longer. He moved in for a kiss and it caught her off guard. She jerked her head back and lost her balance. They tried to grab for each other, but it was too late."

"And then you turned into Superman and saved the day?"

"Not at all. I'm trained to respond. I knew I was in the best position to be tactically proficient."

Unbelievable! He is totally downplaying this entire episode. If he only knew how many times I am planning on telling this story and I guarantee that each time it will become more and more exaggerated.

"What was the second thing?" he asks, disrupting my thoughts.

"Hmm?"

"You said you were thinking a couple of things." *Man, he really pays attention.* I take a deep breath and smile happily.

"I love this song."

I can tell my answer surprises him and he smiles and looks back down at the menu.

Two and a half hours later Sgt. Balzly is handing our waiter his credit card and standing to stretch his legs. The food was delicious (I had shrimp and crab linguine), the atmosphere was amazing (a live band played several sets on the outdoor stage), and my dinner date (was this a date?) was fascinating. It may have been the Mai Tais, but I think Balzly and I really connected

49

tonight. And to be honest, I'm not really picking up on what Bo is so worried about.

Balzly appears to be well-adjusted to civilian life. It wouldn't be uncommon for someone with such a challenging job to struggle outside of that world. He is a trained analyst and his unbelievable mind never stops, but he handles it so well. I observed the way it worked all night. He sat across from me smiling and sipping his beer and asking genuinely thoughtful questions. Any onlooker would have seen that I was the center of his attention. But his eyes would quickly dart around the patio when new people were seated. One quick glance and he had collected new observations. I could see them spinning around in his mind as he worked to file them in their proper place, all the while, never missing a beat in our conversation. The guy was impressive.

And he really didn't seem to have any family-related trauma. He shared a few fond memories of his childhood and what it was like growing up in Mountain Brook. His dad was a computer engineer and his mom stayed home. He was an only child. He seems to be close to his family. He talked a lot about the American Legion post at Camp Hill and the "old timers" as he called Bo and the other vets.

There was only one red flag. I know. I hate this too. Here is a seemingly great guy and I am psychoanalyzing everything he does and says. I tell myself that I am doing it for Bo who is worried about him and needs peace of mind and because he's paying me to help. But in reality, I'm doing this for me. Sgt. Balzly has intrigued me. And I can say with complete confidence that I never had this kind of a reaction to Paul. Which means that after two dinners with Balzly I am more invested than I was with the man I spent the last six months dating (and sleeping with).

When I am around him I feel relaxed. It's hard to explain. He is so cool and calm and laid-back on the exterior, but I just find myself wanting to know everything that he is thinking. So after peppering him with questions, there was really only one thing that I noticed. And I'm not even sure if it's a thing. It's just a concern that I can't mark off my list yet so I make a mental note.

I think the other thing I liked about Balzly is that the entire time I was with him I was the center of his attention. He made me feel like I was important to him, which is hard to pull off with someone you just met. Up to this point all of the dinner dates I've gone on have been able to fit into three categories; awkward, bizarre, and boring. This was something entirely different.

It's my nature to be charming and personable. No drama. No judgment. That's what people can expect from me. I'm comfortable. That's probably why I've always gotten along so well with guys. But, after everything that happened with Jeff, I have my guard up around all men. I worry that on some level this could be my fault. Did I lead him on? If so, I DID NOT intend to. *I still feel an actual wave of nausea when he crosses my mind.*

And that's why I am determined to behave tonight. Balzly is clearly a catch and so good looking that I can't seem to stop staring. But, I have to. No more glances that linger, or moving in a little closer than necessary when talking. I need to control any charming banter or flirting. This is a work relationship. *Even if he has no idea.* He is a client. I am mindfully avoiding anything that could be taken the wrong way.

As we walk off the effects of the Mai Tais on the beach I am careful to leave a friendly two feet between us, which he doesn't seem to notice.

"So, what is it like living in Nashville?"

"I love it actually. Nashville has some really cool neighborhoods popping up all over the place. A year ago I started renting a remodeled house in 12 South. It's two blocks away from South Street which has marvelous shops and restaurants. I'm becoming a bit of a foodie. Plus, I love live music. And the Nashville music scene is really hot right now."

"A buddy of mine from college is a musician. He invited a bunch of guys up for his bachelor party a while back. We walked around downtown, slipped into a place for a beer, listened to a live set and then moved onto the next. It was a lot of fun."

"Downtown can be a fun night. But I'd rather hit up one of my favorite dive bars around the neighborhood. A night downtown is for a special occasion."

Suddenly we are no longer walking, but standing (two feet apart) and looking out at the ocean. The look on his face has changed. I haven't seen it before. It is intense. His breathing becomes louder. *Are his nostrils flaring?* I can tell his mind is somewhere else.

It could have been something I said. Downtown? Dancing? Dive bars? I reach out to touch his elbow and it startles him. He looks at me then, eyes wide open, as if suddenly remembering where he is.

My arms are out in front of me now where he can see them, palms down, fingers spread. "Are you okay?" I ask in my therapy voice.

He blinks. He exhales. He runs his fingers through his hair and turns to look at the ocean. "Sorry," he says. "I ugh, I was somewhere else for a second there. Forgive me."

"Whatever you were just thinking of must be pretty upsetting. I'm sorry you had to endure it." I say in the voice.

He looks at me as if that is the last thing he expects me to say. His eyebrows move slightly together and he takes another loud breath in through his nose. I reach out again and touch his arm in the same place. This time he doesn't jump. He simply moves to wrap his hand around my wrist and holds it there.

Balzly

I t was Memorial Day Weekend in downtown Nashville in 2018, and a good buddy from college had a crew together celebrating his upcoming nuptials. I had just gotten back from a tour in Syria and wasn't in the best place.

So it's nearly midnight and we're at a place called Tootsies Orchid Lounge shooting whiskey and listening to a young band play "Body Like a Backroad" when the sexiest woman any of us had ever seen walks right up to me, wraps one hand around the back of my head and pulls me into a long and hard kiss. As you can imagine, the guys get the biggest kick out of this and start hollering and cheering as if I had just won the Super Bowl. She ends the kiss and her lips find their way to my ear where she whispers, "I want you."

My eyebrows flew up in surprise and I was immediately hard. It was so provocative. I stepped back and took a long look at her. She was younger than me and wore cowgirl boots, a cut-off jean skirt, and a bright pink top. She had long blond hair. My alcohol-induced mind was already made up. It had been a long six month tour on active duty and I deserved a little careless fun. I looked at her and smiled, nodding my head slightly. She grabbed my hand and pulled me away from the guys as they cheered in disbelief. She led me through the crowd and into the ladies room and locked the door behind us. Someone knocked and she sang out, "Occupied." Her voice was slightly raspy. She sat on the counter and beckoned me to her. I walked over and stood in front of her with a stupid drunken grin on my face. She kissed me again and my hands went straight to her thighs where her legs were wide open. I slipped her skirt up around her waist. That's how it started.

And for the next year that's pretty much how it continued for Caroline and me. With an introduction like that I should have known things wouldn't end well.

Tonight was one of the best I've had in a long time, even after what happened at the beach. Brigid is amazing. I'm laying in bed, restless, staring at some rerun, but thinking about the way it felt when she reached out to me. There was absolutely nothing provocative about that touch. Just a friendly, reassuring, and non-judgemental, "I got you." And somehow she was able to keep me from feeling like a complete jackass. She spent most of the drive back to the resort quizzing me on random things, testing my "cool party tricks" as she called them. She'd throw out a question and the answer would immediately roll off my tongue and then she would give some exasperated response and we'd both laugh.

"What was the name of the paramedic?"

"Will Drysdale."

"How much did the lady in front of us at the Casual Corner spend on that ugly bathing suit?"

"$29.15"

"How many words were on the menu at the restaurant?"

"I don't know. I was counting letters... 2,417."

She seemed to get the biggest kick out of me. And it was sort of awkward because I would have liked to walk her to her door and tell her what a great time I had. I would have liked to kiss her. But, instead we were opening the door and walking in together. Neither of us seemed to want the evening to end, but as soon as her Mai Tai wore off and we were alone she put her guard back up.

"Well, thanks again for dinner. It was delicious and Pier Park was really cool," she had said as she laid her purse down on the kitchen counter and dug out her phone.

"Yeah, it was definitely worth checking out," I said nonchalantly.

She said she needed to call her friend Piper and headed to her room. I grabbed a beer from the fridge, locked the deadbolt, and then headed to mine. I grabbed a quick shower and tried to completely clear my head from the flashback I had at the beach. Brigid said she wasn't much of a party girl, which makes her the opposite of Caroline.

I kicked myself again for ever getting involved with her. All I had to do was say, "no." I didn't have to be rude. I could have said, "Thank you, but a beautiful woman like you can do better than me," and then walked away. Instead, in a moment of weakness I slept with a complete stranger.

I learned the next morning, when Caroline woke up beside me in the hotel room that I was sharing with three other buddies, that she was from New Orleans and was working as a bartender that summer in "Little Vegas" and crashing with some friends. She still had another year of college and was studying hospitality management at Tulane.

We went to breakfast and talked long enough for her to pull the basic information she needed from me. I was 30 years old. Single. Born and raised in Georgia. Earned my undergrad degree in three years at Auburn. Four years of grad school at Vanderbilt, where I earned a PHD in mathematics. Enlisted in the Corps and trained at Parris Island. Six years active duty. Five deployments.

I guess she thought that was pretty impressive because she seemed to want our fling to continue. It sounded like a good idea at the time.

I was stationed at Camp Lejeune, which was ten hours from Nashville. I didn't think it would work, but she assured me that it would. I flew her out from Nashville half a dozen times that summer. And it was crazy. I'm not sure what it was, but she unleashed in me something I had never experienced with any of the other girls I had dated. I say girls because I really hadn't had a serious girlfriend since undergrad. From the moment I picked her up at the airport we couldn't take our hands off of each other. We had sex everywhere: the airport bathroom, Onslow Beach, my room on base. You get the point. And it was incredible. She was pretty much up for anything.

When she went back to school that fall we didn't have as many weekends together so we relied on our imagination. We didn't do a lot of talking, but I guess I wasn't worried about it because we had such a strong physical connection. She was always sending me nude pics or calling me from parties where she was clearly drinking. This one time I heard her friend say, "Oh my God. Are you still dating that old guy?"

She just laughed and said, "If you saw him naked you'd understand." I remember thinking that was hilarious at the time.

She agreed to spend her Christmas break with me at my parents' house in Mountain Brook. You can't imagine what it is like to have the hottest woman you've ever seen in your childhood bedroom doing the most unthinkable things to you while your parents sleep down the hall.

I flew to New Orleans on Valentine's Day weekend and got a suite at The Roosevelt to surprise her. I rented a limo and took her to dinner at Compere Lapin. She wore a red sequined dress with a neckline that went down to her navel. I told her that my active duty was up in six months and that I was thinking about moving home and renting an apartment. I asked her to move in with me. The celebration started in the limo on the way back to the hotel. I guess that was a yes.

I flew to Mountain Brook in March to find a place and settled for a two-bedroom, two-bath apartment in the heart of Crestwood Heights. She moved in after graduation that May and I took a week off in June to help her get settled and shop for furniture. And that's where I was when the call came in with my last orders, a three month deployment to Kandahar. Apparently three months was too long for Caroline. If only she had realized that before I left.

Before my head goes to a bad place I untwist the cap on a cold Bud Light and pull out my guitar. Funny, I wasn't even going to bring it. I haven't played in over six months. Everything about the evening with Brigid was so refreshing. I start strumming an old favorite. Unlike Caroline, Brigid seems genuinely interested in getting to know me. We had a great conversation over dinner. Her personality is so endearing.

In every shop we went into, she spoke to the people working there before they even had a chance to greet us. "Hey guys. How is it going?" she would say, or, "I love this shop! These are so cute," as she pointed to something on display. People responded to her as if they had known her their whole lives.

And I like the way she doesn't seem to be afraid to take charge. Like when I'm swimming to shore with the girl that had fallen and all I can hear is her voice shouting out orders. By the time we reached the beach Brigid had already pushed the tourists back and called an ambulance. She had found a nurse in the crowd and sent guys up to the street to flag down the first responders.

So I'm sitting in my room wearing nothing but gym shorts and plucking around on my guitar strings still pretty keyed up from the evening when my phone blasts out "OohRah" which is my text alert. I reach for it and open a message from Bo. He's still learning how to text.

"How did tit go tonight?" *Poor guy.*

"Tit went well. We had a nice time together."

"Oh good. She seems like a sweet girl. And a looker."

"Yes, she is both."

"Do you want to meet us tomorrow at the buffet breakfast?"

"Sure."

"See you at 9:00 a.m. sharp."

"Yep."

After the best night of sleep I've had in a while I'm fumbling around the kitchen in my gym shorts, making a pot of coffee and trying not to wake Brigid up when I hear her phone ringing from inside her bedroom. I try not to eavesdrop, but who am I kidding.

"Hello. I didn't expect to hear from you."

Who is calling her this early on a Sunday?

"Well, thank you for saying that Paul, but I think we both know that this is no one's fault. I acted like a crazy woman in Asheville. I'm sorry. It's Jeff."

Paul. Jeff. My stomach drops.

"I just don't think that's a good idea." Quiet. Then, "I'm actually out of town this week." More silence. "Yep, you called it. Look, I know this isn't what we wanted, but I think we need to be honest with ourselves." Silence. "It is." Silence. "Take care of yourself." And then the call is over.

A few moments later her door opens and she walks out with her hair piled up in a messy heap on top of her head wearing a long sleep shirt and bare legs. *Good Lord, this woman is killing me.*

"Oh, hey." She rubs her sleepy eyes and crosses her arms. "I thought you'd already be gone."

"Nah. The conference starts at 9:00 a.m."

Something about her demeanor has changed. She seems sad. Is it the call?

"Would you like some coffee?"

"Uh, no thank you. I think I'm going to sit outside for a bit."

She walks out to the balcony with her phone. I wants to go out there, but it doesn't look like she wants company. Instead, I throw on some khaki shorts and a blue golf shirt and brush my teeth and head out to meet Bo.

So my day is spent with the guys who finally seem to relax a little around me. Maybe my better mood has helped them to forget about the binge I went on a few days ago back at the post. Instead of giving me grief, they spend most of the day teasing me about my good-looking roommate. The breakfast buffet is surprisingly good. The day is pretty busy with two sessions in the morning, followed by lunch at the poolside bar, and then two more sessions in the afternoon. The speakers do a great job and it is nice to spend some time with Bo and the old timers away from the post. Most of these sessions don't relate to me at all, nor do I really have much interest in the presentations.

Bo can tell. After the last meeting we end up walking down to the bay and checking out the boats. He motions for me to sit down beside him on the dock. I can tell he wants to talk.

"So, I guess you didn't get much out of this weekend after all," Bo says, sounding defeated.

"That's not necessarily true. This has been a great weekend. Throwing back some cold ones with the guys in the sun. Meeting a new acquaintance. It was exactly what I needed. Thanks for helping to pull me out of my slump Bo."

"Slump?" He looks at me with a serious expression. "We both know it's more than that."

I keep quiet, trying not to engage.

"You're drinking too much. You look like hell. Son, what happened in Kandahar?"

I'm not sure, but I think meeting Brigid has made me want to pull myself up out of this shit. For the first time in two months I don't feel quite as heavy.

"You don't have security clearance," I say.

"Not true. The Department of Defense gave me a confidential level clearance."

"That was in 1972."

"Leave out the details." He nudges me.

"You know Sgt. Mike Vianetti, my buddy from Parris Island?"

"Yeah, I've met him. Great guy. Terrible poker player."

It's true. He could not bluff to save his soul. God, I miss him.

"He's gone."

Bo takes a deep breath and lets it out slowly. "I'm so sorry son. That's a hell of a loss." He doesn't say anything else and neither do I. It has nothing to do with his lack of security clearance. I am too ashamed, too disgusted, to tell him more. We just sit in complete silence watching the boats rock back and forth together. There are very few people I can sit beside like this without things getting awkward. He is giving me time to think things through.

There is a formal dinner this evening at 7:00 p.m. in the main conference hall. After that, everyone will be packing up and heading home. Some will stay the night and leave the following morning. Bo has been hoping I will stay for the rest of the week and take advantage of Larry Butter's timeshare. I guess he thinks being alone in my barracks isn't doing me much good. And hell, he's right.

Although I'm not sure I'd be in any less agony here. From what I overheard this morning, it sounds like Brigid is ending things with a guy named Paul because of a guy named Jeff. I should have known that a girl like her wouldn't be single. I wish I had said something to her before leaving this morning. Anything to let her know how much I had enjoyed spending time with her last night. I spent most of the day anticipating what her reaction would be if I decided to stay for the rest of the week.

Just then the sun comes out from behind a white fluffy cloud and the sea breeze picks up. I take a deep breath. This place is therapeutic.

"You know what? I think I will stay for the rest of the week. Hell, I have nowhere else to be. This place is pretty great."

Bo smiles and pats my knee a few times.

"Good. You know, I gave Larry a call about this timeshare mixup. He was pretty pissed. Said he'd call down here first thing Monday morning and give them an earful."

"Ah, it's no biggie. I just appreciate the hospitality."

I stand up and give Bo a hand. We walk back up to the resort and are weaving our way through the island oasis when I hear a familiar voice.

"Hey Sgt. Balzly."

I turn to see Joe Delicot's daughter, Heather, waving. She has her kids in the pool and is talking to someone who looks familiar. The other woman waves. She is shoulder-deep in the water and is wearing big sunglasses. Her hair is wet. Both of the women are holding drinks. The other woman speaks, "How was your day?"

I do a double take. It's Brigid. She no longer looks sad. I give Bo a look. He smiles and nods back to me and then heads off toward his room to get ready for dinner. I walk over and bent down beside the pool as Brigid says goodbye to her new acquaintance and makes her way to the edge.

"Looks like you've had a good day," I say.

"I have. Everyone here is so friendly." She is definitely a little tipsy.

"I bet." I look at Heather and her kids and smile.

"Hey, can we talk?" she asks. She flashes me that amazing smile which somehow leaves me feeling relieved, like what she has to say is going to work in my favor. The way she is looking at me now, staring up from the pool, is different somehow—different good.

"Sure. Let me grab you a towel."

"Thanks."

That was a mistake. I went to grab a towel off of the rack and turn back around to see her pulling up out of the water. Her red bikini leaves little to the imagination. There are strings tied on each side of her hips. Small triangular pieces covering her breasts do little to conceal how cold she is.

Jesus Christ.

I hand her the towel and she dries off in the sun and then bends her neck to ring out her hair. I see a guy on the other side of the pool staring. I give him a stern look as she slips into her cover up and flip flops. We walk out of the pool area and follow the wide-paved path beneath the palms that wind through the resort.

She takes a deep breath and smiles.

"This place is so beautiful. It is exactly what I needed."

"Honestly, me too."

"Do you know what I was thinking about today?" she asks.

"What's that?"

"You. You've been on my mind all day."

"Me?" *Do you know how that feels?*

"Yeah, I really enjoyed your company last night. This weekend has ended up being pretty great. Which is sort of surprising given what I have going on and so I wanted to say thank you."

"If you don't mind me asking, what do you have going on?"

She takes a deep breath. "Honestly, I'd rather not talk about it. It would kill my buzz."

"That's fine. I was just…" I press my lips together and squint my eyes. "I'm just trying to figure you out."

"Ha!" She lets out a laugh, "I thought you already had me pretty much figured out."

"Yes, but… never mind."

"What? What were you going to say?"

"I was just wondering if you are seeing anyone." There. I said it.

"I have been seeing someone for about six months."

Why do these words feel like someone just punched me in the stomach, hard?

She continues, "We actually broke up this week. Paul was a nice guy, but just not a good match for me."

I exhale. I didn't realize that I had been holding my breath.

"Well, that's good news."

"Is it?" she asks sarcastically.

"Yes." I stop walking. She stops too.

"And why is that?"

"Because I would like to ask you out."

She smiles. "What did you have in mind?"

Brigid

I called Piper last night and whispered from inside my walk-in-closet (like a teenager) telling her all about the amazing Sgt. Balzly and our evening together. She totally freaked out about the girl falling off the pier. I knew she would. She made me retell the story for Dave on speakerphone. I admitted how difficult it had been to keep my guard up around Balzly because he seemed so genuine. She did her best to convince me that I was reading all of his signals correctly and that I should just be myself.

So I fell asleep last night to the quiet strumming of a guitar (he didn't tell me he could play!) and woke up to freaking Paul. I'm so pissed that he called. Hopefully he at least got some closure. After the words we had, I am unlikely to hear from him again. Then, I'm bombarded the second I walk into the kitchen with Sgt. Balzly standing shirtless at the coffee pot, offering to pour me a cup. His dark hair was disheveled. *If he stays I'll never survive the week.* Something is wrong. His body doesn't belong here with me. It belongs in some museum exhibit of the Greek gods.

I had to escape to the balcony and wait until he left for fear that I'd jump straight into his arms and he'd wind up being called to testify against me at the school board meeting.

I spend the day bumming around the resort, checking out the spa, and then tanning by the pool. The resort is comping all of my food and drinks to try to make up for the mix up with the room, which is actually pretty incredible since I am flat broke. I read a little more of my book and drink two pina coladas, all while wondering about Sgt. Balzly. There seems to be a connection between us. Does he feel it?

Later in the afternoon I start up a conversation with a friendly woman who is in the pool with her kids. She mentions that she drove her father down for the conference.

"Oh. My resort roommate is at the conference this week," I tell her.

"Resort roommate?"

"Just for this weekend. It's a long story. We got double-booked."

"Who is it?"

"Um, Sergeant Balzly?"

She looks at me and smiles. "Yeah, I know Balzly. He's friends with my Dad. He spends a lot of time at the Camp Hill post when he isn't deployed. Sometimes they get him behind the bar. Mostly, he just hangs out with the old timers."

"Gotcha."

"A lot of the women I know would consider him quite the catch."

To hell with those women. The thought of any woman laying a hand on Balzly makes me want to throat punch someone. Her face is begging for the details on our relationship. But, it's not a relationship. We're just sharing a condo for a couple of days.

I smile. "If that's true why aren't any of them dating him?"

"I'm sure they would. According to my dad, he never gives any woman the time of day. He was dating someone much younger at one point, some college girl, but I'm not sure if they're still together."

"Hmmm. Interesting." I act as if I couldn't care less when in all actuality, my ribcage feels like it has splintered open and is now stabbing into my heart and other vital organs. How is it that this guy is having such an effect on me when I've just met him two days ago? Ah, but what a weekend. It is so refreshing to find someone that you actually connect with. Someone interesting that you genuinely want to get to know better. I hadn't really thought to ask Bo if Sgt. Balzly was dating anyone. He didn't seem like the kind of guy who would ask me to join him alone for dinner twice if he had a girlfriend. But, considering my record with men, I could be wrong.

So I order another drink and talk more with Heather and then the next thing I know she's hollering, "Hey, Sgt. Balzly," and waving him over. He's looking at me like he doesn't know me. It's unnerving. I open my mouth to speak and he finally smiles. I wade over to the edge of the pool to say hello. My heart is in my throat at the thought of him with a college girl. So when he bends down near the side of the pool I follow the advice of Piper (be proactive) and ask if we can talk.

Our leisurely stroll around the resort ends at the door to our condo. Our conversation ends with him inviting me to dinner again. Apparently, the conference is ending with a semi-formal dinner and award ceremony and he asks if I will join him. And this is exactly what I want, but it's also kind of awkward. The dinner is at 7:00 p.m., and it's 4:45 p.m., and this is typically when I would call Piper or another girlfriend over to help me wash all the chlorine out of my hair and pick out the perfect dress and shoes. I'd do my makeup and be looking like a knockout before the guy ever arrived. But, in this situation, we are walking through the door together and he is going to know if I freak out. I have to look amazing without him knowing how hard I had to work to get there.

So I'm slipping out of my flip flops and grabbing a water bottle from the fridge and nonchalantly asking him about what he is going to wear tonight?

He's sitting on the couch, crossing his leg with one arm behind his head looking just about as sexy as any man has any business looking. He turns and smiles at me and says, "I brought a suit."

I walk over and sit on the coffee table in front of him. My heart is pounding, but I need to get this out. "You asked me earlier if I was dating anyone."

"I did," his eyebrows furled.

"Heather mentioned that she thought you were dating someone and I just wanted to let you know that I'm not the kind of woman who would go out with someone else's boyfriend."

He takes a deep breath and sits up. He reaches out and takes my hand in his, rubbing my knuckles and becoming very serious and sincere. "I was dating someone, but I ended it two months ago."

"Was it serious?" I ask.

"It was seriously screwed up."

That answer takes me by surprise. He leans in so that our faces are close and looks me straight in the eye and says, "Just so you know. I'm not the kind of man who would be with more than one woman at the same time."

I look down at my hand and know this is the start of something. I can feel it.

And at this moment, I make up my mind. Jeff isn't going to control me. His accusations were false. This was his problem. And if the school board can't see it, then forget it. I am a brilliant psychologist who is great with kids and can work anywhere. I'm not going to hide who I am around men in fear of another weasel like Jeff. And I'm not going to let this interesting, intelligent, thoughtful, and sexy man that is holding my hand right now think that I am anything less than who I always have been.

So two hours later, I come out of my room finally feeling like myself again. I am wearing the dress I planned to wear when Paul was going to take me to Red Stag Grill—the really nice restaurant inside the Grand Bohemian Hotel. I spend a second imagining how that fancy dinner would have gone and am so relieved that I am wearing it to dinner with Balzly instead.

I didn't have much of a choice. It is the only thing I brought that is semi-formal. It is champagne colored with a short-ruffled skirt and a plunging neckline. The dress is backless except for the thick band that ties together to form a bow midway and the small straps tied around the back of my neck. I bought this dress for a girl's trip to New Orleans last summer and it was a hit. Paired with my dressy, strappy heels and the S wave curls in my hair, I am hoping to make an impression.

Sgt. Balzly is waiting for me in the kitchen wearing a suit that fits him too well and releasing pheromones that made me want to rip it off of him. I'm halfway through this fantasy when the sound of two glasses clinking steal my attention. He pours us both a shot. His chin drops and his eyes travel up and down my body. *He is unraveling me.*

"You are breathtaking. Truly. This was a good idea." He smiles approvingly.

"Was it?" I muse. "Because it looks like we could get into some trouble tonight," I say in the flirty voice he hasn't yet heard directed towards him.

He rubs his jawline and smiles. He lifts his glass and I follow suit.

"What are we toasting to?" I ask.

"To Larry Butters," Balzly says.

"To Larry Butters."

We both take a shot. It burns in the good way that liquid courage does.

"Are you ready to go to dinner?"

"Yes Sergeant."

It is quite a trek to the conference center in my heels, but I don't mind. Sgt. Balzly reaches out for my hand in the elevator and doesn't let go until we are outside the doors of the ballroom checking in at the table lined with name tags. He picks his up quickly and slips it in his pocket, but not before I could see his first name.

He opens one of the double doors and I am a little taken aback. The wall across the room from us is almost completely made of glass and the view of the sound is spectacular. The room itself is elegant; tall ceilings with ivory material draped in a crisscross pattern, accenting five large crystal chandeliers that hang from the ceiling like dangly earrings. Two dozen round tables with white floor-length linens and the most beautiful flower arrangements in the center fill the space. There is a brilliant display of appetizers, a bar along the back wall, and a stage where a live band plays dinner music.

"This is beautiful," I say to Balzly as he begins leading me across the room toward a table where Bo sits with Joe, his daughter Heather, and another older couple I don't recognize.

"You are beautiful."

The words catch me by surprise and I stop walking and look at him trying to read his face.

"What?" he asks. "Did I say something wrong?"

He seems concerned.

"No. Sorry. It's just, I've heard that line before."

His eyebrows immediately look worried and he reaches out and touches my wrist, but before he can speak I continue, "But, it sounded different coming from you."

"Is that a good thing?"

I smile. "Yes."

You are beautiful. Those are the last words Jeff spoke to me before he forced himself on me that night in my office. Ugh. *Don't go there.* Thinking of my current work situation makes me want to scream, so I force it to the back of my mind and focus instead on this last evening with Balzly.

The shot of whiskey has kicked in so it is easy to be myself. Balzly introduces me to everyone at the table and by the time the appetizers are gone I have them all eating out of the palm of my hand. I'm hilarious. Have I told you that yet? My brother Dave doesn't want to admit it, because he thinks he is the funny one, but really I am the one with the power to captivate.

"I'm sure everyone is interested to know just how you happened across this magnificent creature Sgt. Balzly," Joe asks. Heather smiles and winks at me. The other couple at the table who were introduced earlier as Dave and Patricia turn to look at Balzly.

"I'd say the timeshare gods are smiling down on me." Balzly replies with a smile. Joe looks at Heather, confused.

I explain, "Our condo for the week got double-booked. He's had to put up with me the whole weekend."

"Poor guy. That's terrible," Joe says sarcastically. "I'll be happy to take her off your hands, Sergeant," he says, reaching out for my hand. *He is so stinking cute.* I can't refuse him, even though he's leading me to the dance floor before dinner has even been served and there is currently no one else dancing. This is the exact situation that would mortify Paul. But Balzly finds it endearing. I can feel his eyes on me.

"Are you enjoying your vacation so far?" Joe asks as we dance.

"I am. This place is amazing. How about you? How was the conference?"

"Oh, good, good. Plus, it's always nice to spend some time with my daughter and grandkids."

"I bet."

"Our Sgt. Balzly is something else, isn't he?"

"He sure is. Did you hear that he saved a young woman who fell backward off the pier last night? Jumped right in after her."

"Doesn't surprise me. Our Balzly is one hell of a man. You two go together nicely."

"Well. I don't know about that. We just met."

"Trust me. I have an eye for these types of things. And I can tell by the way he is looking at you right now that you have him captivated."

"Maybe so, but he's leaving tonight." I wrinkle my nose.

"Nah. That boy's not going anywhere. Can you blame him?"

The lead singer announces that dinner is being served and Joe escorts me back to our table.

Dinner is delicious. (I had pork tenderloin, stuffed spinach and cheese tortellini, and a salad.) Balzly ordered the same. *Sweet!* My favorite part was when he said, "I'll have what the lady is having." Afterward, the American Legion board members are introduced and then the president is invited up to recognize different post leaders for their outstanding service. He spends some time talking about this year's Charles B. Rigsby Volunteer of the Year Award recipient, which I have a feeling is a pretty big deal because it is one of the last awards given. Everyone is on the edge of their seat when he finally reads the name—Bo Gibson!

As clapping erupts, Bo turns to shake hands with those seated around him, Balzly included, before heading up to the stage to receive his award. The entire room is on its feet cheering for Bo. The people at the table beside us stand to join in the excitement just as a member of the waitstaff walks behind them carrying a tray filled with empty glasses.

In slow motion I watch as everything that hangs in the balance violently hits the floor, shattering into hundreds of pieces and letting off the most terrible high-pitched clinking sound. Almost as audible is the shocked inhale that everyone in the room seems to take at the same time.

Nearly as soon as the glass shatters so does Bazly's face. What was filled with excitement just a moment before haa turned dark. Something is wrong. He is no longer clapping. His eyelids are lower and pulled close together. He is staring right through me. His lips are tightened. Beads of sweat are forming on his forehead. I know better than to reach out and touch him.

That had startled him last night. Instead, I turn my head towards him and say gently, "James. You are okay. You are safe. Take a deep breath. Look around you. You are with your friends. I am right here."

After a few moments, James looks at me and sees me. The realization of where he is kicks in. He looks up to see Bo taking the stage. I can see his heart racing from beneath his white dress shirt. His breathing is heavy. He is squinting his eyes.

"Let's go outside and get some fresh air," I suggest as I reach my hand out to him. He doesn't take it. Instead, he stands and walks across the room to the glass doors that open up onto a patio as I follow.

The night has cooled off some making the temperature sort of perfect. James takes a few deep breaths and runs his fingers through his hair.

"I'm sorry about that. I don't…." He takes another deep breath and then admits, "I don't do well with loud noises. It's stupid. Sorry."

I sit down at a patio table and motion for him to join me. He does.

"Where do you go?"

"Hmm?"

"Where does your mind go when you hear loud noises?"

"We don't have to talk about this now."

"That's true. But, I'd like to know. It may help to tell someone."

James sits down beside me and takes a few more deep breaths. We sit in silence for several minutes and I can feel him weighing his options. In the end, he decides to talk.

"It goes to Afghanistan."

I nod in understanding and give him my best psychologist look. You know, the one that says, "spill it."

He takes his time. His words came out slowly and quietly as if there could be someone spying on us.

"The Province of Kandahar is in the Taliban-contested area of southern Afghanistan. My platoon had been stationed there for two months when one of our NSA handlers brought in a letter that his asset on the ground left during a dead drop."

I think my face must have betrayed me, because he feels the need to stop his story and explain his intelligence jargon and that Russia has been secretly working for the past several years to bolster the Taliban in an attempt to undermine the Afghan government. *I wish I kept up with current affairs. I hate the news.*

"I see." I try to sound encouraging.

"As soon as the intelligence came in I was called to the command center. It was the worst possible moment. I was a mess." He stops and looks up at me, deciding if he wants to keep sharing. With his elbows resting on his knees and his chin in his folded hands he continues.

"I had just found out something upsetting about Caroline. I wasn't in a good place, to say the least."

Caroline.

"Were you able to make sense of the communication?"

"It appeared to be nothing more than a letter written from a young man who was away at university to his uncle. It was written in Pashto."

If he tells me he speaks fluent Pashto I will truly begin questioning my life's purpose.

"There was a message hidden inside the letter—a location and time for a weapons exchange."

"Weapons exchange?"

"The US has suspected for some time now that the Russians have been arming the Taliban with anti-tank guided missiles. My team had been targeting Russia's communication systems and anticipated a weapons exchange. This was the information we needed. So I jumped on it."

"Wow." I look up at the sky full of stars. And then I look at him, sitting here in his dashing black sports coat over a crisp white shirt and black slim tie. And I'm here next to him in my cocktail dress. Through the windows to the ballroom I can make out the shapes of people dancing. A soft ballad is escaping into the night. I'm thinking how absolutely bizarre it must be for him—to be here on such a beautiful night when weeks ago he was tracking black market weapon trades in the Middle East.

"We had six hours to prepare for the op. Our plan was to take two teams, one to guard the perimeter of the compound where the drop was going to take place and the other to raid. I was on a rooftop across the street staring through my M4 night vision scope. There wasn't any movement on the street. The raid team entered, but everything was quiet. Too quiet. I knew in my gut that something was wrong."

He stops talking.

"What?" I ask. "What was wrong?" I am on the edge of my seat.

"I thought back to the handwritten letter I had analyzed earlier in the day." He takes a deep quivering breath. "And then I saw it."

"What?"

His eyes meet mine for the first time since we walked outside and I can see the pain in them. I can see how hard he is trying to hold back tears.

"My mistake." His voice is barely audible.

I reach out and place my hand on the center of his back and he begins to shake. It starts small but works its way up to his chest. He exhales. A few minutes later he continues, but his voice has gotten much quieter.

"I was looking so hard I didn't see what was right in front of me. The last sentence of the letter read, 'may god give you health brother.'"

So I'm sitting here in my pretty dress holding James Bond in my arms and wondering what in the hell is so suspicious about that when he explains to me that Afghans only refer to each other as brothers if they are addressing someone of the same age. A young man away at University writing to his uncle back home would have taken a more respectful and formal tone.

"Okay. So what does that mean?"

"Our asset wrote that sentence because he wanted it to stand out. It should have jumped out at me. It was meant to be a warning. He was wishing us good health."

"How is that a warning?"

"He was wishing us good health because he knew we were in danger. The location and time we decoded weren't signaling a drop. They were signaling an attack. He was trying to warn us of an attack."

As I am beginning to make sense of the story, James stands and walks a few feet away staring into the night.

"I ordered an immediate evacuation. The team came running out of the compound as the entire place blew up. Our asset had been made, but not before uncovering a plot to blow up one of the Afghan government's largest weapons cache."

Tears are stinging my eyes. I stand and walk to him, wrapping my arms around him from behind. "And your team?"

"American Soldier Killed During Failed Operation—Bad Intelligence to Blame." He turns in my arms and buries his face in my shoulder. We stay like this for a long time. I am devastated for him. His loss. His guilt. The trauma of it all. But at the same time it feels so good to be the one holding him. The one comforting him. The one that he finally opened up to. The one.

Finally he pulls away, uncomfortable with his own vulnerability—his own grief. He runs his fingers through his hair and takes a deep breath.

"I'm sorry. I don't know why I just told you all that."

I reach down and slip out of my heels, picking them up with one hand and slipping my other hand into his. "Let's go for a walk."

The way he looks at me is so endearing. Like he is grateful that I understand—there is no way he can go back in that ballroom.

It is a beautiful night to stroll the grounds and we take our time weaving through the lush landscape.

"It's inevitable. No one talks about it, but everyone knows it. When you're doing some of the most dangerous work in the world and dealing with the most dangerous characters—it's inevitable. But, not Mike. I never thought it would be Mike."

I squeeze his hand.

"We started out together. Met at Parris Island during basic, chose the same MOS, ended up on the same team. I don't remember the last time I ran an op without him. I knew before it blew up that it was going to happen. I realized my mistake, but no matter how loud I screamed orders for the evac, how fast I moved in, it was too late. Mike's gone and it was entirely because of me."

I can feel his heartbreak. I want to fix it. I want to heal him. And in that moment of grief and vulnerability only two words pop into my head—conjugal prayer.

When I was a kid it was easy to tell when a phone call brought bad news.

My Mom would stretch the phone cord from the living room to her bedroom (in the middle of Jeopardy) to talk in private. One night the bad news came when Piper was sleeping over. We couldn't take the suspense so we plastered our heads up against the door. *My uncle had lost his job and they weren't sure how they were going to make ends meet.* I'll never forget what my mother said. "Conjugal prayer! Fixes everything. All he needs is some conjugal prayer. Just love him through it." She sounded so upbeat and confident.

Piper and I exchanged glances and smiled and pretended to know what she was talking about. From that moment on our fix for every life problem was conjugal prayer. Bike tire flat? Conjugal prayer! Failed a test? Conjugal prayer! Didn't make the team? Conjugal prayer!

It wasn't until later in life that we realized what she was suggesting. We never laughed so hard.

But it is here, in this moment with James, that I finally understand my mom's advice—how loving someone through it, prayerfully, is sometimes all a person could do. I want to take that broken piece inside of him and add to it my own and make something between us feel whole again.

Instead, I say what I always do in these situations. "I'm so sorry that this happened. I can't imagine how difficult this is for you."

"It's like I can't move past that moment. And I know I don't deserve to. I can't sleep. Every time I close my eyes I dream about it. And then sometimes everything is fine and then I hear something or see something and I'm suddenly right back in that moment—trying to stop the inevitable and being completely incapable of doing so."

"It helps to have someone to talk to," I say. "What you're going through isn't uncommon. There are lots of things that can bring back strong memories and trigger your brain to make you feel like you are back in that exact moment. It must be terribly painful to relive this again and again. How do you cope?"

James looks at me, "Not well."

Balzly

*J**ames.** She had called me James. She must have seen my nametag. No one calls me James anymore—not since I became a Marine. There was something in her voice when she said it that made me feel more like myself than I have in a really long time. Maybe that is why I decided to open up to Brigid. And miraculously, it seemed to help. She was so easy to talk to that by the end of our conversation I felt like the weight of the world had been lifted off of my shoulders. I'm not sure if that makes any sense. Someone finally knew what I had done—how badly I had screwed up. I had said it out loud. I had been trying my best to shake this, reminding myself that I can handle anything. When in reality, my survival has more to do with the large amounts of alcohol I've consumed and less to do with any level of mental toughness I presume to have. When Brigid Taylor tucked her arm in mine, I felt like maybe I could survive this; Caroline, Mike, being stuck inside my head.

After our talk on the patio I was mentally drained. I worried that if our evening together continued, I would just mess it up even more. I think she could read my mind because she yawned and suggested we go for a walk, complaining that her feet were too tired for dancing. I felt bad, especially because she looked so damn beautiful. I reminded myself not to call her that again. It seemed to upset her. Man, I would have liked to have danced with her, to have felt her body in my arms. Instead, she held me while I whimpered on like a complete idiot. Not exactly what I was going for. Any interest she had in me went out the window when she recognized me for what I am—damaged goods.

When we finally made it back to our condo she thanked me for dinner and gave me a quick, tight squeeze before tucking into her room. She had left her phone on the counter. I stayed in the kitchen nursing another whiskey when a text message from her friend Piper came through on her phone. I read it before I realized that I probably shouldn't have.

"How was your evening with Prince Charming?"

I wanted to respond, "Total nightmare. This guy has some serious issues to work through." Instead, I took my tie off and picked up my glass. I unbuttoned my shirt and went outside for some fresh air.

On the balcony I heard music—someone was singing. I searched the night, but it was late, and there was no one out and about. *The music was coming from her bedroom.* The drapes were pulled, so I pressed my ear to the glass sliding door that led to the master suite. I'm standing there, picturing her on the other side of the glass, lying in bed, wearing that oversized t-shirt and listening to Jewel sing "You Were Meant for Me". She falls asleep with music on. She's listening to nineties soft rock. *I think I could love this girl.*

I woke up this morning ready to move on—to begin putting the pieces of what remains of my future back together. And it begins with an apology to Brigid. I ruined our entire evening. So I'm making her breakfast, and will know the minute she walks out of her room whether or not I still have a chance.

Her face will help me make the decision—either leave today or stay for the week. Regardless, when I do leave, I won't go back to base.

It's 9:00 a.m. when I finally hear her wake up and turn on the shower. I am making bacon, eggs and toast. I pour two glasses of juice and set the table outside for breakfast. Then, I sit on the couch with my cup of coffee staring mindlessly at the local news and wait. At 9:24 a.m. she walks out of her room wearing navy blue shorts and a striped tank top. Her hair is still wet but braided down one side. She has no makeup on. Her feet are bare. She looks directly at me.

"Morning, James."

And there it is. The smile. *She's mine.*

"Morning. How did you sleep?" I ask.

"Pretty blissfully actually."

"Good. Come outside." I stand up and slide open the heavy door leading to the balcony.

"What's all this?" She is genuinely surprised, which pleases me more than I anticipated.

"An apology breakfast."

"Not necessary," she begins to say.

"Last night did not go as I had hoped," I admitted, pulling a chair out for her.

"Really? Because it went exactly as I had," she said nonchalantly.

I am standing on one side of the table with both hands on the back of her chair reading her face and analyzing her body language.

"It's obvious that something has been bothering you. You trusted me enough to share an important part of yourself. I was happy to be a friend."

Friend.

I had hoped she couldn't see my lungs explode in my chest as I exhaled slowly or that my face was the epitome of unrequited love. *Okay, yep, she could tell.* Immediately she was walking towards me. Her hazel eyes locked on mine. She didn't stop until she had her arms around my lower back and her head on my chest—on my heart. I wrapped my arms around her. God, she smelled good. Her shampoo was an aphrodisiac. She didn't say anything, but she didn't let go either. This wasn't a friend hug. Not that I had lots of experience with friends hugging me. Not that I really had much experience with female friends. But still, this hug lingered. I dropped my chin to rest on the top of her head.

"Do you know what I think?" she asked, still hugging me.

"What's that?" *I was in paradise.*

"I think you are pretty incredible." She pulled her head off of my chest, released her arms, and leaned up and kissed the place where my neck meets my jawbone.

It sent off a frenzy inside of me and it took every ounce of my being to control it. I wanted this girl badly. Suddenly Caroline and the night at the bar popped into my head and I took a step back and forced myself to sit down at the table.

"Thank you for saying that. Hey, I want to talk to you about something. I came down for the conference, but have no real reason to rush back to base. I was thinking of staying for the rest of the week. I would get my own condo of course. I've imposed on you long enough."

"Oh good. I'm glad you're staying. This place is amazing, but not as much fun when you're alone." She crunches a piece of her bacon and pulls her foot up in her lap.

"I don't know if I'm crashing your party, but you aren't bothering me a bit. Actually, I feel a little bit safer knowing that you are here. I know that sounds silly since I live alone, but I usually have Fitz to protect me." She makes an adorable face.

"Fitz?"

"My bichon frise." She pulls up a picture on her phone of a white fluffy puppy and hands it to me. You can flip through them. There are a few more. I see her dog lying on the back of a gray couch. Her living room has a bright yellow rug and yellow throw pillows. There is a large abstract painting hanging on the wall. The next picture is taken from the porch where large planters are filled with flowers. The puppy is sprawled out in the sun.

"Fitz is cute." I swipe to the next photo and see a close up of Brigid's face as she lies on the grass.

"So are you." I handed her the phone. "Are you sure you don't mind me staying?"

"So long as you don't mind being stuck with me."

"I don't mind," I say.

"Besides, who would feed me if you left? This breakfast is so yummy."

I smile and ask her what I should have asked her on Friday night, instead of assuming I knew every detail of her life. "So, tell me more about yourself. What is your life like?"

She thinks for a second and swallows a bite of toast. "Well, my life is pretty great actually. I had a semi-normal childhood. My parents are Steve and Karen. They live in Edgefield on the east side of Nashville in a blue bungalow where Dave and I were raised. It is an older home with gorgeous architecture and my parents filled it with large pieces of artwork and music and plants. My parents are very visual, creative people. They own their own marketing firm now, but when I was a kid Dad worked and my mother spent most of her time gardening and putting together flower arrangements in my aunt's flower shop. Dave is my only brother. He's a car salesman, which pretty much means he is full of shit and will talk to anyone. We've always been close. My best friend in the world since forever, Piper, married Dave seven years ago and they have three daughters who I adore."

"Do you see your family often?"

"Yeah. Sunday is sort of our day. We go to church together and then have brunch. Sometimes that turns into heading to the farmer's market or the park. Through the week I'm pretty busy. Some nights I cook and some nights I meet friends from the neighborhood for dinner or drinks. I'm only about two miles from work, which is nice because I can bike when the weather is warm."

"You like to bike?"

"I'm not a serious cyclist who trains for races or anything, but I have a nice bike and I like the exercise."

"Well, you're cooler than any teacher I ever had." As soon as the words leave my mouth, her lower lip tucks between her teeth again, and then she's quiet.

I decided to change the subject. "So, how did you meet Paul? Is he a friend from the neighborhood?"

She smiles and lets out a small chuckle.

"Nice pivot to my love life."

I shrugged my shoulders. "Can't a guy be curious?" She finished chewing her bite before responding.

"No. Paul is an insurance adjuster. I met him through a friend."

"So, you just broke up huh?"

"Yes, but there is 0% chance we are getting back together. It wasn't that serious. I guess my friend thought opposites attract, but in this case, not so much. Paul is this really serious kind of guy and super focused and organized, and I am more of a creative, outgoing, sort of a passionate person. We weren't clicking."

I rubbed my jaw and was reminded that I needed to shave when her phone buzzed from the kitchen. *Another text from Piper?*

"Sorry. I better check that. This was delicious, by the way," she said as she collected the plates and headed back inside.

I grabbed our glasses and followed her in and started loading the dishwasher while she checked her phone. A quick text and then she was beside me at the sink, scraping the pan I fried the bacon in.

"Hey, do you want to do something today?" she asked.

"Actually, I was going to see if you wanted to go boating."

"What time were you wanting to go?"

"I figured we could head down to the marina at 11:30."

"Sounds good. Let me finish getting ready."

She is back in her bathroom brushing her teeth when her phone dings again and I can't help but look at the screen as it lights up.

"How was your evening with Prince Charming?" Sun 11:04 p.m.

"Hello?" Mon 10:01 a.m.

"Absolutely perfect." ♥ Mon 10:03 a.m.

"Oh good!" Mon 10:32 a.m.

I am used to this word. *Perfect.* It describes my SAT score and that last kick in the soccer finals senior year. I can speak five languages perfectly and write the perfect essay. I have perfect pitch. I can do a perfect pushup. But Brigid Taylor using that word to describe being with me, well, it feels perfect.

Brigid

He's staying. I knew I wasn't making this up. Bo and the others are leaving, and James is staying, which can only mean one thing—he thinks we might have something here.

Last night was a major breakthrough and I knew I would have to tell Bo, which kind of makes me feel bad in a way because James was so vulnerable and I hate to disrespect that. But, I've treated too many kids with PTSD. I know James needs a support system.

I was awake half the night tossing and turning thinking about how good he looked in that suit and how incredible it felt to be led into a room by him. He shared a part of himself with me that he hasn't even shared with Bo. I debated whether or not I should sneak into his room and slip under the covers beside him. There was something about his vulnerability that was so sexy. In the end, I fell asleep before I could make a fool out of myself. When I woke up to that incredibly sweet breakfast and an invite to go boating my mind was made up. Sgt. James Balzly is a man worth pursuing. But, there was something I needed to do first. I called Bo's room and asked if we could speak privately before he checked out. We agreed to meet in the lobby bar in ten minutes.

I told James I had to grab a few things at the resort market, grab my purse with the envelope full of cash, and head down to meet Bo.

This is so covert and exciting. Too bad I suck at being sneaky. I'm trying to disguise myself at the bar behind a drink menu like a Charlie's Angel, but I probably look more like Melissa McCarthy in that spy movie.

"Hey darlin." Bo comes up to me from behind and scares the shit out of me. I let out a panicked, "Good night!"

"Sorry."

"You scared me. It's fine. I'm okay. I'm so glad I caught you before you left. I need to give this back to you." I get the envelope out of my purse and set it on the bar.

"Why? You didn't discover anything?"

I'm making it my mission to discover everything.

"I actually did. It's just that, it doesn't feel right taking the money. James and I are becoming close." I slide it in his direction.

"I see," he said with a slight smile.

"Well, what do you think is going on with him?"

"I think you are right. He seems to be suffering from post-traumatic stress disorder (PTSD) from an event that happened during his last deployment."

Bo's eyebrows were drawn together. I could tell that confirming his fear was upsetting news to him.

"He confided in me yesterday that one of his fellow Marines didn't make it home. Did you figure out what happened?"

"I did and there is more to it than that."

"Well?"

"We don't have time to get into all of this right now. I told James I was running to the resort market and I'm a terrible liar so he might be suspicious," I say as my eyes dart nervously around the room, "but let me put my contact information in your phone."

He hands me his flip phone and I let out a quiet chuckle as I begin entering my contact info using his numeric keypad.

"Okay, look. It's right here under Brigid. I am going to text myself so that I have your number in my phone. I will try to find a quiet moment to call you this week, but he has decided to stay, so I'm not sure I'll get the chance. If you don't hear from me by the weekend, call me or text me."

My phone buzzes and I know the text came through.

Bo pats me on the knee saying, "Thank you girly. You sure have gone out of your way to help this old man and it is appreciated. I'm glad he's going to stay. That already tells me that he's in a much better place than he was

Wednesday night. Do you think he is going to be okay?"

"I think he will be. His case is mild. With some treatment he can improve his symptoms and learn some coping skills. I'll call you when we can talk in depth."

"Sounds like a plan. Listen, you enjoy the rest of your week in paradise."

"I will," I assure him as I stand and throw my purse around one shoulder and my arms around both of his. We say our goodbyes and he wheels his luggage across the lobby. For some reason I feel sad that Bo is leaving. I've formed a bit of a connection with him and it is weird to think I won't ever see him again.

An hour later James is loading a golf cart with the cooler and I am having a mini freak out about my finances. James said he called down to the marina this morning to reserve a boat, but is it fair for me to assume he is going to pay for it?

I'm sitting on the front seat digging through my bag for my phone so I can pull up my Chase app to see how close I am to reaching my credit card limit when I feel it. Bo put the thick envelope full of cash back in my bag. *That sneaky son of a bitch.*

I am already feeling so incredibly guilty that I ever agreed to this in the first place. Don't get me wrong. Meeting James seems like it could be one of those life changing events that I look back on and recognize as the moment my entire universe pivoted. After everything he shared with me last night and how intimate our friendship has become, I feel like a big jerk that has just taken advantage of him. I'm going to tell him. I'm going to give the money back to Bo, again. But, I think I'll need to wait to see how this boat rental goes down first.

So we are in the bait shop on the pier and James is at the counter in the front signing for the boat (which he completely insisted on paying for) and getting an oral lesson on how to drive it (which he swears later was totally unnecessary) while I am meandering through the aisles checking out all the trinkets for sale. There is a step down into a small room in the back filled with clearance items and I am there turning a rack filled with magnets when a couple of guys walk up and start spinning the rack next to mine. One is kind of skinny and the other is, well, not—but they both look a little rough and smell like a mixture of fish and gasoline. And I'm thinking these guys really don't look like they belong on these private docks when one says, "I found the rack we're looking for."

I look at him. He is wearing sagging jeans and a dirty t-shirt. Both of his arms are tattooed, and he needs a haircut. He is staring directly into my cleavage.

I roll my eyes and turn to leave. The other guy steps into the aisle blocking my exodus.

"If her nipples were any harder they could pierce your other ear," he says to his friend. I let out a disgusted "ugh" and turn back to walk in the other direction but Skinny Tattoo is there and he grabs my arm and is staring down at my breasts. And that's when I realize—he is high as a kite. My heart is in my throat and the feeling returns. I hate this feeling. It's so helpless. I am trapped. And just when I realize that I'm not breathing I hear it.

"Get your hands off of her."

I recognized the voice, but not the tone. I turned around in time to see James' fist connect with the guy's jaw, releasing his grip on my arm, and sending him staggering into a display of sunglasses. James' brows were pulled down and his eyes were wide open, glaring in a way I hadn't seen before. He turned back to Fat Fish Guy who was backing up in the aisle. "Don't you fucking touch her."

His hands were up, feigning innocence. "Dude. We were just messing around."

James reached out and grabbed my hand. "Not with her."

And in a flash I am pulled away, back outside, with his arms around me and his heart pounding audibly and his whispered apology in my ear.

"I am so sorry."

Before I could catch my breath he had scooped up the cooler with the other hand and was ushering me down the dock towards our boat. At the end of the dock he jumped onto one of the speed boats, sat the cooler down, and then turned to reach for my hand. I stepped down and went to wrap my bag around one of the captain's chairs while he fired up the engine and untied the ropes and buoys from the dock.

Thirty seconds later the engine was roaring and we were flying through the no-wake zone and away from the marina. He stood in front of the captain's chair with both hands on the wheel. I studied him quietly. His jawline was stiff. His Carrera sunglasses probably cost more than my entire outfit. They were seductive as hell but were making it very difficult for me to read him. I saw a pair of Under Armour sliders in the front of the boat and looked to see that his feet were bare, which was a nice surprise for some reason.

I am watching the speedometer rise and realize we are flying. The boat is slicing through the waves and my hair is whipping against my shoulders and face. James is speechless but I can see his chest heaving. I'm not sure if he is upset with me for getting in that situation or what, but the dynamic between us has changed and things are suddenly awkward.

After I realize he isn't going to speak to me I focus on the spectacular view. The bay is gorgeous. Every shade of blue dances across the water and into the sky. I rest my chin in my arms on the side of the boat and close my eyes to embrace the sensation of the wind blowing on my face and try to forget about the sick feeling in the pit of my stomach.

I am so pissed right now at those assholes. I am sick of guys thinking they can just manhandle me. I decide to sign up for a self-defense class when I get home when suddenly the engine dies and we aren't moving. I look up to see that we are in the middle of one of the small coves that outline the bay. James' seat is turned towards me. He runs his fingers through his hair and then looks at me, piercing my heart with his eyes.

"Are you okay?" he asks, and it is so sweet that I can hardly stand it. *He is worried about me.*

"Those guys were just being jerks. I'm used to it." He flinches as if I had just slapped him across the face.

"You're not okay. You're shaking."

I look down and realize he was right. I am shaking.

James reaches out and pulls me towards him and in a second I am sitting on his lap resting my head on his shoulder and he is stroking my back and whispering things into my ear like, "It's okay. You're safe now."

I feel the lump rising in my throat but before I can control it the tears come. I know. Idiot. Complete idiot, especially since my crying is not that attractive. Let's call it what it is, ugly. I'm an ugly crier. And I don't even understand why I suddenly have this wave of emotion. Maybe it's that everything with Jeff has me so messed up, or maybe these are tears of joy. *So this is how it feels when a man protects you.*

After a few moments of pure bliss I raise my head and apologize. "I'm sorry. I don't know why I'm crying. I just don't like the way those guys made me feel." There. Chalk one up to honesty.

"It's okay. You have every right to be upset. I hate it when guys act like that. You're safe now."

"Thanks to you."

"I wish I had noticed them messing with you a little sooner."

"That's sweet, but I feel pretty good about your response time." I smile and he wipes the tears from my cheeks.

"Are you ready?"

"Yes." I began to pull away but he turned me around on his lap and put my hands on the wheel and began teaching me how to drive the boat.

His hand rests on top of mine and we push the throttle forward, revving the engine, and steering out of the cove and into the open waters. He's explaining to me all about the kill switch and how to adjust the trim and I am smiling and feeling more alive than I have in a long time.

"Do you know everything about everything?" I tease him.

"No. Of course not."

"Really, because it seems that way so far."

He laughs out loud. "I understand engines," he says as humbly as he can.

I smile. "Teach me about engines."

"Engines require three things; compression, air, and fuel." I listen as he explains the inner workings of the engine and the difference between internal and external combustion engines. He has a knack for taking something difficult and making it sound easy to understand. I love the way he knows

86

everything but doesn't make me feel like he's smarter than me. I mean the guy has cooked for me, poured his heart out to me, apologized to me, saved me from a couple of creeps, and gone out of his way to plan surprises for me. Suddenly my heart feels like it could burst out of my chest. I am still sitting on his lap. My hands are on the wheel and his hands are on mine. I can feel his breath on my shoulder. And I wish that I was the kind of woman who could have sat there on his lap, feeling his breath tickle the back of my neck, and debate whether or not this relationship is professionally unethical. But, I'm not.

"The basic principle behind a reactionary engine is Newton's Third Law." I pull back on the throttle until we come to a slow stop, then twist sideways in his lap. Our faces are inches apart.

"Basically if you blow something with enough force through the back side of the engine it will push the front end forward."

Suddenly, I need my lips on his. So I risk it. Everything. I push his sunglasses to the top of his head and try to read his face. His eyes are piercing mine and he swallows. I bite my lower lip and look at his mouth, but before I can move in, his lips are on mine. Soft. Slow. Perfect. Gentle, but full. Heat rises from my stomach to my chest. His hand grips my knee and the other is caressing the back of my neck so softly I think I'm melting. I wrap my hands around the back of his head and nestle them in his hair. I wasn't sure if I had dreamt this moment into existence or if it was really happening. It seemed so unlike any kiss I'd had before. Then as quickly as his lips were on mine, they were gone and I was on the dark side of the moon.

"I'm sorry." He says as he pulls away from me. Suddenly his hands are nowhere to be found. "I shouldn't have done that. I'm sorry." He turns his head to look out over the water. Every rising emotion in my chest just fell, the way my stomach does on a roller coaster. Why am I still sitting on his lap? I take two deep breaths, but he is still staring across the water away from me so I stand and walk to the front of the boat, anything to avoid sitting in this awkwardness. I act busy digging around in the cooler for a drink before laying back on a bench seat in the front with a water bottle. The boat is bobbing lifelessly in the middle of the open water when I hear James exhale and make a move to come and sit on the bench seat opposite of me. His elbows were on his knees and his head in his hands again. I had seen this posture before.

"I'm not sorry that I kissed you." He looked up at me and rubbed his jaw. "That was incredible."

And I can see in his eyes that he meant it and breathed a quiet sigh of relief.

"I just," he stumbles to find the right words. "I think you should know that I know what's going on."

Shit! Shit! Shit!

"I don't know what you're talking about."

Did I tell you that I'm a terrible liar? If Piper were here right now she'd be pointing out that my face has turned three shades brighter and I'm ending my sentence with a frontal lisp.

James reaches out for my hand and begins playing with my knuckles. "I know you're not a teacher. I know that you're a psychologist and I think I can guess what you are doing here."

And there it is. I feel like I've been punched in the stomach. I'm bracing for another impact when I look up at his face, but he doesn't seem angry, which is weird, so I'm thinking maybe he is willing to hear me out.

"I can explain." But, I can't. There is no excuse for my behavior. What I've been doing is completely unethical—accepting an obscene amount of money from a complete stranger, taking on a client without their consent, and then letting him stick his tongue in my mouth—and liking it. I've crossed a line.

"You don't have to explain anything. I think I can put two and two together."

"What do you mean?"

"I googled you. I found your picture on the student support services site for MNPS. You're a child psychologist with the words "status pending" beside your name. I know something upsetting has happened to you—you've said as much. It must be work related. I scrolled through the rest of the staff pictures and that's when I saw him."

"Who?"

"Jeff McAdams."

"How did you...?"

"I'm trained to read people. And that guy has 'douchebag' written all over him. Look, something obviously happened and I just regret kissing you without asking your permission first."

I don't know if I'm more relieved that James is still in the dark about my deal with Bo or impressed that he was able to deduct this on his own.

"I'm not sure what you're thinking happened." I said as my mind raced.

"I can guess. I'm good at reading between the lines, remember. After seeing your physical reaction to those guys in the bait shop, I'm thinking something must have happened with your boss."

I look the other way, out across this beautiful day and wonder how something so ugly could have caught up with me. I can't escape it.

James comes to sit at the end of my seat and lifts my feet onto his lap. It is such a sweet gesture that my eyes are beginning to tear up again.

"What happened?"

"Pour me a glass of wine."

He reaches down into the cooler for the amateur charcuterie board that we had thrown together and two glasses while I ditch my water bottle. He pours us both a sweet red.

"What happened?"

I take a long swig, then another. When I feel my head begin to swim a little I begin.

"About three weeks into the school year I assessed an eight year old boy and diagnosed him with Asperger's Syndrome. It's a neurodevelopmental disorder. AS kids find it difficult to communicate and fit into social situations. It wasn't until I met with his parents that I put two and two together. His father was the superintendent of MNPS—my boss' boss. I was super nervous about having to deliver the news of the diagnosis because it can be pretty upsetting. His ex-wife sobbed and he sat stone faced and listened as I explained the tests I conducted and the behaviors I observed. They were upset, but couldn't disagree with my observations. They had experienced them. They were desperate for solutions.

I began working with their son twice a week on cognitive behavioral therapy. I also suggested family therapy and was surprised when only Jeff

89

showed up to my sessions. I had a gut feeling that something was wrong, but I told myself that lots of the families I worked with were one parent households and that his ex-wife must not be on board with therapy or maybe her schedule didn't allow for it. We began meeting once a week in my office, which is on the third floor of the admin building.

After a couple of weeks he started stopping by unannounced, always with a question for me, or an issue that came up with his son that he really needed my opinion on. It was kind of awkward because that's not really how my department runs. We don't usually do drop-ins, but I figured since he was the super, it was okay."

I look up to see James holding my feet in his lap. His thumbs are rubbing tiny circles around my ankles and he is staring at my toenails. I can see the wheels spinning in his head, but I can't tell what he's thinking.

"Our HR department plans a big back to school bash for faculty and staff every Labor Day weekend. This year it was at the Bell Tower, which is sort of this historic church that has been transformed into a modern venue. So there were like 700 people there, mostly female teachers, and they had food and a cash bar and a great band. I was on the dance floor with my group of work friends when Jeff shows up and sort of works his way into our circle and hands me a drink. And this is where Paul thinks I went wrong, but I accepted it. In a moment of pure awkwardness, the song changed and a couple of my friends went to use the bathroom. I was left with just him and he was all over me. And I am totally buzzed, but still thinking this is completely inappropriate. Ugh. God, I can still feel his breath on the back of my neck. When the song was over I made an excuse to go find my friends, but I could feel his eyes on me all night, and not in a good way. It was a red flag.

When our family therapy meeting came around the next week he acted completely normal. His son started joining our sessions and I was seeing some real progress.

Then it happened. My big mistake. A couple of weeks later I emailed him to see if he could stop by before the end of the week. I had gotten some observational feedback from his son's teachers that reported some real growth and I was hoping to share the good news and go over some adjustments I wanted to make moving forward. He had emailed me back Friday morning and said he had a meeting with some board members at 5:00 and would I still be around after for a quick chat. I dreaded having to stay late on a Friday but there is so much paperwork in my line of work that I am constantly behind. So I spent the afternoon and evening buried in it, playing catch up. Before I knew it, it was 8:30 and the lights on the third floor had been turned off for the night, except for my office. So I am packing up my things and thinking I will just catch him next week when he bursts in the door. It's obvious that he is tanked. He sits down on the couch in my office and I take a seat at the other end. I start in on the news I wanted to share with him and he suddenly interrupts and says, 'How do you do it?' And I'm like, 'How do I do what?' And the next thing I know he is sliding towards me on the couch and he says, 'Fix my kid? Fix everything?' I could smell the bourbon on his breath. Every part of my body tensed up. I felt super uncomfortable so I'm trying to blow past the awkward moment by saying, 'Just another day at the office.' I tried to get up, but as I was beginning to lift off the couch his hand reached out and landed on my knee and squeezed."

I looked up at James then and he was sitting perfectly still, my feet still in his lap, listening intently and staring at the small circles he was still rubbing into my ankles. I take another sip of wine.

"So Jeff is telling me how much he appreciates my work and I am trying to read the situation and I can't tell if he is coming on to me or if he is just feeling like we totally bonded as friends throughout what has probably been a pretty emotional time for him, dealing with his son's issues and all. But then, the knee pat turns into him gripping my leg and his hand sliding up as he leaned in to press his lips against mine. And he says, 'You are beautiful,' and I tried to pull forward, to get up, but he leaned into me, pushing me back. I thought I was going to throw up. Before I could even scream for him to stop, his lips were clobbering mine. I felt like I was drowning. It was all I could do at that moment to catch my breath. I pushed his shoulders back and he looked at me with this face that I'll never forget and said, 'You know you want this,' and the next thing I knew his hand was sliding up beneath my skirt. I screamed for him to get off and finally kneed him in the balls as hard as I could and ran out of my office. I didn't stop running until I was out of the building and several blocks away. I had left my purse and phone in my office. I had to pry open the side window of my dining room and climb on a bucket to get back into my house. I took a shower but I couldn't get the smell of him off of me. Bourbon and expensive cologne. I stayed up half the night writing everything down. I typed up a full report of all of my encounters with him and took it to the HR department the first thing Monday morning. Instead of support I was handed an envelope. Inside of it was a letter saying that an accusation against me had been filed stating that I had acted unprofessionally by offering sexual favors to an administrator in exchange for a promotion. It was his word against mine. The school board had already been notified and I was placed on leave while a thorough investigation could be conducted. My paychecks stopped coming. I had to hire a personal attorney and put a huge retainer down. I'm getting nowhere. I may lose my job over this, while he walks free to do this to some other poor woman."

I opened my eyes. I hadn't realized they were shut. James waited a moment to make sure I was finished and then began calmly coercing more details from me.

"What is your lawyer saying?"

"Not much, apparently patience is required. He helped me document it by filling out a report with the police. He filed a civil suit against Jeff. I think that pissed Jeff off even more, but my lawyer said it would be better to file before Jeff did."

"He was right. That was smart," James agreed.

I went on to tell James all about how I was interviewed by members of our HR department and the non-partisan committee that deals with these types of issues in the district. Apparently they might also be reaching out to other people in my department.

"You don't deserve this, especially after everything you did to help his son."

"Thank you for saying that. It's so unnerving to think that someone could make up a lie about you at any time. I still feel threatened by him. The thing is, I love my job and I'm good at it. I would absolutely hate losing it, but I know I could find work, maybe something with a private practice. What I can't stand is the lingering feeling that this whole situation has left me with."

"Which is?"

I take a deep breath, not sure I want to share everything, but there is something in the way that he is looking at me right now and so I continue.

"Paul said maybe I need to tone it down. And I'm thinking maybe he's right. I can be a little much. I'm outgoing and passionate and friendly and I treat everyone like I've known them for years and I worry that in some small way I invited this upon myself."

James gently sits my feet back down on the bench seat and stands up. He reaches out his hand for me and I take it. He pulls me up and I think he might kiss me once more, but he doesn't. He simply puts his arms around me and pulls me into his embrace. His chin rests on my shoulder and I can feel his head nodding back and forth as he says, "This isn't about you. This is about him. Trust me. I've been around. I know guys like this."

He keeps his arms around me, but pulls back a little so that he can look down at me. Again, I think he is going to kiss me and I'm standing there realizing there isn't anything I want more in the entire world than his lips on mine. But, he doesn't lean in. He simply looks at me with those piercing brown eyes, slightly squinted, and says, "He should be ashamed to call himself a man."

Balzly

I t's been raining all night. Storming actually. I should know. I have been sitting on the balcony watching the lightning crack and listening to thunder roll across the bay. Sometimes I do my best thinking in the rain.

When I was eight years old my parents drove me north to spend the day with some doctors who were going to "help us learn more about my special brain." It was a long drive and it stormed the entire way. I was complaining and asking when we would arrive when my mother told me to look out the window and think about what I had learned at school so I would have something to talk to the doctor about. This was before kids were handed ipads to keep them occupied and before headrests had built in flat screens. So "think" is exactly what I did. I sat in the back seat of my parents Subaru for four hours and thought about everything I had ever learned at school.

My mom had read an article about a couple of doctors who worked with gifted kids and one day later I was on the waiting list for a full cognitive assessment.

I remember thinking the building was amazing with its contemporary style and bright colors everywhere. The office they took me to was filled with toys and puzzles and interesting looking pieces of furniture. I can still hear my mom saying, "Just do your best to show those doctors what you know." But I didn't see any doctors. Just a couple of guys came in and we hung out playing with toys and talking. I talked mainly. After all, my mother told me to tell them what I had learned at school. I had learned a lot. By the end of the afternoon I was exhausted. My parents took me for a steak dinner at Ponderosa and let me make my own ice cream sundae at the dessert bar.

Mom was too scared to drive home in the bad weather so Dad rented a room at the Holiday Inn Express. The latest hurricane had hit the coast and as it moved over land it turned into a hellacious tropical storm that spun up several tornadoes across the south. The warning sirens went off as we were watching a black and white rerun of Andy Griffith on the television in the hotel room.

"Everyone to the bathroom," Dad had said. Mom got into the tub and pulled me onto her lap wrapping her arms tightly around me. Dad sat on the toilet seat as the tornado sirens squealed. An hour later it was all over. Half the town was destroyed.

I slept between my parents that night, which was an odd treat—I wasn't in the habit of crawling into bed with Mom and Dad. I remember having my eyes closed and pretending to sleep, but really I was listening. I was curious about what went on in my parents room at night.

"One thirty-nine," my dad whispered, sounding amused.

"I told you," my mother said. A few minutes of silence and then Dad said, "I've got to be honest. All that information they gave us. I'm feeling a little overwhelmed. With the new IBM project. I just…"

"I know. Don't worry. I'll handle everything."

And she did. My mom made it her mission to feed my brain. She filled out my application for membership in Mensa the next day.

My IQ was 139—impressive. My EQ, on the other hand, left much to be desired. I was seemingly oblivious to other people's feelings. It was annoying to have to try to figure them out. It's not like I was a robot or anything, it's just that my mom's way of "handling it" had more to do with supporting my off the chart abilities for logical reasoning and abstract thought and less to do with teaching me how to relate to anyone socially.

Music saved me. When I was eleven, I became interested in playing the guitar. My mother had read that gifted children are often musical prodigies so she drove me to guitar lessons every day after school. My guitar instructor was this really tall guy with long hair named Seth who only had three fingers on his left hand. It was crazy watching him play. He taught me that music was its own language and that each emotion had its own sound. At my first recital, I played Gran Vals by Francisco Tarrega and my mother cried. I guess he was right.

Seth introduced me to another instrument—my own voice. Before long, I was playing and singing the kind of music that I loved the most—soft rock. Eric Clapton, Bryan Adams and Dave Matthews Band were my favorites. When I was fourteen, my parents bought me a notebook filled with blank sheet music and I began writing my own stuff. The lyrics were a little cheesy, but I found a way to express my feelings and listening to music helped me understand others.

By the time I started high school, I was more self-aware and approachable. I could empathize with others. I could handle being critiqued, although I rarely was. I was probably the only fifteen-year-old reading *The Language of Emotional Intelligence,* but it paid off.

And maybe that's why I'm out here, alone, watching the storm—wide awake. I am still reeling from what Brigid shared with me today. My heart is breaking over what my girl is going through.

I've known Brigid for four days and already I'm thinking of her as mine. And the thought of that guy forcing himself on her and then trying to ruin her when she said no—well, it makes me want to put my fist through a wall. She acts all whimsical and adorable and carefree, but I can see it—the hurt. This asshole really did a number on her. And to have Paul, the guy she was seeing, jump on board the blame Brigid train is shitty. That dude better hope he never runs into me.

So here on the balcony with the rain pouring down across the bay and the wind blowing the mist in on me, I decide that Brigid would be better off with me. I know. I'm damaged goods. But I'd treat her a hell of a lot better.

The day we just spent together was incredible. I want to be sleeping, dreaming about the way her lips felt when I drew her to me, reliving that moment. But I can't sleep, so instead, I've been wide awake for hours as my brain pours over every detail of the incident that she described, searching for some way to help her. Around 2:00 a.m. it occurs to me—maybe everything I need to help her has been right in front of me the whole time. I look through the window and see her phone on charge in the kitchen. She's been sleeping for hours and even though the odds of her waking up and catching me conducting a total breach of privacy are rare, I decide to dig into this in my room. I grab the small notepad of resort stationary and the pen off the table near the door and head to my bed. I think back to earlier when she had her phone out on the boat. *How did her fingers move as she unlocked her screen?* The memory comes back to me and I repeat the pattern. A few tries and I am in.

In under three minutes, I have gathered all the intel I need to put together a case. I opened her email app and searched "law" to discover the name of the lawyer she is working with. A quick read through those emails gives me an update on the case and the hefty retainer fee before forwarding them to my account. I flip through her photo roll and text myself all of the pics she took the night of the staff party. I open her google drive and search McAdams and find the file on his son. I downloaded it. Lastly, I read back through her text conversation with Piper and find their discussion the day of the event. I took a screenshot of the conversation and texted it to myself. Then I erase any evidence of my snooping and return her phone to the counter.

Anyone else in my shoes would have fallen asleep hours ago minding their own business, but not me. This is what I am programmed to do. Collect. Process. Exploit.

Now that I have something more to go on I can finally call it a night. I passed out around 3:00 a.m. surrounded by my laptop and three dozen pages of resort covered stationary scribbled with notes from my investigation.

Somewhere in the early morning hours there is a loud and terrible explosion and I am back in Kunduz watching while my guys scramble to get out of the building as it goes up in flames. I can hear Mike screaming from the inside so I run toward him, except I'm not really moving. My heart is pounding and every muscle in my body is flexed. I can't breathe. I am working harder than I ever have but am getting nowhere. I watch the entire scene fold out around me in real time, but I'm stuck. I'm trying to get to Mike, but I can't.

Then, there is a second blast that throws me to the ground and knocks the wind out of me. Someone is standing over me, trying to wake me up, trying to get me to safety—but I don't recognize them. I'm not Balzly to them. My eyes are searching for facial recognition but their face is a shadow in the utter darkness. My head's spinning like a rolodex trying to place the voice.

"James. James, get up."

Brigid.

One deep breath and my brain is on solid ground again. It was only a dream. I steady my breathing and try to orient myself to what is happening. I am with Brigid in the condo. It's been storming. *Oh shit.* I sit up and close my computer, throwing the blankets back. I stand up and Brigid takes a step back. It's pitch black. *God she smells good.*

"Sorry to wake you. Did you hear that explosion?" she whispers frantically.

"Yes," I say as I get out of bed and walk back through the living room and out onto the balcony to take a look around before heading back into the kitchen where she stands gripping her phone—flashlight on.

"It's been storming all night. Those loud booms were probably just transformers blowing. The power will be out for a while."

She is standing outside the door to her room bouncing slightly on the soles of her feet with her arms wrapped across her chest. She's holding her phone. The flashlight is illuminating her terror-stricken face. She looks at me and simply says, "I don't like storms."

My heart is pounding again but this time it has nothing to do with a bad dream. Brigid is bewitching. She's wearing a pair of pajama shorts and a tank top. No bra. Her hair is a little wild—resting on her shoulders. And I think about what it would be like to wake up next to her every morning. I smile.

"Why are you smiling? I am freaking out here." Our eyes are locked, but before I can respond both of our cell phones begin making that awful beeping sound from the National Weather Center informing us that a tropical storm warning is in effect until 9:00 a.m.. All citizens should stay put and take shelter in a small interior room. This puts a new look of panic on Brigid's face and she turns and runs back into her room. I follow.

98

This is the first time I am stepping foot in her room. It's a little bit disastrous. Her bed is unmade, of course. There is a small pile of dirty clothes on the floor. A bowl and spoon and cup are next to the bed and makeup is strewn all over the counter. I trip over a pair of shoes.

"Sorry. Watch your step," she says as she frantically begins reaching for the extra pillows and blankets from the shelf at the top of the closet and throwing them into the tub. "Get the ones off my bed," she gestures to the far side of the room.

I follow her lead, pulling off the thick comforter and pillows and tossing them into the tub.

"There," she said. She stepped in and sat down and then staring at me asked, "Well?"

"What?" I said.

"Get in!" She screamed as if we were seconds from being swept away by a twenty-foot storm surge. The truth was this entire resort was built to withstand hurricane force winds in order to meet code. And this wasn't even a hurricane—just a bad storm throwing strong winds and lots of rain across the bay. But when I stepped in and sat down beside her and she looped her arm through mine, I decided I'd hide out there all day if it meant being close to her.

"I'm going to turn off the flashlight to save my battery."

I want to tell her that I have a fully charged portable power bank in my room that could power five devices for two days but there was no way I was letting go of the moment.

"Good idea," I say instead.

In a split second the bathroom is a fortress completely impenetrable from all light. Suddenly, I am hyper aware of our proximity. My right shoulder is touching her left shoulder. Her arm is looped under mine and our bare wrists are touching, but not our hands. My right leg is touching her left. I shift my body slightly and can feel how smooth her leg is. I want to turn towards her and slip my hand up under her shirt. I want her lips on mine. I want to explore every inch of her in the dark.

Damn it. I remind myself to show some self-control. She's scared and all I can think about is taking her in this oversized bathtub. I need to do something before she becomes aware of just how turned on she is making me. Quickly, I think about the last time I was taking shelter in a tub. I remember my dad sitting on the toilet and my mom squeezing the life out of me. That does the trick.

"Sorry to be such a baby. I don't like storms. I thought I was just dreaming, but then I heard it again. Are you mad that I woke you?" she whispers.

I smile, but only the darkness sees. "No. Of course not."

"I used to become a real freak show in storms. Super anxious. They would scare me to death."

"When did you get over the fear?" I asked.

"When you stepped into the tub." Her hand slid down into mine and I thought my heart would explode.

"I'm so tired," she said and I heard her yawn. She looked at her phone. It said 4:25 a.m.

"You are safe now. Go back to sleep." She leans her head on my shoulder. I close my eyes. I'm exhausted from last night's investigation, but I won't sleep. I don't want to miss a second of this moment with Brigid in my arms. I'm reminding myself that I just met her four days ago and that at the end of the week we will go on our way and may never see each other again. Not to mention that I have other fish to fry. But, I'm not even listening to my own argument. It is overruled by my heart which is screaming that this girl is the one.

Brigid

Some far off noise jostles me awake but I'm having that total out of body experience where I truly can't remember where I am. It is completely dark, except for the smallest bit of light creaking in from somewhere across the room. Then, I heard it. The sexiest sound. A quiet but masculine groan. Something beside me shifts slightly. *Ahhh.* I'm in the bathtub with James, which explains the crick in my neck. My head is on his shoulder and his body is turned in towards me, his arm wrapped around my middle. I have no idea how long we've been in this pillow and blanket cloud. He smells so good. Woodsy. I lean my face up into his jawline and take a quiet, but deep breath, hoping he doesn't notice. *God, this is my happy place.*

He speaks. "Good morning."

My instinct is to apologize for the ridiculous situation that I have put us in, but I can't, because the moment is completely unblemished and I'm not sorry.

He kissed me yesterday on the boat. Okay, so maybe I totally invited it, but still, he kissed me. And then I panicked and spilled my guts about Jeff and the entire ordeal. It felt good to tell him. But, it changed something. He hadn't kissed me again. Hadn't touched me again. He was a perfect gentleman the entire day, and it was driving me crazy.

But now, he is holding me and I don't want this moment to end. I tell myself to think of some way to keep him in this tub, worried that if he steps one foot out the moment will be gone.

"Thank you," he says.

"For what? Dragging you out of bed in the middle of the night and squishing you in this tub and then passing out on you?" I whisper. Not an inch of me moves.

A small chuckle was released into the darkness. "Thank you for being a safe place during the storm."

"I saved your life. You're welcome."

He chuckles again.

"What do you want to do today?" I ask.

"This." He doesn't move, just pulls me a little closer to him and takes a deep breath. God, he is wonderful. I can't help but wonder if I have ever felt as safe in another man's arms. James is majestic and incomparable.

I'm lying here thinking about making love to this man and wondering if he is even on the same playing field. His arms are around me, but I want them all over me. I imagine his lips on mine. I imagine his wandering hands lingering over every inch of my body. I want him to lift me out of this tub and carry me to my empty bed and have his way with me. Slowly. I want to roll around with him for hours, our arms and legs tangled together. And then I want him to throw back the curtains and do it all over again in the daylight.

But instead, I am lying here on my side, my head on his chest, his arm around my back and he isn't even moving. *Has he fallen back asleep?* I wait a few minutes and listen to his breathing. His eyes are closed. *What is he thinking?*

My inner psychologist kicks in and I remind myself to take a deep breath and notice how I am feeling in this moment. It is a mindfulness technique I use with my kiddos. I take three deep breaths. *Restless. Super restless.* I tell my students not to judge their feelings, to just notice them, but I can't help but judge my own feelings. I am disappointed in myself.

Here I am in this perfect situation with this perfect man and he is holding me and I can't even enjoy it, because I want more. I want him to be ravishing me. *What is wrong with me?* I think this is what Paul was trying to explain to me. He was always making comments like "the real world isn't a rom com Brigid" or "every moment can't be the climax of a Spark's novel."

And just when I'm thinking I should lower my expectations and quit trying to "write" every scene of my romantic life his voice interrupts my thoughts.

"Bridge?" he whispers.

"Yeah?"

"I'm not really sure how to say this, after what you've been through."

My mind is racing to think where he is going with this. *After what I've been through with Jeff,* he means.

"What is it?" I whisper in turn.

"The way you felt, yesterday, with those guys in the bait shop, like just a piece of ass. You said you are used to feeling that way."

Silence.

"I don't ever want to make you feel that way."

"You could never make me feel that way." I say confidently, immediately.

And there's that masculine grunt again. "If you only knew what I was thinking right now. What you are doing to me. What I've wanted to do since I first laid eyes on you at the pool bar. God. You are killing me, woman."

My heart is in my throat and my mind is spinning trying to remember that moment when out of nowhere the clock radio beside my bed roars back to life startling us both. The power is on and Coldplay is singing "Fix You" into the darkness.

"There is one major difference," I say.

My hand that was resting gently on his chest is now slipping under his shirt and caressing his lower stomach. The tips of my fingers tuck beneath the band of his shorts and his belly quivers. My right leg crosses over his and I reach up to gently whisper in his ear, "I want you too."

The guitar solo begins the emotional lift to the chorus and I smile as he unleashes his craving pulling me into a deep kiss. This is different than yesterday. It isn't soft or slow. It's exciting. Strange. Magnetic. Rare.

His hands slide up my torso taking with it my tank top as he explores every inch of me with his lips.

"I love this song," I say breathlessly.

He stops kissing me long enough to pull his own dark t-shirt up over his head and tosses it out of the tub along with a pillow that threatens to suffocate us. "I was just getting ready to say the same thing." He smiles and

TRY TO FIX YOU

then his lips are on mine again and I am no longer able to think - only feel. My heart feels like it is going to explode and I say, "take me to bed."

He lets out a laugh, "God, I thought you'd never ask."

And in an instant we are untangling ourselves from the nest of blankets we've been snuggled in for God knows how long.

I hopped out of the tub willingly, but then he opens the door to my room and the sunlight floods in along with the reality of what we are about to do.

I promised myself I'd change but apparently I can't be in close quarters with a man for more than a few days before I'm acting like a sex craved teenager. I think James senses my hesitation because he slows everything down.

"Come here." He walks and stands in the middle of my messy bedroom wearing nothing but gym shorts. His dark hair is disheveled, but his arms are wide open so I walk right into them. He leans down and kisses me slowly and softly again, his teeth softly tugging at my lower lip. He releases my lips and rests his chin on the top of my head. His hands are on my bare back gently stroking up and down. My arms are wrapped around his waist, my head resting on his heart. I could feel it pounding.

"You have it, you know."

"What?"

He hugged me tightly.

"Everything."

I take a deep breath. When I don't respond he lifts my chin with his finger and gazes into me with those dark brown eyes.

"If you want it." This is a question.

Suddenly I am thinking about Bo and the deal we made and the envelope full of cash sitting in my top dresser drawer just feet away. I think about that night at the awards ceremony when he shared a part of himself with me. He trusts me. I tell myself I have to be honest with him, but the only truth I can muster enough courage to say is, "I want it."

He takes a step back and pulls down his shorts, kicking them to the side. And I think about the first moment I saw him walking out of the lobby into the sunshine looking like a dream. And now he is standing here in my messy bedroom like an underwear model with his black boxer briefs covering his evident excitement with a look on his face so intense it is unrecognizable.

He hasn't even made love to me yet and I've already decided I can not live without it.

Balzly

I t rained the entire day. The storm early this morning soaked everything, wiped out the power, and wreaked havoc on the entire resort. But, I didn't care. I was experiencing something totally new, something I didn't even realize existed. And I'm glad I didn't know about this feeling before because I wouldn't have been able to breathe without it, to live without it. To know something like this was out there and it wasn't mine would have been excruciating.

My life has been a privileged one—I'll be the first to admit it. Growing up, academics were a breeze. I had a soccer pedigree other guys would have killed for. I never had to worry about finding a date for prom or homecoming. I easily graduated at the top of my class. I watched others work their asses off in AP classes, studying constantly, as I aced every exam. I got invited into a highly competitive PhD program in mathematics while others applied year after year hoping for one of the coveted spots. The Marine Corps recruited me to work with the brightest and most talented men I've ever met in a job where I get to play Superman.

It's funny. I thought I had it all. But now, lying in this bed beside Brigid, watching her chest rise and fall, I realize just what I've been missing—the person I'm meant to share it with.

Caroline pops into my mind and I feel utter shame. How could I have wasted so much time with her? Our entire relationship was based on nothing but sex. I had spent months convincing myself that our connection was so strong. How could I have been such an idiot? After each time we spent the weekend together the guys would beg for all the provocative details. And I was happy to oblige, feeling more like one of them than I had in six years.

The ironic thing is that, even though I always prided myself on my sex life with Caroline, it doesn't even compare to the night I just spent with Brigid.

When I was a kid I remember always praying for those who lost loved ones at church. I remember standing in line with my mother to pay our respects at funeral visitations. Lots of people around me had lost someone they loved. The summer I turned fourteen (the year of my emotional revolution) my Grandpa died. To say we were close is an understatement. It happened suddenly, a heart attack, and I remember my father picking me up from school early one afternoon and breaking the news. I was devastated and for weeks stayed in a complete fog. The one thing that kept running through my head over and over again was that I had no idea life could hurt so badly. For the first time in my life I was experiencing the emotion of grief, feeling pain like I never had before. I suddenly had an entirely new understanding of what others around me had already experienced.

And that's how it is with Brigid now. Until last night, I had no idea what it meant to make love to a woman. I had no idea that sharing myself with someone could feel this way.

I think I realize why my mother has been so worried about me—why Bo has been so worried. They knew what I didn't. I was alone. And being alone in my head is not a great place to be, especially since Kunduz. No one has been able to understand me like Brigid does. She sees me. She gets me.

We spent the entire morning making love. And just when I think I know every inch of her body—every facial expression—every sound, I discover something new—something brilliant. And the best part is she seems to be sharing this experience.

At some point I drifted off to sleep from pure exhaustion. When I woke up she wasn't beside me. I panicked. And in that moment I realized the double edged sword that this new and incredibly blissful happiness brings with it. Now I have something to lose. And that scares me more than anything else ever has. I throw back the covers and slip into my gym shorts. I don't hear her in the kitchen and am praying that she's out on the balcony painting or listening to music and letting me sleep and not regretting everything and retreating back into her mysterious shell.

The light is on in my bedroom. *Fuck. Fuck, fuck, fuck, fuck, fuck.*

I rush to the doorway and see her sitting on my bed with my laptop open, surrounded by what now in the daylight seems more like hundreds of notes—not dozens. I don't recognize the expression on her face and would give anything to know what she's thinking.

"Brigid."

She tilted her head quizzically and then peered up at me intently.

"It's not what you think," I said. "Please don't freak out. I can explain."

She begins picking up the notes one by one and reading through them. "Good. Because it looks like you've gone a little Russell Crowe on me," she says.

I have no clue what that means.

"A Beautiful Mind?"

Nothing.

"Oh my God, you've never seen that movie? You'd love it. I think it's on Netflix. If the rain doesn't clear up we can watch it later."

I was so confused. She's not mad. She's not panicking as if I'm an obsessed stalker, which, let's be clear, is exactly what this looks like.

"So you're not freaked out?" I sit down on the bed beside her.

"It looks like you've gone to a lot of trouble to try and find a way to help me, which is pretty much something no one else has done, including my lawyer, who I am paying. So, no. Why would I be freaked out?"

I pull her into my arms and hug her and send up a silent prayer thanking God that she seems to understand what I was trying to do.

She pulls me back on the bed and we are lying face to face and the tips of her fingers are gently resting on my cheekbone. "You have a beautiful mind James Balzly, and you should never be ashamed of it."

"I've fallen for you."

It was a completely unintentional response. A reflex I couldn't control. For a second, I wasn't sure if I had said it out loud or if my heart was just screaming it. Either way, I meant it with every fiber of my being.

Her face is inches from mine and I can see her mind reeling, reading the implications of what I just said. She isn't saying anything, just staring at me, thinking. Deciding something. Deciding on me. I have been less scared during live combat.

Finally, she leans in and kisses my cheekbone, her lips brushing the end of my lashes and whispers, "I think the feeling is mutual."

We spent the next three days in a cocoon of happiness, slipping into a domestic routine. Each morning she would yawn and stretch every muscle in her body and make these incredibly adorable soft grunting sounds and then she'd roll towards me and place her cold hand on the flat of my stomach, her fingernails always slipping below the waistline of my gym shorts, but just barely. I would respond immediately to her touch and we'd make love. It was slow and sleepy and would sometimes involve neither of us even opening our eyes.

She never seemed to get tired of being intimate with me. But it was so different from what I had with Caroline. Brigid had a way of making every moment seem affectionate. Like when I'm making us coffee in the kitchen and she can't walk past me without patting me on the butt. Or when we're watching the morning news on the couch and she's holding her coffee with one hand and stroking the hairs on my leg with the other.

With the stormy weather behind us we spent our days outdoors in the sunshine. I rented us bikes for the rest of the week and we spent over an hour each morning just cruising around the waterfront neighborhoods near the resort. Then we would lay by the pool, which was pure torture because I was expected to help rub sunscreen on her back and then lie beside her and that red bikini while she read her book and I searched for apartments on my iPad.

After lunch we would get restless and choose some resort activity to try out. On Wednesday we played nine holes of golf and on Thursday I rented a jet ski.

Brigid helped me to discover that apparently there are several things I am terrible at after all—bumping a volleyball, watercolor painting, and identifying flowers.

In the evenings we would shower and head down to Sunset Grill for a romantic dinner. Afterward, we would sit out on the balcony until it was late, holding hands and talking.

One night we were sitting outside together when she looked over and batted her eyelashes at me.

"What?" I smiled.

"Just thinking."

She was up to something.

"That sounds dangerous."

"Not at all, just wondering when you're going to get out your guitar."

"Ah."

"I heard you playing the other night. You're good."

I smiled sheepishly. "It's something I like to piddle with when I'm alone."

"You never play for anyone?"

"Not since I was a kid. I took lessons in middle school. We'd have recitals." As confusion spread across her forehead, I clarified, "I played classical guitar music then."

"Gotcha. And now? Are you too shy to play in front of a crowd?"

"It's got nothing to do with nerves. I just." I really wasn't sure she'd understand this. "I'm not like you." She just listened. "What I'm feeling doesn't always come out naturally. I've always had to work at it. Music is different. When I'm playing it all comes pouring out. It's so personal."

"So you think my feelings come out naturally?"

I just smiled and reached out for her hand. "Yes, you're easy to read. You wear your heart on your sleeve. You speak your feelings fluently." I got up and walked inside leaving her chuckling on the balcony, enjoying my analysis.

I returned with my guitar and sat adjusting the capo and tuning my C string. As I plucked the instrument back into submission I looked at Brigid sitting there across from me on the balcony. She was totally at ease. Barefoot. Hair wild. I spotted that birthmark on her right shoulder blade.

"I thought you said you don't play in front of people."

"No. I said it was personal—the way I show my feelings. How about this one?" I began strumming Savage Garden. After all, I knew I loved her before I met her.

We both shared a passion for music. Before long she was making requests. Funny thing was she couldn't actually remember the song titles or often the group name that she was requesting. She would just start singing these random lines and then ask, "Can you play that one?" This game went on for hours and then we slipped back into her room and fell asleep holding on to one another.

The next night she introduced me to the question game. She had this list of 32 questions that supposedly were proven to help two people get to know each other in the deepest possible way. Your answers had to be brutally honest for it to work.

"What is one thing that people assume about you?" she asked.

"Hmmm. People have always assumed that I'm good with women."

"I could verify that assumption," she said smiling.

"No. I'm serious. I've actually always been kind of shy around girls."

"Really? Because you have the face of someone who was probably pretty popular in high school."

"In high school I was popular in the sense that a lot of people knew me, but that was mainly because I played midfield for our varsity soccer program, which was nationally ranked. I sort of hit this crazy growth spurt the summer before junior year, and suddenly there were always girls hanging around trying to get me to notice them."

"And did you - notice them?"

"They made it pretty hard not to. I went out with a few girls, made out with a few girls, but I never really had any desire to have a girlfriend. My head was always in other places."

"What about college?" she asked.

"Pretty much the same. I dated a couple of girls off and on, but my schedule was too busy for much of a commitment."

"Where did you go? What did you study? Did you love it?"

I smiled at her eagerness to know everything about me.

"I got a scholarship to play soccer at Auburn and I graduated in three years with a computer engineering degree. And yes, I loved it, but not as much as I loved grad school. Grad school was the first time in my life where I felt mentally challenged and was surrounded by a bunch of people that were more like me."

"Gifted."

"If that's what you want to call it."

"Did you do grad school at Auburn?"

"Actually I was in your neck of the woods. I went to Vanderbilt and lived on campus."

"Oh wow. We really were neighbors. I went to Belmont. My girlfriends and I had an apartment in Hillsboro Village. Did you like living in Nashville?"

"I did. It's a great city. Not sure it ever quite felt like home to me though."

"Hmm." The way she looked at me made me realize that I may have just made a mistake. After all, she's from Nashville and that's most likely where she will always want to be. I silently prayed that I hadn't just ruined the possibility of a relationship with her working.

"I was raised in Mountain Brook, Georgia. Between college and my deployments, I have lived in more than half a dozen places."

"So where do you feel most at home?" she asked.

I stood and pulled her up and into my arms. "Honestly? Right here."

Brigid

I'm lying in bed refusing to open my eyes. When I do it will all be over. And after the best week of my entire life—I mean Earth-shattering good—I can't stand for it to end.

I'm so glad Paul pissed me off. If I hadn't lost it on him I would have probably spent the weekend in Asheville walking through the motions and having mediocre sex before returning to my shitty circumstances where I may or may not have employment but am definitely broke.

Instead, I am here lying beside a brilliant man who is kind and spontaneous and sexy and easy to love. I have been telling myself that I'm not afraid to be alone—that I don't need a man. But, the truth is, I want one, especially if he likes my music and thinks I'm pretty and makes me feel like everything I do or say is an adorable surprise. Especially one whose body fits so perfectly with mine.

Everything changed the night I invited him into the tub. *Okay, dragged him.* If I were starring in a romantic comedy the last three days with James would have been the video montage. You know, the part where the song "I'll Stop the World and Melt With You" plays in the background as different shots of us falling in love are juxtaposed to compress time and advance the narrative.

I haven't texted Piper since Monday morning, even though she's been blowing up my phone for days. She is probably freaking out, worried I'm lying dead somewhere. I just can't bring myself to call her because when I do I'm going to tell her everything. And I don't want to jinx this.

"Good morning."

And just like that, it's the beginning of the end. I open my eyes to see James

113

hopping out of bed without a care in the world and I can't help but notice that he doesn't even give me a chance to rub his belly.

"Morning. You jumping in the shower?"

"No, I think I'm going to go for a quick run. Be back in a short bit." And a minute later I hear the condo door slam shut. *Something is wrong.*

Check-out is at noon and I am still lying in bed freaking out because we have no plan. For one, I haven't even booked a flight yet because my credit cards are maxed out. I'm sure Dave would cover the cost and let me pay him back, but since I haven't called to fill them in on recent updates, like how I fell in love with the guy I'm getting paid to psychoanalyze, I might come across as even more of a mooch than I already am. At least James hasn't seemed to notice that I have literally spent no money since I've been here. He's paid for everything without even blinking or thinking twice. I am feeling like a complete loser.

I get up and head to the kitchen knowing damn well I'm going to stress eat, but I don't care. Ugh! There's no food left in this place anyway. My stomach will thank me later. I peek in at James' room. It's neat as a pin. His luggage is already packed and sitting on his bed. *Did he pack last night?*

What am I doing? Did I actually think that this week was going to last forever? *Stupid. Wake up Brigid. Get your shit together.* This weekend was fun—amazing actually—but it is over. Maybe we'll keep in touch, give the long distance thing a try, or maybe I will never see him again. I've got real issues to deal with at home, in the real world. *It was just a fling.*

Thirty minutes later I am attempting to pack up all my clothes when James comes back in from his run. He is standing in front of the fridge, stretching his calves and chugging a glass of water. He's happy as a lark.

"Hey," I say, sort of giving him the cold shoulder on my way to grab some more of my clean clothes out of the dryer.

"Hey, you're up." He smiles.

"Yep." And I walk back past him with a pissed look on my face. *Why am I being such a bitch right now?*

"Did you eat?"

"Nope," I announce as I dump the small pile of clean clothes onto my bed and start folding. He is standing in my doorway looking confused and asks, "Are you okay?"

"Yep." I say nonchalantly. "Just getting packed up to leave."

"I thought you didn't have a flight." He looked worried.

"I figure I'll book one from the cab," I lied. *That would have to be one hell of a long cab ride for me to figure out how to book my own flight online.*

"You called a cab?" He looked hurt.

"It will take me a little while to pack up. I scheduled an Uber." I lied again. *Why am I sabotaging this?* "Don't feel like you have to wait on me. You've got your Jeep. Your bags are packed. I can take care of checking us out."

I am hurting him right now and can see it. But, he hasn't mentioned one thing about our relationship moving past this week when we go back to our own lives, which by the way are totally separate.

"Brigid, would you please stop folding those clothes and come sit down?"

I don't want to have this conversation. I know what he's going to say, and I can't handle it. It will kill me. So I'm acting like I don't care if I ever see him again. At least I will leave here with some dignity intact. I keep folding frantically.

"Brigid, stop." I look up at him. His eyes are sincere. "Come sit outside with me." *Why did I have to look up?*

So we're on the balcony and the white fluffy clouds are floating over a spectacular day. Just another reminder that this place is paradise and I am about to leave.

"I had to go for a run this morning to clear my head. Sometimes there's so much noise up there. Running helps me think." I was sitting at the table with my feet in my seat and my arms wrapped around my knees and my sunglasses disguising the fact that I'm about to start crying at any minute.

"I need to tell you something and I don't want it to overwhelm you." My muscles are tightening and I am bracing for the worst. I think I could throw up.

"I spent seven years in college before the Corps recruited me. My six year commitment is up next month. I love being a Marine. I love my job—my brothers. Hell, I don't even mind my shitty room on base. They want me to

115

re-up for another six years. They want me to be a lifer."

He pauses and just stares out over the water contemplating while I am freaking out. What's he getting at here?

"I don't regret a day of it, but I can't help but feel that it's kept me from starting my life. I'm 31 years old. The only thing I own is my Jeep. Hell, when my dad was 31 he had a wife, a kid, and a mortgage."

"What are you trying to say, *Balzly?*" His eyes flinch when I call him that as if I'd hit him across the face. He knows my guard is up. I'm distancing myself from him—preparing for the blow.

"What I'm trying to say is that it is time for me to start a new chapter in my life. I thought that was going to be with Caroline, but it's not."

"Oh, well, sorry things didn't work out for the two of you."

"Bridge, stop. I'm not saying this right. It's not Caroline. She's nothing to me. She's nothing compared to you." He says this in an intense tone I haven't heard him use yet.

"I've got to go home and clear out our apartment and try to figure out what my next step is."

"Wait. I thought you lived on base."

"I do."

"You just said our apartment."

"We never moved in together. I rented the place and she was staying there until my time was up."

"But you didn't make it that far?" Everything was beginning to fall into place. *He and Caroline were serious.*

"No. We didn't. And I can't stand to keep the apartment, after everything that happened. I need to head back to Mountain Brook and move anything I want to keep out of the apartment. I want you to go with me."

"So, let me get this straight. We have to check out in about an hour and you choose this moment to ask me to go home with you to help you clean out the apartment your girlfriend has been living in?" I walked back in the condo and went to my room, slammed the door and locked it. *Why am I being so unreasonable?*

He's on the other side of the door shouting now.

"She's not my girlfriend, Brigid. I already told you that we broke up months ago. And besides, how are you mad at me when this time last week you were on a weekend getaway with Paul?" I don't even recognize this side of him. He is pissed.

I opened the door to face him. "I told you Paul and I weren't serious. I told you why it didn't work. Paul is not a threat." *Why am I screaming?*

"And Caroline is?"

"According to Jennifer everyone back home thinks you two are still together." I'm doing air quotes with my fingers.

"Well, we're not and that's no one's business."

"What about me? Do I have a right to know what happened? After all, you must have been pretty serious if you were planning to move in with her. You know what, don't tell me. I don't care. But, don't you dare ask me to clean up after another woman." *Who am I right now?*

And then James is losing it. He's breathing heavily, sweating, and walking away from me holding his head.

"Mike is dead because of that cheating bitch." He swings and puts his fist through the door to his room. "Fuck!"

"Good Lord, calm down before you break your hand."

He slams what's left of his door in my face. How did this go so badly so quickly? We don't even have our toes in the water yet and we're already drowning.

He stays in his room and I hear his shower start running. I call the front desk and request a late checkout. I let them know that the door will need repairs and that they could charge the credit card on file. Dave will pay Larry Butters back.

Vacation Brigid is amazing. Apparently real world Brigid is a bitch who pushes away the only good thing she has going right now.

I had to get out of that room so I walked down to the pier to look at the boats. Something about their gentle rocking was comforting. I sat down and hung my legs over the side.

I thought about what James said—about Mike being dead because of Caroline. She must have cheated on him. I think back to the story he shared with me at Sunday's dinner, about the call with the intelligence coming in just as he had learned something upsetting about Caroline. She is the reason he made a mistake—one that ended up costing him one of his men. I needed more information on the circumstances of their breakup, but for the first time I think I am beginning to wrap my head around why James is struggling. And in that very moment a shadow looms over me and I feel someone sit down beside me. After a few minutes, he speaks. This time in a much calmer tone.

"I was so excited about the apartment. It was in this great neighborhood close to my parents' place. Caroline and I had been dating for a year, but it was totally unconventional. It was a long distance relationship from the start. She was twelve hours away. We probably only saw each other a dozen times. Our connection was completely physical and I was too blind to see that, until now. My contract was almost up and I wanted to feel like I had my next step in place. That was the biggest draw with the apartment. Anyway, she graduated in May—she's nine years younger than me—and the week I was helping her move in I got called up for one final tour in Afghanistan."

It's like I'm listening but all I'm really hearing is, *I spent a dozen wild weekends sleeping with a 22-year-old.*

"Before I left I had installed a bunch of smart technology around the place—because, well, obviously I'm geeky like that. I had these motion sensor cameras that only began filming when they sensed movement. I would get short clips on my phone app whenever an Amazon box was delivered or a neighborhood cat peed on my front porch. Anyway, one day the guys and I are talking about this smart technology and I start bragging about my setup. I cast my phone to the big TV in the rec room on base and opened my app. The guys are loving this so half my crew is in there checking it out. And while I'm showing them, a new video pops up and I'm watching live as Caroline picks up the camera from the kitchen and carries it to the bedroom. And I'm about to shut it down because who knows what she's trying to send me when all of a sudden I hear it. A man's voice. And so I think she's being robbed and I am panicking and then all of the sudden she is on the bed taking her clothes off and the voice is fucking my girlfriend."

I turned to look at him for the first time since he sat down. His eyes are wide open staring out across the water. I know it is taking him a lot to trust me with this information.

"She cheated on me. And she went out of her way to make sure I saw the entire thing. The images. I can't get them out of my head. They haunt me. And this other guy in my home with what I thought was mine. I was paralyzed. Completely helpless—something I had never been before. And that's when the intelligence for the op came in."

I lean my head on his shoulder and we just sit there in the sun with our legs dangling off the edge of the pier.

Finally, I speak. "I'm sorry. I can't imagine anyone treating someone they love that way."

He takes his sunglasses off and stares into my eyes. "That's just it. She didn't love me. And if I'm being honest with myself, I didn't love her. I think I loved the idea of her. From the outside looking in everything seemed great, but something was missing. Now I know that it was something pretty important." He put his hand on my knee and began making tiny circles on my skin with the tips of his finger. "I'm sorry about the door. And I realize I have no right to ask, but I really don't want you to fly home today. I can't be without you."

"No, I'm sorry. I panicked this morning when I saw your bags packed and we hadn't even talked about what came next. The truth is, the thought of losing what I found in you this week is making me a crazy person."

Balzly

Once I was traveling from a base in Kabul to a military airport in Kandahar with three of my men. We had orders to deliver some supplies and then we were heading out for a week on leave, flying to Germany to spend our time off there. Things were pretty rough at the time and we always traveled expecting trouble, so we drove an MRAP - Mine-Resistant Ambush Protected. Its size was so massive and appearance so menacing that you couldn't help but feel unstoppable. Driving that beast was a bit of a rush. Barreling down the dusty old roads with those huge tires, feeling like the world was yours and that nothing could stop you.

That is how I feel with Brigid in my Jeep right now.

The GPS on the screen in my dashboard tells me I have exactly 4 hours and 44 minutes (288 mi) to figure out what in the hell I am going to do to keep this girl. And let's be clear - I have to keep this girl.

"So, tell me about Mountain Brook." She has kicked off her flip flops and tucked her feet beside her in the front seat. Her dirty blond hair sweeps across her shoulder and her sunglasses mirror my stolen glances.

I'm just happy that she agreed to go with me on a whim. The last thing she needed was to head home into the shitstorm that was waiting for her in Nashville. If she stays with me I can protect her from any immediate fallout.

"It's a pretty cool place. A medium-sized town in the low mountains of northern Georgia. Lots of hiking and backpacking. There is a lake in town so watersports are pretty big. It's a nice place. The people are amazing - lots of southern hospitality."

BALZLY

Her eyes are dancing with excitement and it occurs to me that there doesn't seem to be a nervous bone in this girl's body. She is spontaneity. I reach out and she slips her hand in mine and I think about how much my mother will love her.

"So my parents are Tony and Melinda. Dad is a semi-retired computer engineer. He still does some consulting and teaches a computer science class at my old high school."

"Oh wow. That's cool."

"Mom, who everyone calls Mel, spends most of her time volunteering at church and on the town council."

"Is she into politics?"

"Not exactly." I wanted to explain that my mother was a force of nature—that she had her hands in the middle of everything happening in the town, from coauthoring the latest city ordinance to organizing the town's entertainment series, Live at the Lake—but I didn't. I told myself it was because I didn't want to overwhelm Brigid with too much information, when really I didn't want to tell her the truth. My parents don't have the greatest marriage. My dad spends most of his time in his own little world. I think my mom gave up trying to keep his attention and, since I've grown up, has instead poured all of hers into the town.

It's like Brigid's reading my mind or something because the very next thing she asks is, "So, what is your parent's relationship like?" She's using 'the voice' again and I can tell she's probably good at what she does because even though I had already decided not to dive into the deep end where my parents are concerned, that's exactly what I do.

"I have a lot of respect for my parents. We are a very close family, but if I'm completely honest," I search for a way to describe this without being too dramatic, "What they have is different from what I want in a marriage."

"What do you want in a marriage?"

Suddenly a ten pound rock lodged itself in my chest and I silently take my own pulse. I glance over again and find my reflection in her sunglasses and I realize that she's hanging on every word that I am saying.

"I want to marry my soul mate."

121

And then there is that smile.

"I know it sounds cliche, but I want to marry the one person that I can't live without—can't breathe without." I squeeze her hand.

"And that's not how your parents are?"

"No. They love each other and respect each other and have accomplished a lot, but it doesn't seem like they've accomplished much of it together. Does that make sense?"

"Actually, it does."

"My parents have always kind of lived their own lives. My dad is a lot like me I guess—always stuck in his head. He's not easy to talk to, or get close to. And now looking back, it doesn't seem like my mom did much to try. Instead she poured all of her time and energy into me."

"Well, I'd say she did a fine job."

"She did. And I have done a fantastic job of screwing it all up."

"Why would you say that?"

"Because it's true."

"How?" I could tell her question came from a very genuine place.

"It's hard to explain."

"Try."

I take a deep breath. "It's like I have this gift, and I am supposed to be doing something incredible with it."

"You are," she says convincingly. She sees the skeptical look my eyebrows make and adds, "You've been using it to serve your country."

"I'm an embarrassment to my country." This is the first time I've said aloud what I've been telling myself over every shot of whiskey.

"I am so lost. This whole thing with Caroline was shameful. The only real relationship I've had in my adult life ends with such a terrible miscalculation. Mike is dead because of me. It was my job to make sure my guys got back safe and I completely failed."

"You're right." Her answer catches me off guard and my hands tighten around the steering wheel. "Your job was to get your guys back safe and you failed. Now what? You're not perfect, despite what your Mom or every life experience has led you to believe. Caroline was a mistake. She wasn't worthy of you. She proved that the minute she screwed you over. What happened with the intelligence—that was a mistake. What's making this so difficult is your limited experience with failure. You're not good at making mistakes, because you haven't practiced."

I fixate on her words and they ring true. *A hard truth.* I put miles of highway behind us before we spoke again. Finally, her hands went to the radio and she scanned until she found a good station. Her hands went back to her own lap and for a long time she looked out the window, but the tropical bay views were long gone. Alabama isn't as pretty—just flat farmland and run-down towns on both sides of the interstate. After quite a bit of silence I began worrying that Brigid was regretting going along with this whole thing.

"You're awfully quiet." I probe as I reach out and take her hand back in mine once again, where it belongs. "You okay?"

"Just busy studying license plate numbers." She smiled. I laughed and then realized that for the first time in a long time, I wasn't. I was too absorbed in my thoughts of her to remember any numbers. Her joke broke the ice and we ended up talking the entire rest of the way home which was a completely new experience for me. I think I shared more with her in that one conversation than I ever have with anyone—my college roommates, Caroline, even my Marines. I told her everything about my adolescence from my weird obsessions to all of the crazy stuff my mother did to feed my brain. I opened up to her about my deployments—my experiences in the Middle East—more details about Michael, and about the drinking that followed as I searched for ways to get out of my head. The flashbacks—everything. She didn't flinch. Nothing I said seemed to scare her. The opposite in fact.

"Okay, back to the question game," she declares. She opens the app on her phone and reads, "Would you ever want to be famous and if so, in what way?"

"Hmm. That's a tough one. You go first while I think."

"I don't think I'd want to be so famous that people everywhere recognized me. Flashing cameras and no peace—that might be fun for one weekend. And I wouldn't want to be famous on the internet—too fleeting. But I guess it would be kind of cool if I was famous in my own town. You know, to be recognized for some great work or deed and to have a park or a fountain or the wing of a building named after you."

"And what would you be famous for doing?" I asked.

She thought for a moment, "Helping children. Helping them find joy." I smile and then she goes on to explain how hard life is for some kids. She tells me about all of the special needs that kids have and how we don't spend enough time or resources on strengthening their mental health. She talks with her hands like she does when she gets excited. She's describing some of the kids she's helped, and the feeling it gives her and I'm thinking that her whole theory on the 36 questions that lead to love is a pretty good one. With one answer, she shares everything she aspires to accomplish in her professional career—helping kids better understand themselves and how they learn, how to advocate for their needs, giving them the tools they need to reach their full potential. She has the most noble and beautiful dream and by the time she has answered the question I am picturing her future and realize that I want to be a part of it.

By the time we stopped for gas she had completely cracked me open and nothing inside seemed to scare her. So I'm standing at the gas pump and she is leaning against my Jeep and I ask her to tell me more about her life. Her response cracks me up and I wonder how long these adorable surprises will last.

"The best way to truly get to know me is to listen to my soundtrack." She smiles and every part of me wants to be alone with her. Instead I settle with backing her against the Jeep and kissing the hell out of her. Her full lips drive me crazy. Just when I think I can't stop the gas pump clicks and she pushes my chest off of hers and smiles and says, "Come on. I'll play it for you on the ride."

As we settle back in, she pulls out her phone and connects the Bluetooth to my stereo.

"So, this was a project I had to do in grad school when I was taking a class called Music Therapy. The idea was to use music as a means of communicating your experiences, your feelings, with others."

"So, does it work?"

124

"Honestly, you're the first person I'm sharing it with."

Do you know how that feels?

I spent the next 35 minutes in silence hanging on to every word and by the end the only thing I knew for sure was that I loved this girl. She was meant to be mine. I had worried for years that my life was passing me by and that I was missing the opportunity to build something meaningful. I had the nagging thought that I should be making plans, moving forward. And in a split-second decision to follow Bo for a weekend away, I ended up finding my everything. As I listened to every note I decided that I would do anything to not lose her. I would go wherever she was. I would be whatever she needed me to be.

Growing up, I never felt like I belonged. Even when I was adored by my peers, beloved by my teammates, respected by my men. I never really belonged. Brigid is where I belong. Everything is entirely different with her. By the time we reached the end of her playlist she was looking at me with big questioning eyes waiting to hear what I thought. Totally putting herself out there. The face of vulnerability. She was waiting for a response.

I pulled off the road in a dusty gravel driveway that seemed to lead nowhere important.

"Well?" she asked, turning towards me.

I smiled and tucked a loose strand of hair behind her ear.

"It's missing something," I said.

"What?"

I take the phone out of her hand, open the Youtube app, and type in Coldplay. And then it's playing—the song from the radio the first night we made love. The song that has been playing in my mind on repeat. The song that's making me believe Brigid might possess the power to fix me.

"The next track."

Brigid

oly shit. He underplayed his hand. James has intentionally told me just enough about his parents and where he's from to lure me into thinking his background is normal. *And it's not.*

First of all, Mountain Brook is this absolutely charming lake town—totally upscale. The streets are lined with bungalows from the 1920s that have undergone million-dollar renovations and have meticulously landscaped lawns. Flowers are blooming everywhere. *My mother would love it.* James rolls down the window and I can't help but stick my head out.

We turn and drive underneath a large metal archway with the words Lakeshore Drive and suddenly a marina appears with the most gorgeous boats and a stretch of beach where groups of people are gathered together enjoying the late afternoon. A large expanse of grass stretches around the beach underneath the shade of full-grown magnolia and cypress trees. Outdoor lights are swooping from one tree to the next and I can only imagine how magical this place is at night.

The downtown area makes my hip, up and coming neighborhood in Nashville look small and unexciting in comparison. Every block is lined with alluring boutiques, interesting restaurants, and other shops. I can't hide the smile on my face. *I love this place.*

"What's that?" I asked as we drove past a beautiful entrance and a sign that said Anderson Gardens.

"That is a resort complex. It has everything—lodge, an 18-hole golf course, walking and biking trails, its own private beach."

"Wow. Did you spend much time there growing up?" I asked, eyeing him curiously.

"You could say that."

We take a left hand turn and begin climbing up a private drive beneath a canopy of sycamore trees. When they opened up, an incredible house with breathtaking views of the lake stood before us. So, yep, the second thing is, his parents are loaded.

"What are you thinking?" he asked nervously. I could tell that he recognizes this is a lot to take in and is giving me a moment to digest it all.

"I am thinking this place is magnificent," I say as James pulls up to the front of the house and turns off the ignition.

"My Uncle Jim is an architect and specializes in making what's new appear old."

"What year was the house built?"

"1987."

"It feels more like 1907."

"He is a talented guy. You know I've seen this view millions of times, but it never gets old." He leans in to steal one quiet moment with me in the car before the inevitable happens.

When a side door on the front porch opens I see a middle-aged, well-dressed woman sauntering out to greet him. *His mother.* He steps out of the car and walks around to open the door for me but his mother's embrace finds him first. She is sobbing and saying, "Thank God," and hugging him as if he was just raised from the dead. And then I realize this is probably the first time she has seen him since he returned from Afghanistan and my heart melts a little. She is blotting away tears when she notices that I am in the car and immediately breaks into a big smile.

It's obvious James didn't mention that I was coming with him, or maybe that I even exist. I have to cut the guy some slack, considering the way I've totally ghosted Dave and Piper this past week. Which reminds me, *I've got to call them tonight.*

Here goes nothing.

"Hi," I say with a bright smile as I step out of the car.

"Mom, this is Brigid Taylor," James says as he steps beside me placing an arm casually around me and a sweet kiss on my cheekbone.

There was about a half second when I didn't know how this woman was going to react. She looked at James, reading his face in some familiar way. Then suddenly, she reached out for my hand and pulled me into a full embrace, patting me on the back.

"Well, isn't this a surprise? It is so nice to meet you Brigid."

"You as well Mrs. Balzly."

"Actually, my last name is Anderson—when Tony and I married, I kept my maiden name. Nonetheless, call me Mel."

Anderson.

"Brigid is going to help me with some things in town tomorrow," James explains, somewhat vaguely, as he leads me up to the porch and into the house. "I was hoping we could crash here tonight."

So James didn't even tell her that he was coming into town. No wonder she seemed a little surprised—albeit pleasantly. There was something hilarious about him using the phrase "crash here" when "check into our suite" seemed more appropriate.

"Perfect! Do you have plans for dinner tonight?" she asked.

James put his arm around his mother and said, "Yes. With you. And then I thought we could head down to Live at the Lake."

James led me into the beautiful Georgian style home before I had a chance to count all of the windows placed symmetrically across the front facade.

"Why don't you take Brigid upstairs and show her where she can put her bags and then give her a tour of the house while I get started on dinner." *She should have said estate.*

"I think this is the most unique staircase I have ever seen." My mouth was practically hanging open. The walls in the foyer were covered with wainscoting from floor to ceiling, and a beautiful crystal chandelier hung from the second story.

James led me upstairs and down a long carpeted hallway with heavy wooden doors on each side and opened one with windows that faced the lake. The room was impressive.

I set my bag down on the bed. I had an opportunity to play it cool in this situation, to act like nothing unusual was happening. *We all know I didn't take it.*

"I can't believe you didn't tell me this," I said with an astonished look.

"Tell you what?" he asked.

"What? Hmm, I don't know, maybe you could have given me the heads up. Like, hey, I was actually raised in an ostentatious utopian society, and my parents are billionaires. My real name is James Gatsby."

He laughs at the hint of sarcasm in my voice and walks back to the door. I hear the key turn in the lock. (Yes, there was an actual iron key in the lock.)

"Would it have changed anything?" He reaches out for me seductively, pulling me closer.

"Yes."

He seems nervous for a second.

"I would have worn a nicer shirt."

He chuckles and then grins down at me with his hands around my waist. "Let's take care of that right now."

So, after what will later be referred to as the time we had sex in his parents' guest suite, we headed back outside to walk around the property.

"So really. Why didn't you tell me about the money?"

"I don't know. People tend to treat me differently."

"So your dad makes a lot of money. Who am I to judge?"

"My dad has done really well, but most of this has more to do with my mom's money." He's pointing out over the vast acreage.

"I thought you said she was a stay-at-home mom." My picture of his childhood has drastically changed in the last twenty minutes.

"My grandpa owned Anderson Gardens. He died when I was in middle school and my mother was the beneficiary."

That explains that. I'm trying to think about whether this new information changes anything, but it really doesn't. Mainly it just reminds me that there is a lot we still don't know about each other.

"I'm sorry about your grandpa. I'd love to see Anderson Gardens." Without warning James looks uneasy. *Is this place a trigger for him?*

"I'm not sure we'll have the time."

"Speaking of time, I really should find some to call Piper and Dave."

"Now works. I'll just head into the kitchen to help Mom with dinner."

"Great. I'll be right behind you," I say from the back porch.

I couldn't muster the courage to call Piper because, well, I was a chicken. So, I texted her instead.

"Everything is fine. Sorry I have been MIA these past few days. As you may have guessed, I've fallen for Hotwheel. Are you pissed?"

"Yes! How could you not tell me that Ross sleeps with Elizabeth?"

It takes me a second to register this, but then I remember she is binge watching Poldark on Netflix, per my suggestion.

"I know. I hated him for like four episodes, but it gets better."

"Ugh! I HATE her!"

"IKR!"

"Good thing you finally answered my text. Dave was ready to call the local police to do a "safety check" on you."

"Is that even a real thing?"

"Apparently so. Where are you?"

"Okay. Don't freak out...."

"Freaking out a little."

"I'm with Hotwheel in Mountain Brook, Georgia."

And just like that my phone is blasting out the famous *Golden Girls* theme song. I should have known this wasn't the kind of thing she'd let me explain via text.

"Hello."

"Spill it."

"Okay, I've pretty much just had the most incredible week of my life. Turns out Sgt. James Balzly is this amazing guy and we completely hit it off. We ended up spending the entire week together and by Friday morning we just really didn't want to be apart."

"Oh my God! Did you sleep with him?"

I'm wondering how I should answer this. I've always been 100% real with

130

Piper, but ever since Dave and her got married, it's like anything I tell her I have to be okay with Dave knowing.

"You slept with him!" Piper is screaming and I hear Dave in the background asking who she's talking to.

Shit.

"It's Brigid. Shhh. I've got to hear this. Go on."

"Okay, so he is a Marine stationed at Camp Lejeune, but his time is almost up. He had a few weeks of leave and needed to take care of things in his hometown and he asked me to join him. He is super intelligent, very kind-hearted, and good at everything."

"I don't like him," Dave screams at the phone.

"Seriously. Shut up." I hear Piper walk away from the domestic noise. So, how long are you staying?"

"Honestly. I'm not sure. We just got here about two hours ago. I've met his mom. She seems really nice. We are going to listen to some live music tonight."

"Awesome. He sounds amazing."

"But?"

"I know this is the last thing you want to deal with right now, but I need to tell you something. God, I've been calling you relentlessly for four days."

My heart drops. *I know this tone in her voice.*

"What happened?"

"Nothing is wrong. It's just that your mom found out that Jeff McAsshole is being interviewed Sunday morning."

"What do you mean, being interviewed?

"He is going on *Inside Tracks* Sunday morning."

"You have got to be kidding me." I walk away from the house and out into the yard, in case I have to throw up.

I was hoping that the school board would move their asses and actually set a hearing date so that we could settle this and I could get back to work. This is exactly what I worried would happen. He's making this political. The school board is made up of elected officials. He is going on that show to try to win the support of the public, hoping that they will have to side with him.

131

He's going to trash my reputation on live television.

"So, what are you going to do?"

"I'm not sure. But I probably need to call my lawyer. Ugh!"

"Listen. Dave and I are here for you, whatever you need."

"I know. Let me hop off here because we are about to eat dinner. I'll be in touch."

"Are you okay?"

"I'm okay. Love you. Mean it. Bye."

"Love you. Mean it. Bye."

I am not okay. I know this sounds crazy, but I've always had this fear of making a mistake and ending up in prison. I once knew a girl who had just gotten her driver's license. She popped over a blind hill going too fast and hit and killed a motorcyclist on the other side. She didn't see the stopped traffic. She was stuck in a crazy legal battle and ended up doing jail time.

It's not like I'm worried about going to prison over this; it's just that I hate the idea of making a stupid mistake. I went against my better judgment and continued to meet with Jeff alone, even after I was having a gut feeling that something was off. I should have never agreed to meet with him that evening after hours. Because of that mistake, it feels like my entire life is being taken from me. Jeff is such an asshole. He's going to go on public television and make me seem like a whore.

And that's when I threw up in Mel's backyard. *Thank God no one saw that.* Wait. Nope. *James definitely saw that.* He is running out towards me now with a look on his face that I haven't seen before.

"Sweetheart. Are you okay?" he asks, helping me to my feet. I didn't realize I was still kneeling on the ground. I'm crying and my hair is stuck to my cheek and he pulls me into his arms and guides me away from the spot where I just got sick.

Tears are pouring. My head is lying on his chest and maybe it's the way his arms feel around me or the fact that he just called me his sweetheart, but I say to him what I couldn't even admit to Piper.

"No. I am not okay."

"What happened?" he asks, but I get the sense that he already knows what

I'm going to say before I say it.

"This whole thing with Jeff is about to blow up. He is doing a TV interview on Sunday morning. My name is going to be splashed around all over Nashville."

James is taking slow and deep breaths, but I can feel every muscle in his body flex. He is resting his chin on the top of my head.

"If you don't want that interview to air I can make it disappear." He said it so seriously that it sent a chill through me.

"What are you talking about?"

"It can't be hard to figure out, for someone who is good with computers."

He meant for someone who breaks ciphers to ensure our national security.

"Don't even think about it. I won't let you do something illegal."

"Fine. I'll call them, see how much they're paying Jeff to do the interview, tell them I'll double it if they cancel."

"No reputable news program pays for interviews."

"What about setting up an interview to tell your side of the story?"

"I could never go through with it."

"You're stronger than you think."

I wanted to tell him that I'm really not and that if I were at home alone I would be lying across my bed screaming into my pillow while my music blares through my surround sound speakers so loud that my house would be shaking. That was, after all, what I had been doing before Paul whisked me away to Asheville for the weekend.

But instead, I take a deep breath and start walking back towards the house. His mother is a gracious host and I should make the most of it.

Balzly

B rigid looks entirely deflated. It started after she found out the news about Jeff's interview and lingered all through dinner. Despair is written all over her face, though she is doing her best to hide it for my mother's sake.

My mom has been acting a little weird too. She completely skipped over the part where she pumps me for details about my deployment and instead goes out of her way to ask us a lot of personal questions.

"So, how did you two meet?" It sounds innocent enough, but the way she says it makes me feel more like we owe her an explanation and less like she is genuinely interested in how our paths crossed.

"This is actually a pretty funny story," I say.

Brigid perks up at this question. She sits across the table from me smiling with her eyes, obviously enjoying my perspective. I am giving her a hard time about not noticing me in the manager's office, assaulting me outside our condo, and freaking out about the InstaCart delivery guy. She is giving me the *I'm going to kill you later* look.

But, when I turn my eyes to my mother, she isn't smiling.

She says, "So you've only known each other a few days," and she sounds content with that knowledge. "Tell me Brigid, what do you do for a living?"

"I am a school psychologist."

"I see." *What is my mother's issue right now?* "And where do you live?"

"Nashville."

"How lovely. And how long until you head home?"

"Mom." I had to intercept this one. *Why is my mother being so mean?* Brigid

134

is everything and my mom is practically asking her when she's going to leave. She's sending me some sort of crazy signal with her eyes, which even I cannot decode.

"Our trip here was a bit spontaneous, but we are going to talk more tonight about our plan moving forward."

This did not please Mel Anderson.

In the end, I'm not sure that either of the two women in my life made the best first impression on each other. Luckily, Brigid was so preoccupied with the news of Jeff's interview that she didn't seem to notice how rude my mother's questions were.

I am beginning to doubt if my plan to protect Brigid would work out the way I had hoped. She has already found out about the interview. And even if it does work, will she ever forgive me for getting involved? Apprehension fills my guts.

Despite Brigid's mood, she wouldn't give up on the notion of going to Live at the Lake. I suggested we stay home, but I could tell she welcomed a distraction.

My mother mentioned having a few things to take care of, so she shooed us upstairs to get ready. That is when I was reminded how different men and women are.

"Ugh. I'm running out of clothes. I can't stand to wear this one more time."

Even though I could tell you what Brigid had worn each day since we met—and yes, on some days those clothes repeated—I didn't really register this as a problem. But, apparently it was. I heard it in her voice. She wished she had all her things. She was ready to be home. I know that feeling all too well.

I had to fix it.

"It's only 6:45 p.m.. The band doesn't start playing until 8:00 p.m.. Let's stop and do a little shopping in town."

I could tell she was wrestling with this idea.

"Come on. A little retail therapy might be good. Let me spoil you."

We drove to Main Street and ended up at a women's clothing boutique called Thistle. It went a long way in lifting Brigid's spirits. She tried on several items. When she walked out of the dressing room wearing pants—high-rise button-fly jeans that she referred to as trendy (I wouldn't know) —and a gray ribbed tank top with a flattering cut, my heart was in my throat. She was dazzling.

"Please let me buy that for you so I can have the pleasure of taking it off you later," I whispered in her ear. She kissed the corner of my jaw and I had to count backward from ten to keep from following her back into the dressing room.

While she tried on different pieces I looked around a bit. I wanted to find something to surprise her with, but nothing seemed worthy enough. Then I came upon a table with handmade sterling silver jewelry and found a necklace with a turquoise pendant. It was perfect. Simple. Natural. Delicate.

"How much?" I asked the sales clerk.

"It is originally $369.99, but all of our sterling silver pieces are 10% off right now."

"That's fine. I'll take it."

I slipped the box into the pocket of my jacket.

An hour later, we were settled in our lawn chairs with our Coronas, listening to the first set. It felt right. Being here with Brigid felt more like home than it did without her.

"Are you sleeping?" I asked when I noticed her eyes were closed. She looked so relaxed.

"No, but I could be." Her eyes remain closed. "I love falling asleep to happy noise."

"Happy noise?"

"You know, some people like ocean sounds or rain or crickets."

"Right."

"Me, I could pass out on the couch in the middle of a big family Christmas party. I fall asleep to happy noise."

I lean my head back in my chair and close my eyes.

"Just listen. It sounds happy right?"

I knew exactly what she meant. The music was playing. People's voices and laughter filled the air. Kids nearby shrieked playfully. There was a light breeze coming off of the water, which made a soft smacking sound when it hit the beach.

I opened my eyes and reached into my pocket. I placed the small box on her lap.

"You are my happy noise."

She opened her eyes.

"What's this?"

"Just open it."

"James, I can't…"

"I insist."

She opened the box slowly and her eyes took one look at the necklace and then found mine. She stood up from her chair with the box and in an instant was kneeling down before me, wrapping her arms around me, and burying her face in my chest.

"I love it. I'll never take it off."

I thought back to the biggest moments in my life. It was ironic. I've put so much time and effort into every accomplishment. But somehow, nothing has made me feel as fulfilled or as happy as I am at this moment. I have earned the admiration of this incredible woman and all I had to do was be myself. Suddenly, I want to give her everything. I want to spend the rest of my life taking care of her and pleasing her. I think I finally know what it means to be in love with someone.

I was pondering over this idea as her phone beeped and she left my arms to dig it out of the purse that was slung across the back of her chair.

"Ugh."

"What is it?"

"My lawyer." She replied to the text, then threw her phone back down on the chair. I hated that she had to deal with this right now, especially since the entire reason I brought her here was to avoid the interview.

She clasped the necklace around her neck and it fit her perfectly. She asked where the ladies' room was, and I'm pretty sure she just wanted a chance to look in the mirror. Her fingers were still gracefully holding the pendant. I pointed her to a shelter house across the lawn.

She wasn't gone long when her phone beeped again. I didn't think twice before reading the text. I felt pretty confident that anything she discussed with her lawyer would be shared with me.

Boy was I wrong.

I'm holding her phone in my hand like a grenade as the message explodes before me, ripping my heart in two.

Brigid

I don't like being ambushed. I'm trying my best to enjoy this time with James, but how can I, when I just found out that, in like thirty-two hours, Jeff is going to ruin my life.

James suggested I be proactive and tell my side of the story, but the truth is—I'm never good on the spot. Part of me is thinking I should have agreed to let James do his voodoo computer hacking on *Inside Tracks*.

Jeff's one of the most well-known public figures in the city. He has a good reputation and most people like him. Honestly, before my "run-in" with him, I was one of those people. He has done a lot for the district—balancing our budget and bringing us out of the red, increasing the teacher's retirement benefits, and implementing a new after-school program that has helped kids in low-income areas.

For the first time since finding out about the interview, it occurs to me that my students are going to hear about this. I doubt they will be up watching local news on a Sunday morning, but I guarantee this will end up on the internet. I can already see myself as a ridiculous meme gone viral. And all of the families I've worked so hard to build up trust with will most likely want to be assigned to another psychologist. That is, if I get to keep my job.

I'm staring into the mirror in a building way too nice to be called a "shelter house" and admiring the necklace James bought for me. He said I looked dazzling. I sure don't feel it.

I close my eyes and take three deep breaths, in thru my nose and out thru my mouth. *You can't control his actions. You can only control your reaction. What happened with Jeff doesn't define you.*

139

I'm in the middle of this mental health check when the door opens and a young woman walks up and stands at the sink beside me. She begins digging around in her purse before finding lipstick and reapplying. Some college kid wearing a white polo shirt with the logo for Anderson Garden embroidered on the front pocket.

"You work at Anderson Gardens?" I asked. I may be in the middle of a personal crisis, but hey—I'm still friendly. "I hear it's paradise."

"Yes, I do. And, yes, it is. You should check it out." The girl said with a smile. "My boyfriend's parents own it."

Hmm.

"I thought Tony and Mel owned it."

"They do. How do you know Tony and Mel?"

My stomach dropped. I looked at the girl again in the mirror. She was wearing a nametag. *Caroline.*

What the frick!

For the first time in my life I was completely speechless. Confrontation isn't my strong suit, so instead of losing my shit, I went into "work mode" and calmly began asking prompting questions in an attempt to gather more intel.

"I just met Mel today. I'm here with James."

"James who?" She looked confused and it occurred to me that she may have never known his first name.

"Sgt. James Balzly, her son."

This is when her entire demeanor changed. Suddenly, she understood something she hadn't before. I became a threat to her. Her smile disappeared and she stood up a little straighter. For the first time, I turned and looked at her—not her reflection. We both stood a few feet apart sizing each other up. *She was a complete knockout.*

I couldn't really make out much of what she said next. Her raspy southern speech became artillery fire. Maybe I was in shock. My eyes completely glazed over and suddenly her voice sounded like it was coming from some far off place. All I could do was stand there, leaning against the counter, trying not to picture James with this girl, and failing miserably.

By the time I came to, her red lips were in my face and she was interrogating me. "Are you sleeping with him?"

"Excuse me." I took a step back and tried to remain calm.

"Did you sleep with my boyfriend?"

"I think he stopped being yours the minute you betrayed him while he watched helplessly from across the world."

There! For once in my life I was able to say exactly what I wanted to say when I wanted to say it!

"I don't know what he's told you, but you know nothing about our relationship." This came out sounding bitchy.

"I know the most important part. It's over." With that, I turned and headed to the door. I was visibly shaken and couldn't get away from her fast enough.

But just as I reached for the handle she said, "We never broke up. Yes, he's pissed at me about the video. But he asked me to do it you know. To make that kind of video."

I stopped with my back to her, still facing the door. Something in her voice had changed.

"I gave him exactly what he asked for and the only reason he got pissed is because his friends saw it. That part was on him."

She sounded desperate—victimized even.

I turned to look back at her, and in that moment, recognized someone I knew—myself. She wiped a tear from her cheek.

"Trust me. Whatever you think you know about him, you don't. He's not back here with you. He's using you to get back at me."

Balzly

I left Brigid in the bathroom and stormed off with one thing on my mind. *I need a real drink.* I ended up at Bar Harbor a few blocks up the street. The place was a little touristy compared to the Rusty Pelican, but I didn't care. I needed a place to think. I sat down at the bar and ordered a double shot of top-shelf whiskey. Then, I ordered another. The bartender looked as if he was about to ask, but the expression on my face must have warned him not to. I opened her phone and read the text again.

"Good evening young lady. I assume you made it home safely. I wanted to thank you again for taking on Balzly as a client. Call me when you have time to talk about his diagnosis. And don't you go try to return any of that money. You earned every bit of that $3000."

My mind is spinning, trying to make sense of this message from Bo. And then, I see it.

The older man approached Brigid at the pool bar and handed her something. She looked down and then spoke with a new disposition. He got defensive and made a rebuttal. Then she stood up and threw one arm over his shoulder. He turned and I recognized him.

He handed her an envelope full of cash and she tucked it in her purse.

She lied to me. She has been lying to me since the moment I met her. Our time together starts playing through my mind like a movie reel, except this time, I catch it. The voice. The questions. The comforting way she accepted all of the absolutely crazy shit I've told her. The hesitation on her face before we slept together. I was never supposed to find out that she wasn't a school teacher.

I ordered another shot and wondered what in the hell Bo was thinking. I mean, I drink too much one time and he thinks I need an intervention. I already admitted that I let things go too far. I should have never called him that night to come and get me. If I knew he was going to completely overreact I would have just driven myself back to base. Instead, I woke up at the Legion Hall in Swansboro with a killer hangover and no memory from the night before. According to Bo, (and I don't remember this so who the hell really knows) —I was drunk out of my mind and altogether out of control.

My head is spinning and I'm beginning to sway a little on my stool. A waitress comes by to ask me for my food order, but I don't even acknowledge her. I can't. I can barely even breathe. My chest feels heavy.

How could Brigid make me think that I meant something to her? That we had a future? Part of me wants to march back down the street and demand an explanation. But I don't trust myself to look at her right now.

How far did Bo go to trick me? Did he hire Brigid to act like she was on vacation? Did he arrange this entire timeshare mixup? And where did Bo get that kind of money?

And suddenly, it all became clear. *My mother.*

I sit at the bar and wonder how I could be such an idiot.

Ten minutes later, I'm still brewing when the stool beside me gets pulled back. I could smell her perfume. I could hear her legs cross seductively. I could feel her breath on my neck. And then it came, her raspy voice.

"Hi stranger."

I've dreamed about this moment and what I would say if I ever saw her again. For weeks my anger raged—betrayal seething through my blood. Then it dulled. During this past week with Brigid, it finally began to disappear.

I am a statue.

"Are you seriously going to ignore me right now?"

"What are you even doing here Caroline?" I get nauseous hearing myself say her name. *This night seriously couldn't get any worse.*

"Waiting. I've been waiting for weeks. We need to talk."

143

"I have nothing to say to you."

"I know you do or you wouldn't be back here."

"I thought you were long gone."

Her shoulder pressed into mine. "I couldn't very well leave when your mother offered me a job and begged me to wait for you."

I wanted to accuse her of manipulating my mother, just as she had manipulated me, but instead I took a deep breath and stared straight ahead at the bar. Caroline is like Medusa. Once you make eye contact with her you're doomed. The more I kept quiet the more frustrated she became—the more juvenile.

"You told me to send you a sexy video. I did."

I exhale and stretch my fingers and then place them around my cup. *I want them around her neck.*

"You left me alone for months pinned up in that tiny apartment in this boring town."

I didn't flinch.

"Is this about Owen? Because he's just some guy I know from work. He doesn't mean anything. I just needed him for the video that you told me to make. God, any other guy in here would have gotten off on that."

I motion to the bar tender for another. *Show self-control.*

"I saw that woman you're with."

Shit.

"You can pretend all you want, but you know she'll never fuck you like I do."

The reality of what she said bubbled to the surface and suddenly I couldn't breathe. Yes, I was pissed at Brigid. Maybe she was playing me. Maybe she was lying to me for the money. But deep down I'm not sure I really believed that, and I wanted to give her the chance to explain herself. I need to find Brigid. But first, I need to be done with Caroline once and for all.

"You're right. She doesn't "fuck me" like you do."

I throw a fifty-dollar bill down on the bar and scoot my chair out to leave. When I turn around, Brigid is standing right behind me.

Brigid

Everything I thought I knew about Balzly—intelligent, well-intentioned, honorable—all a lie. Either that, or Caroline is one amazing actress. I storm back over to our seats, ready to assail him, but he's not there. I head to the bar thinking maybe he's getting us another round, but I don't find him. I spend the next twenty minutes searching the entire venue only to be back where I started and still no Balzly. He seems to have completely disappeared.

I knew this was going to happen. *I knew it. I knew it.* I tried to warn myself not to get involved with another guy. I tried to make this trip all about me, and instead it ended up being all about how gullible I am. *I knew this was too good to be true.*

I'm pacing back and forth in front of our chairs, searching for his face in the crowd, willing him to turn up, when it occurs to me that he may have seen Caroline. He may be off somewhere talking to her right now. Would he have left with her? No. He wouldn't have left me here. Unless. Was this his mission all along? Was I here just so that he could flaunt our relationship in public to make her jealous? I didn't think that sounded right, but I'm starting to doubt whether or not I really know Sgt. Balzly after all.

I walk back to where we parked. His Jeep was still there on the street where we left it. It was later now, around 10:00 p.m., and dark out, except for the matching streetlights with the hanging baskets of cascading flowers lining the sidewalk. The shops were closed. Only a few lights were on. There was a two-story brick building on the corner with the words BAR HARBOR lit up. Something told me he was there.

I flung my purse around my shoulder and started marching up the sidewalk in my strappy heels. I pushed my way in through the heavy wooden door and scanned the room quickly. It was not at all what I was expecting.

It was a shotgun style building with high ceilings covered with antique metal tile. A group of college girls were sitting in the weighty chairs made from reclaimed steel with arms the shape of wrenches. Down one side was a wall of exposed brick covered with large pieces of industrial art. Booths lined the wall, and pub tables stretched down the center of the room. The bar ran down the left side of the building and had more bottles of liquor than I had ever seen in one place. In the very back a crowd surrounded a stage listening to what appeared to be a five-piece nineties cover band. They weren't bad. All in all, the place was pretty upscale for a bar. In this town—figures.

There have definitely been moments in my life when I've felt completely humiliated. Starting my period at prom and bleeding through my dress, getting a speeding ticket in the school parking lot in front of the entire football team. I literally tripped on my graduation gown and fell on my way up to receive my high school diploma.

Still. Nothing has prepared me for this moment.

I am collateral damage.

There they are. Together. Sitting shoulder to shoulder at the bar with a line of shot glasses before them. *She was right. He was using me.*

I had spent the last twenty minutes telling myself that the only explanation for Balzly being MIA is that he saw her and was off somewhere with her. There was no other reason for him to leave me high and dry out of the blue. I had tried to prepare myself.

I just stood there, frozen, in the middle of the room, willing myself to do something—anything. I searched their body language, but he was facing forward, both elbows on the bar, hands on a glass—unmoving. She was sitting, long legs crossed, playing with a straw. Twice she leaned in to nudge him with her shoulder, but he was steel. He didn't seem too happy to be with her. The opposite, in fact. He seemed pissed, and if he was throwing back shots, I thought maybe, just maybe, I could be reading this whole situation

146

wrong.

I caught a quick glance of myself in the mirror above the bar. The good news is I look much better than I feel. Maybe it's my strappy heels giving me confidence, or my cleavage in this new shirt, or these high-waisted jeans making me look thinner than I actually am, but I look good—put together. I found enough courage to confront him. He owed me an explanation.

Just as I stepped up to the two of them, he turned to face Caroline and opened fire, his words assaulting my ears as he admitted, "You're right. She doesn't fuck me like you do."

He turned then and saw me—witnessed my face turning to glass and shattering. I clutched my stomach as if I had just gotten sucker punched.

Behind me, the bar door flew open and a rowdy crew pushed in, momentarily distracting him. I watched as his eyes left mine for a split second, just long enough to collect intel on the abrasive sound. When his eyes turned back to me, I was gone. I had turned on one heel and headed down towards the stage. So yeah, I panicked. But I didn't want him to see me cry.

I feel like a vacation toy. You know what I'm talking about. As a girl, whenever my family arrived at the beach we would buy a massive bucket filled with beach toys, a couple of skid boards, massive pool floats shaped like dolphins, and new goggles with snorkels. At the beach we couldn't live without these must-haves, but by the end of the week, with limited space in the car, we usually left them behind for some other kids to use. So yep, I'm a vacation toy.

I ordered another Corona from a passing waitress—my third of the night—and stood right in the center of the crowd, a few feet in front of the speakers, letting Matchbox 20 tell me that it's 3:00 a.m. and I must be lonely. My heart was pounding, but the liquid I was pouring down my throat was helping slow it down.

I should leave. Now. But I'm not sure wandering around in the dark would accomplish much. Besides, I want to punch back. I want to hurt him. I want to scream expletives and make him feel bad for how he's treated me—for what he's done. But if my past weekend with Paul has taught me anything, it's that anger doesn't look good on me. So instead, I'm going to make him feel like the vacation toy that he is.

Two songs later the waitress is back handing me another bottle. (I opened a tab.) *It's going to be that kind of night.* I glanced behind me to where they were sitting together at the bar.

He's gone.

I scan the room quickly.

He's gone.

Forget him.

Why do I already miss him? His large hands and how they feel so soft against my body. Those eyes that stare so intently into my soul. His immaculate chest. His shirt is like a second skin. I've basically started a cult to worship James's body and that is hard to shut down. The Kool-Aid has been drunk.

So as I drain my next beer I must admit, I am a bit of a lightweight. My head starts to float around. The band starts playing Green Day, who I love, and before I know it I am jumping up and down to "Basket Case" along with everyone else who has crowded close to the stage.

These guys are good. The lead singer is impressive. I get lost in the music. And as I dance alone in the middle of a crowd I realize that I have no plan. I am in the middle of nowhere. I have no car. I don't know a soul. I wanted spontaneity. I got it. But it's impossible to be unhappy or worried about anything when you're buzzing and this song is playing and so I am smiling and my arms are waving in the air and my Corona bottle becomes a microphone. It's exhilarating.

Then the band starts playing "Creep" and I close my eyes and let Radiohead remind me that I don't belong here.

That's when I notice the hooligans that entered earlier. They are gathered around a pub table and eying me—probably a bachelor party. One of the guys is really cute and apparently pretty shy because it has taken several encouraging nods and a push to the back from his buddies before he reluctantly heads my way with his Oktoberfest bottle in one hand and the other tucked safely in the front pocket of his jeans.

"Hey." He leans close and screams in my ear over the band. "I was enjoying watching you and didn't want to continue gawking. Would be rude."

"I'm glad you joined me instead. Want to dance?"

Maybe it's the alcohol or the desperation to feel desired, but Sgt. Balzly has left with Caroline and I'm here to drown myself. I give him a smile and lean in a little closer. He's not as tall as Balzly. *Who is?* And his hair is longer and sort of shaggy. But I like the way he smiles and so I smile back as a familiar guitar note kicks off the next song and a new wave of cheers from the crowd fill the air. The music is blowing out my eardrums and I pull him closer to me.

"You need to loosen up," I scream and he begins swaying back and forth next to me. By the end of the song he is jumping as high as I am and screaming out the words to "All the Small Things." And it goes on like this for hours. I drink three more beers and have successfully forgotten where I am and who I'm with (or not with), and after an eventful trip to the bathroom, where I lose my footing and fall hard against the counter—*Am I bleeding?*—the band announces the last call from the bar. *Can that be right?* I open up my purse to check the time and realize my phone is gone. *Great.*

"What time is it?" I scream at the guy.

"What?" He is looking down at me and smiling, and I'm thinking what a great job I've done loosening this guy up.

I point to my wrist.

"What time is it?" I scream again.

He pulls the phone from his pocket and shows me. 1:50 a.m. *How the hell did that happen?* I stumble back a step and he grabs me around the waist to steady me. I lean back into him and my body feels so heavy. He wraps his arms around me and I no longer have the strength to stand alone. He slips his hands down into my front jean pockets. We are swaying back and forth to "My Chemical Romance" when his lips find my neck. They feel weird. They aren't *his.*

My eyes are closed. The music speeds up, but we have slowed down. I have lost all ability to reason. All I know is that I feel a whole hell of a lot better than I did when I walked into this place. His fingers are rubbing small circles on my lower abdomen and he is whispering in my ear, "You feel amazing.

Do you want to get out of here?"

I turn to say yes, but he is ripped away from me and thrown across the room. Suddenly, everything is spinning the way it does when I'm riding the Tilt-a-Whirl at the county fair. Images flash quickly before me, but before I can perceive them they are gone. The band. The lights. The bar. The guy. Somewhere men argue. A barstool gets knocked over. Someone gets punched in the jaw. Screaming. When the ride stops spinning I am being carried out of the bar while the band sings "Closing Time". That's the last thing I remember.

Balzly

I am a warrior. I am trained to search for any vulnerability that could be used to break the enemy. The only weapon I ever needed was covertly hidden beneath my helmet. I was guarded—unsusceptible to attack. Safe.

This week, Brigid has completely unmasked me. My heart has been exposed for the first time in my life. Her deception with Bo pricked it, but watching Brigid's face as my verbal daggers—meant to hurt Caroline—were misinterpreted has completely punctured what's left of it.

I stopped drinking the moment she walked away from me. Nothing sobers you up quicker than hurting someone you love. Even if they hurt you first.

I told Caroline that under no circumstances would we ever be together again and I was sorry my mother had wasted her time.

After she stormed off, I went for a walk to nurse my wounds—leaving Brigid to blow off steam. After a while, I ended up down at the lake. I gathered up our chairs and loaded them in the back of my Jeep. Then I headed back up to Bar Harbor to try to negotiate a peace treaty.

The minute I opened the door I spotted her. It's funny. I used to close my eyes and see mathematical formulas, algorithms, and patterns. Now, all I see is her. Her carefree smile. Her fingers running through her hair. The way her body moves.

I know how to resist interrogation. Survival. Evasion. Resistance. Escape. Nothing has prepared me for the kind of torture Brigid puts me through over the next four hours.

She is completely obliterated. She's dancing barefoot. Drink after drink, song after song, she lets herself go. And I'm the sorry son of a bitch who hurt her. I am who she's trying to escape. I don't even think she knows that I'm here—watching. There's something captivating about it—watching her when she thinks she's surrounded only by strangers. This time last week, she was actively trying to close herself off—be someone she's not—out of fear that she had somehow welcomed Jeff's assault. What Paul saw as embarrassing, I think is amazing.

Then this guy approaches. First, it's slightly obnoxious. After a while it becomes nauseating. Now, his hands are on her and he's whispering in her ear and I'm about to lose it. When his lips press against her neck, my primal instincts take over.

Thirty minutes later, as I'm tucking her into my bed back at the apartment, I'm glad she is too drunk to remember my complete lack of self-control. I'll make it right in the morning.

Brigid

y bladder is saying wake up, but my brain is sending the opposite message. *You can't move.* My head is pounding. My shin is aching. My eyes peel open, but I don't recognize where I am. It's dark except for a small beam of light coming through the window. I roll over to see that I'm lying alone. The spinning of the ceiling fan above me reaffirms my need to vomit. My mouth is cotton.

I'm frantically trying to remember what happened last night and how I ended up here, but I can't. I close my eyes again and try to swallow. Then, it comes to me—the words have been seared into my brain. *She doesn't fuck me like you do.* Alone in the dark in this strange place, I let myself hurt. Tears stream silently down my face as I think about how he left me alone in the bar.

My brain slowly begins to put the pieces together. Drinking. Dancing. A guy. *Oh shit!* That's where I am right now, at his place. I sit up and search for remnants of sex, but the only evidence points to a caretaker. A glass of water and a bottle of Advil sit on the table beside the bed. A trash can is on the floor.

I think I'm going to die. I'm not wearing my clothes but instead an oversized T-shirt that smells vaguely familiar. I take three long, deep breaths and then drag my feet to the floor and use my elbow and momentum from the roll to push myself up into a sitting position. I have to pee. The alarm clock next to the bed is blinking 6:07 a.m.

A new wave of nausea rises up as I stand and turn on the lamp. My cell phone is sitting on the dresser next to my folded clothes and purse. I grab it and use my thumbprint to open it—seven percent. *Great!* My charger and all of my stuff is with Balzly at his parent's place. *I'm not going back there.*

I sneak into the bathroom with the lights out, trying to avoid disturbing whoever is here with me.

I open my Google Maps and see that I'm on South Harbor Street—a few blocks from the water. It looks like I'm about a mile or so down from Lakefront Drive.

I made a decision to get out of Dodge. I need to be home. I may not have my things, but I have my purse with the wad of cash from Bo and a phone that is on life support. I open my Uber app and try to remember how to request a pick up. Epic fail. No one is in the area. It's too early and I'm in no man's land.

So I google the Atlanta International Airport and use the last bit of power to check out my ground transportation options and I'm able to request a taxi to pick me up from a coffee shop about a half mile away.

I quietly slip back into my own clothes, throw my sling purse around my shoulder, and open the door to see a spacious apartment. It's still dark out, but I can tell that it's well furnished. There's a body sleeping on the couch with a single blanket pulled over it. A tinge of guilt passes through me, so I decide to leave a note.

I think this may be the first time in my life that I've actually taken the walk of shame. I never really went through a wild partying stage—even in college. I had a serious boyfriend for a while. And yes, I went out and had fun with my friends, but I never hooked up with someone I met at a bar.

This is completely humiliating. Just when I thought I had reached an all-time low, I find myself walking in strappy heels with a busted-up shin, underneath the same pair of pants that I wore yesterday, in a town where no one knows me. The sun is rising and the temperature has dropped. I have no jacket, barely any belongings, and my hair is a mess. My phone is now officially dead. I could vomit at any moment. I'm crumpled inside and out.

And it doesn't escape me that at this very moment Caroline is probably lying in bed with her pretty little head on James's chest. If only I could continue life under the alcoholic-induced daze of last night. I think that '90s cover band may have saved my life.

I need a reset.

I need a professional and personal reset.

It feels a little weird limping into the coffee shop, obviously disgruntled, two minutes after they opened, but after I downed a water bottle and two chocolate chip muffins, I don't look quite as near to death. Of course, there is the completely awkward seventy-two minutes that follow, where I have nothing to do but wait. I can't bring myself to make my usual cheerful banter with the two young ladies working. Ten minutes in I notice a bookshelf by the fireplace filled with board games and a few random novels. So I'm on chapter six of John Grisham's *The Firm* when, through the grace of God, a taxi pulls up.

I swing my purse back over my shoulder and walk into the cool October morning to take a final look around this charming little place. My prospects for a future with Balzly looked a lot brighter pulling into town than they do leaving. I'm sure I'll never see him again, and after what he did to me, that's okay. On the bright side, I should have an easier time getting through airport security.

Balzly

Caroline is poison. I silently curse the day I met her. Deep down I know that I should take part of the blame. My infatuation with her was screwed up from the start.

My dad and I just finished hauling off the last load of furniture from the apartment. My entire life is now shoved into a mini-storage unit off of Highway 123, and if I never see any of it again, I couldn't care less.

Dad took off without saying much—what's new—and I'm lying alone in the middle of the empty living room in the apartment I never lived in, watching the ceiling fan spin around and around and around.

Completely alone.

Tomorrow I will drive back to base. I should probably hang around here a few more days and make things right with my mom, but honestly, I can't even stand to look at her right now.

In hindsight, I should have told my parents what happened between me and Caroline from the get-go. It was just so humiliating. Giving them details was really never an option.

I am trained to see patterns. The most obvious one was right in front of me and I completely missed it. Deb Anderson lives in fix it mode. You've heard of helicopter parents, right—the kind who hover over their children and become overly involved in their lives? My mom is more of a lawnmower parent. A new breed of overbearing, always plowing ahead—micromanaging—with one goal and one goal only: to protect me from failure.

I completely missed it. Of course she wasn't going to let Caroline get away.

After all, she was the only woman I had ever brought home. We were moving in together. Mom's heart was in the right place, but I'll never understand why she wasn't honest with me from the moment I arrived home with Brigid. She should have told me that Caroline was still in town. And worse, that she had convinced her to stay until I returned from my deployment so we could work things out. She had even helped her get a job at Anderson Gardens. Just a little heads up would have been appreciated. Instead, I walked straight into a landmine.

If I'm being honest with myself, I hate the way last night went down. Yes, I was feeling betrayed, not just by Brigid, but by Bo too. I was at least hopeful there was an explanation—that it wasn't all a lie. After Brigid heard me talking to Caroline at the bar, all hope was gone. The way she looked at me said it all.

Once in Syria, I was running a security detail with a fellow Marine when four targets came at us quickly. I shot a man close up. I saw the look on his face. The surprise. The pain. It's the same look I saw on Brigid's face last night. I hurt her.

I fell asleep telling myself that everything would be better in the morning once Brigid and I had a chance to talk. But when I woke up, she was gone, and all that was left of our week together were some pictures on my phone and a note sitting on the counter.

Thx for taking care of me last night. You've been a welcome distraction, but I really need to get back home. I'm sorry if I led you on. Forgive me.

Brigid

I allow myself one day. One day to wallow around the house in self-pity. One day to soak in my clawfoot tub and listen to U2 sing "Stuck in a Moment" on repeat while I rotate between gentle sobbing and dramatic wailing. One afternoon where I lie on the rug in my living room, in the spot where the sunshine beams through the front window, surrounded by used tissues and scrolling through pictures of Balzly and I on my phone. One evening of overindulging in carry-out food and binge watching *This Is Us* until I have cried myself to sleep.

One day.

As promised, on Sunday morning, I wake up and hit the reset button. I am determined to make it through brunch at mom and dad's and Jeff's interview on *Inside Tracks* without a meltdown.

"There's my girl."

I walk up the back stoop and into my dad's arms. There's a familiarity to this hug. Not only because he's been holding me like this my whole life, but because James has been holding me like this all week. It's protective. Intimate. Safe.

"Hey Dad," I say and give him a kiss on the cheek. "Sorry I didn't make it to church this morning. It's been quite the week."

"That's what we hear," my dad says as he helps me out of my jacket and leads me to a seat at the counter. Mom has a fresh mimosa waiting for me.

"Steve, put her coat on the hook. I made some homemade cinnamon rolls too, your favorite." Mom gives me a sympathetic smile.

"So I guess you guys have talked to Dave and Piper." My parents exchange a guilty look. I take a big swig of mimosa and then bury my head in my arms.

"Ugh. What is wrong with me? Why is my life such a trainwreck?"

"It's not a trainwreck," my mother says encouragingly. "So things didn't work out with Paul." She's throwing her arms in the air like there's nothing to worry about.

Okay, maybe they don't know the whole story after all.

"Or Hotwheel," Dad chimes in.

Ugh!

"Just look at the bright side, honey." My Mom sits down beside me at the counter.

"Which is?"

"Jeff's interview will be over soon and if he makes one slanderous remark about you, we can sue his ass for damages."

Just then the front door opens and Mom and Dad go to greet Dave and Piper and the girls. The noise level changes almost immediately.

I look around the house and think about my parents' marriage. I'm seeing what they built together with a new appreciation. It isn't some impeccable million-dollar home in some parasitic town, but it's real and they built it together.

The girls scream and run into my arms and I am surrounded by my little sweet blondies.

"How are my girls?"

"Good," they say in unison.

"Did you bring us anything back from your trip?" Abigail asks.

"Did I bring you anything? Of course I did! Go get my bag out of the car and take it to Gram and Pop's room. Dig around and see what you find." At that, the girls took off.

"You didn't have to do that," Piper said as she threw her arms around me.

"It's nothing much, a bunch of free stuff from the resort."

Just then Dave comes up from behind and gives me a bear hug. He's

159

famous for them. As much as I don't like being pitied, it does feel nice to be surrounded by people who I know love me no matter what.

A few minutes later, the girls return sporting ball caps and sunglasses with the resort logo and lathering suntan lotion on themselves.

"Wow. What's all this?" my mom asks.

"Aunt B got it for us." They were so proud.

"Let's go out into the sunroom and set up an area for you girls to draw with your new pens and stationery.

"This is bullshit. I've spent $1,000 so far on Christmas gifts and they are perfectly happy with a bunch of free crap," Dave jokes.

"Yeah, you're an idiot," I fire back. "There's a koozie in there for you."

"Sweet."

"Everybody get a plate. We've got about 45 minutes until show time." Mom orders us around and we know better than to argue.

"I love how Mom can put a positive spin on everything," Dave whispers under his breath.

"She makes it sound like we're headed to a Broadway show, instead of preparing to watch my professional career implode on live television," I agree.

"Come on. Maybe it won't be that bad."

"In what world is that possible?"

"I still have time to make it down to the station. I'd like to give that asshole what he deserves." My dad looked just pissed enough to make good on his threat.

Thankfully Dave speaks up, "Dad, he's going to get everything he has coming to him."

"Is your lawyer watching this?" Mom asks.

"Yeah. She's going to call me after the show."

"Good."

We all crowded around the small table in the breakfast nook and ate cinnamon rolls and drank mimosas. Mom brought the girls their plates and turned on one of their shows in the sunroom.

"The girls are settled," Mom said matter-of-factly as she sat back down.

"Okay, go ahead. Fill us in."

Everyone at the table was anxiously waiting to hear about the events of the week. There was no use in trying to get out of it. So I spilled my guts—well, almost all of my guts.

"So, first of all, it was never going to work with Paul."

At that, my entire family let out a sigh of relief and exchanged happy glances.

"Seriously? If you hated the guy that much, why didn't any of you tell me?"

"We didn't hate him," Dad offers up.

"We just hated him for you," Mom clarifies.

"Anyways. I guess I had known it for weeks, and when we were in Asheville together he just pushed me to my limits. His temperament is just so different from mine. He had this way of always making me feel like I was doing something wrong. I sort of unleashed a lot of pent-up feelings."

"How did he take it?" Mom asks.

"Honestly, pretty well. I was dropping f-bombs and totally losing my shit and he kind of gave me the 'you're such a child' attitude and ended it. So I'm freaking out thinking I'm stuck with him and that's when I call Piper."

"Well, that's when I remembered that Dave had won that timeshare for a week and we weren't able to use it," Piper chimes in.

"So, I booked a plane ticket—Merry Christmas sis—and the next morning she was in paradise." Dave adds.

"Yes, and thank you Dave. And it was paradise. You guys wouldn't even believe this place. Remember that time that Granny and Pap took us all to Orlando and we stayed at that Hilton resort?"

"Oh yeah. That was a great trip," my dad's smile is filled with sarcasm because my brother and I were in middle school and argued during most of the drive down.

"Sorry Dad." I say.

"Sorry Dad." Dave says.

"The resort was sort of like that Hilton. Remember that big oasis area?"

"That was perfect."

"This place was too. The landscaping everywhere was so tropical. I felt like I was in Hawaii."

"Sounds like we should have tried harder to use that timeshare," Dave jokes.

"So anyways, I'm sitting at the pool bar, swearing off men and waiting for my room to be ready, when out walks this really tall, dark-haired guy wearing sunglasses. One minute I'm checking him out at the pool, and the next thing I know, I'm sitting in the manager's office being told that our condo has been double-booked. I'm freaking out and he's offering to share the room with me because he's only staying three nights. And so, of course, I'm thinking, *No way in hell*, but then I'm so intrigued, I agree."

"Sounds like serendipity." My mom is such a hopeless romantic—apples don't fall far and all that.

Of course I didn't tell them the entire story. I may have left out my quid pro quo with Bo and how my actions were completely unprofessional and pathetic.

"I thought so too, honestly. And I did my best to keep my guard up and give him space and focus on myself, but we just ended up hitting it off. He invited me to dinner and it was wonderful. We just connected. He is absolutely amazing. So, long story short, he decided to stay the whole week and we ended up spending every second together." I got out my phone and passed it to Dave and Piper. "Scroll right."

"So he's a Marine?" Dave asks.

"Yes. His six years are up in a couple of weeks actually. He's a code breaker. He's crazy smart. You should see what he can do while he's driving."

"Okay. TMI," Dave says.

"Okay, that's not—never mind. Anyways, he is sweet and fun-loving and handsome. And we had an amazing week."

"So what happened?" Piper asks.

"I feel like the end of the week came way too fast and neither of us were ready for it to end. He was still on leave having just gotten back from a tour in Afghanistan. He said he needed to go home for a bit to take care of some things at his apartment. He invited me to go."

"Where is he from?" Mom asks.

"Mountain Brook, Georgia."

"Sounds wonderful honey."

"Yep. I thought so too. So brace yourself." I start to tear up. *Damn it.*

"What happened?" Piper asked with one arm around me.

"One minute I am having dinner with his mother and thinking I am falling in love with him and the next minute I'm being ambushed by an ex-girlfriend and he's leaving with her. So, it turns out the entire week was just a ruse. I think he was just using me to make her jealous. He said some pretty terrible things and I overheard and instead of coming after me and apologizing, he left. And I'm pretty sure he left with her." The tears are starting to flow now and I'm glad they have no other follow-up questions.

My mom pours us all another round of drinks and then she and Dad and Dave go into the sunroom to check on the girls.

Piper puts her head down on my shoulder. "So, you didn't talk to him before you left?"

"No."

"So what if this was all a big misunderstanding?"

"It wasn't. Besides, he has my number. He hasn't texted or called. Who does that to a person?"

"I don't know honey, but this just proves he's not good enough for you."

"The thing is, he was incredibly good." *Earth-shattering good!*

"If it's meant to be, it will work out. Maybe he'll call. In the meantime, you need to stop putting so much pressure on yourself to find the one. It's going to happen."

And maybe that's good advice, but I'm 31 years old, all of my friends are married, and I just spent the most incredible week of my life finally getting a taste of what everyone else has—so this is like the last thing I want to hear right now. But I don't blame Piper. She's my ride or die and I know she means well.

"It's ten o'clock, girls. It's on," my mother calls from the other room.

Great.

I thought watching the interview with Jeff would give me that sick feeling in the pit of my stomach all over again. But, for some weird reason, seeing him didn't have the same effect on me. Something has changed in me this week. Despite my relationship with James ending badly, I will say that he helped me through a pretty tough time. I think I came away feeling a little bit more confident in who I am.

There was nothing unusual about the interview until the very end. The last question. The reporter said, "You filed a complaint against an employee two weeks ago regarding her conduct towards you during a private meeting. Our records show that she has been on unpaid administrative leave while the school board looks into the matter. What was the nature of this misconduct and what would you like to see happen moving forward?"

I'm holding my breath.

Jeff swallows hard. His eyes dart away from the journalist just long enough before he answered. It was so quick I almost didn't catch it. There was someone else in the room—someone he exchanged a glance with before responding.

"That complaint has been dropped. It was the result of a terrible misunderstanding that has since been cleared up. Thank you."

"Thank you Superintendent McAdams. I'm Stacy Rose wishing you a wonderful week."

"Stop. Rewind this. Take me back a bit." I'm barking out orders to Dad before I grow impatient. "Actually, give me the remote," I say.

I rewind the interview and play it again. This time I pause it just as his eyes dart away.

"Are you seeing this?"

"What?" everyone asks.

"It's like he turned to look at someone before he answered. He's trying to decide whether or not to be honest. Someone in that room is giving him warning eyes. I can almost see a reflection in his pupils."

And just like that my parents and Piper are up at the TV, squinting and trying their best to make out the figure that I'm seeing in his eyes.

"Okay," Dave says, as he grabs the remote out of my hand, "someone has officially spent too much time with Detective Hotwheels."

"First of all, he's not a detective—he's a cryptanalyst. And second of all, I can't help it. I've spent all week with someone who notices what no one else notices. It rubs off on you. Besides, even you have to admit that something must have happened for Jeff to change his story so dramatically. Someone is behind this."

"Maybe he's getting some good advice from his staff," my mother suggested.

My phone starts ringing and I look at the caller. "Incredible timing."

"Who is it?" Piper asks.

"Is it Paul?" wonders my Mother.

"Is it Hotwheel?" asks Dad.

"It's my lawyer," I say, hopping up as I walk out of the room to take the call.

Two weeks later and I'm finally "invited" back to work now that the HR department has formally wrapped up their investigation. And thank God because I can't stand another minute alone in my house with my phone willing it to ring. I stop at The Frothy Monkey on the way into work and grab a caramel mocha latte. I'm wearing my black power suit (the only one I own) so that I appear to be the professional that I very much am. I'm grateful that my first day back is a Friday. It's making it much easier knowing that I have the weekend to recover from the embarrassment and shame that will no doubt come with the return.

I have to say, the Human Resources department was pretty professional when it came to keeping my reason for being off work under wraps. Unfortunately, anyone who watched the interview with Jeff is on to me. It wasn't too hard for them to figure out who the "work colleague" in question was. I am the only person who has been missing in action for a month.

It was a good idea to get to work a half hour early. Most people hadn't arrived yet, leaving me to endure only a few awkward encounters on the way to my office. I am silently congratulating myself when Katie Burck steps onto the elevator. The 90-second ride feels more like 90 minutes. Katie is going on and on about how much everyone has missed me around here. She hopes I am doing okay with everything. She is here for me if I need anything at all.

The only thing I need is to get to my office and lock the door.

165

I love the office I've had for the past eight years. It's a great space, albeit a little awkward. It's narrow and long. I have one side set up with a couch and a bookshelf filled with games and toys. I bought a bright rug and paintings at IKEA that make the space feel friendly. On the other end of the room I have a desk that matches all the other office furniture in the building. Behind it is a big window with a view of the parking lot. At least I get good light.

I unload my bag, putting my Panera Bread soup in my mini fridge and setting up my computer on my desk. I spend two hours going through emails. I watch a twenty-minute video on what to do in case of an intruder, which is apparently a district wide requirement. Run. Hide. Fight. All things I did when Jeff intruded on my personal space. *Ironic.*

After the interview my lawyer called to tell me that she had been contacted by Jeff's legal team. He decided to drop the complaint that he filed with the HR department and wanted to settle the civil suit out of court. He agreed to pay $10,000 damages to cover my legal fees and time off work.

"What does he want in return," I had asked. I held my breath, waiting for her to say that I had to drop my complaint to HR, but she never did. Apparently he didn't want anything in return. Dana suggested I let my original complaint play out in the MNPS system and that I keep her on retainer in case I need her to help represent me to the school board.

So something has happened. What it is, I'm not sure. Regardless, I should be happy. The truth is I'm not sure I'll ever be able to work for Jeff again. Even my office, which I've always taken pride in, feels dirty.

All of my current students were handed off to Jackie or Brenda while I was away. No evaluation applications have passed my desk today. In a school corporation this large, that's rare, but I remind myself that no one really knew until yesterday that I was coming back. And yes, I'm happy to be back at work, but I'm starting to wonder if that has more to do with getting back into a routine (Yay! I brushed my teeth before 9am!) and less to do with being here.

By lunchtime I couldn't stop staring at my couch and reliving the memory of that night with Jeff. I could feel his hand on my leg. I could smell his breath. Ugh.

166

I decided to try and face my fears by lying down on it and trying to create a more pleasant memory—a psychology trick. I grab a copy of *Psychology Today* off the bookshelf and lie back for a little reading. Maybe immersing my brain in something will be therapeutic and inspiring. The feature article entitled "How to Disarm Internal Triggers and Improve Focus" catches my attention. *Seriously, universe?* I turn the page. "How Does Trauma Hijack the Brain?" *Oh my gosh!* I flip through the article and take a deep breath. *Let's try again.* "Five Reasons Why People Ghost You." *And that's enough of that.* I'm closing the magazine and sitting up when something catches my eye. There was a full page advertisement for the Brain Institute. Their logo was a side profile of a human head. It was open so you could see the brain on the inside. If you looked closely you could see the back of the head was actually a hand that appeared to hold the brain. *Clever.* Below there were two professional photographs of doctors in their early sixties looking calm and decisive. There was a map of the southeast and a star in each city where the Brain Institute currently had locations. Apparently Dr. Broady and Dr. McIntire are hiring psychologists for their new locations. Intrigued, I ripped the page out of the magazine when the phone on my desk rang and the screen said 114 - HR.

By two o'clock, I'm in the formal meeting room on the second floor, surrounded by seven other people from human resources.

"Welcome back Ms. Taylor. We wanted to meet and let you know that Mr. McAdams has officially changed his statement on record regarding the events of September 29th." The lady at the end of the table spoke for everyone. I forgot her name.

She passed me a letter and they all watched obnoxiously as I read it carefully.

Ms. Brigid Taylor
7900 Scheller Ave.
Nashville, TN 37011
Dear Ms. Taylor,

This will confirm that we met with you on October 1 to discuss your allegations of possible sexual harassment by Mr. McAdams. This letter explains our MNPS policy as well as what state and federal laws require us to do once we receive such a complaint.

MNPS does not ignore sexual harassment in the workplace and is committed to preventing, investigating, and, when appropriate, taking disciplinary and other action in response to incidents of harassment. We consider your allegations to be serious.

Our harassment policy, aligned with Tennessee law (Section 4.21-302), requires that we consider both parties' understanding of the events in question. Accordingly, we have conducted an investigation regarding the allegations, and have interviewed Mr. McAdams and other individuals who have knowledge regarding this matter. We have done our best to conduct this investigation in as sensitive and confidential a manner as the circumstances allow. The investigation is now complete. We have found that Mr. McAdams acted inappropriately and we will testify to the school board within the next thirty days providing a full summary of our findings, along with our recommended consequence that he be suspended from his position effective immediately until he completes a training and counseling program.

In the meantime, please be assured that you will not be retaliated against because you complained about sexual harassment. It is in all parties' best interest that disclosure of the allegations be limited only to those individuals who have a need to know them. Enclosed is a copy of the MNPS sexual harassment policy for your information.

Sincerely,

Sandra Brown

Human Resources Department Chair

615-246-9764

sbrown@mnps.org

Sandra. Her name is Sandra. I remember now. Something interesting is happening in my chest and I realize I just took the first easy breath I have in almost a month. *They believe me.* They investigated and somehow, miraculously, found the truth. Even if the school board doesn't take their advice, even if he ends up getting off scot-free, I think just knowing that my claims have been supported makes all the difference.

"Ms. Taylor, you do understand that no final decisions have been made and that ultimately the school board could choose to act against our recommendations?"

"If that's true, why tell me now? Why get my hopes up?" I ask bluntly.

"Our district policy requires us to give a copy of our decision to the complainant within three days."

I feel like I'm on Judge Judy.

"It says here that 'disclosure of the allegations should be limited to those individuals who need to know.' Did you watch the morning news yesterday? Did Mr. McAdams sound like he was limiting the individuals who know about the allegations when he answered a question on live TV to the entire population of Nashville and their local viewing area?"

"That was very poor judgment, but since your name wasn't mentioned he technically wasn't divulging anything," another young man explained.

"So, where do I go from here?"

"Back to the fourth floor. Back to having a positive impact on our students," Sandra suggested cheerfully.

"I mean in regards to working under Mr. McAdams," I clarified.

"You have officially been taken out of his chain of command. You will report solely to Nancy from here on out. She is your supervisor and you are to have no dealings directly or indirectly with Mr. McAdams."

"But, I still have to wait to see if the school board approves your recommendation. When will that be?"

"The board meets on the second Tuesday of every month. This proposal will go before them on Tuesday, November 9."

"Do I go?"

"No, actually, it's a closed-door meeting."

"So basically I'm just waiting to hear if the consequences you propose will be accepted? What if they disagree?"

"Our report makes suggestions, but ultimately the school board is in charge of making the final decision. You should know by the end of that evening what they decide to do."

By late afternoon, news that I was back had made its way around the office and my inbox started filling up with random welcome back messages—a few of them more nosy than nice. Every office has that one person who likes to meddle in everyone else's business. Our office has two. I didn't respond to either.

A few new evaluation requests hit my inbox and I began the review process for a nine-year-old boy with ADHD who has been struggling with reading and writing. His parents feel he is dyslexic and that he needs to receive special educational services. He probably does. My heart goes out to the poor kid, but the truth is, he passed his state tests and his grades don't look half bad - in a system this big, he'll never qualify for services. Ugh! I may hate paperwork, but this is the toughest part of my job, having to deny these parents' requests for my time. I thought again about the ad I had seen earlier in the day for the Brain Institute. Part of me is extremely interested in moving to the private sector, especially after everything that has happened. Even if the school board does take the advice of the HR team, Jeff would still be our fearless leader, and I'm not sure I could move past this. I think about James and the huge step he is about to take. He is finishing a six year commitment and gets to totally reinvent himself. Suddenly that sounds pretty appealing.

I told myself I wouldn't do it. I told myself I'd make it through the entire workday without checking my phone, but I couldn't stand it. I'm flipping through the pictures from two weeks ago wishing I had taken more. The selfie of us with our bike helmets on is my favorite. He's standing behind me and has his arm around my middle. God, I can still feel the heat that rose in my chest when he touched me. The next few I took of him when he wasn't paying attention. He was at the pool bar sipping a drink. One look and I can feel the stubble of his jawline as it scratched up and down my body.

I should be happy to finally be back at work. I should be grateful that this mess with Jeff is becoming less threatening. Instead of feeling balanced,

I have never been such a mess. My heart has been holding out hope that I might still have a future with James, although all evidence points to the contrary. I remind myself that the last time I saw him he was ditching me for his drop dead gorgeous ex-girlfriend and proclaiming that I could never fuck him the way she does. *What is wrong with me? The relationship is over.*

I'm sitting at my desk telling myself that I need to move on - from this job, from him. But the truth is I'm not sure I can until I get some sort of closure. I haven't had any communication with James in over two weeks and it's driving me insane.

I have nothing to lose. I decided to text him. And of course I recruit Piper to help me with my strategy. I know she will keep me from doing or sending anything that I will regret. I get out my phone and type, "Got a minute?"

"Yep. How's the first day back going?"

"It's going. I've decided to text James."

"That's huge. Try it out on me?"

"Yep."

"Shoot."

"Hope you are happy with Caroline. At least ship me my luggage."

"Too snippy."

"The week went by so fast. Great getting to know you."

"Too breezy."

"Any word on when you will be back to pick me up?"

"LMAO. I mean seriously. Who does that to a person?"

"Excited about who I thought you were, disappointed in who you obviously are."

"Good one."

"Too bitter?"

"Maybe."

"Let's talk."

"Too vulnerable."

"Not sure what happened between us, but I want you to know that I hate how it ended."

"Perfect."

"Should I send it?"

"Send it."

I sent the message and exhaled. Seventeen seconds later, I am still staring at my phone, willing it to respond when I feel a glimmer of hope—the dancing dots. He is working on his reply. I guess part of me didn't think he'd respond. My heart is pounding, and I'm thinking a quick response means whatever he says will at least be honest.

"You mean that you couldn't fix me."

"Fix you?"

"….."

I wait. I wait for the dancing dots but eventually they disappear and no message comes through. Then my gut starts to burn, tears fill my eyes, and a terrible thought crosses my mind.

You mean that you couldn't fix me. Shit! Shit! No. No. No.

I need to talk to Bo. I opened a new text to him and looked at my stream. I had missed his last message.

"Good evening young lady. I assume you made it home safely. Want to thank you again for taking on Balzly as a client. Call me when you have time to talk about his diagnosis. And don't you go try to return any of that money. You earned every bit of that $3000." The timestamp is Saturday 9:07pm

NOOOOOOOOOO! Everything suddenly falls into place. James saw the text while I was in the bathroom. He most likely left fuming. He needed a drink. Caroline tracked him down before me. He thinks I betrayed him.

I did betray him.

I begin frantically throwing things in my bag. I have to get out of here. It's only 3pm but I know myself well enough to realize that I won't be able to get anything else done. A few people notice as I walk out early, obviously distressed. The Lord only knows what they're thinking.

I call Piper from the car but she doesn't answer and I figure she's at preschool picking up Olivia from her afternoon class. I can't go home. I don't want to be alone right now so I park my car in front of the house and walk two blocks back to The Frothy Monkey. This is my absolute favorite neighborhood place. It's sort of this all-day eatery slash coffeehouse where

172

people naturally gather. And today is no different. This whole neighborhood is dog friendly so I walk past two pooches tied to the front step drinking from the dog bowls they have set out. It's too chilly to enjoy my usual spot outside so I grab a two-top near the front window and order my usual.

To anyone passing by I appear to be a young professional enjoying a bowl of shrimp and grits and drinking endless caffeinated sodas, but on the inside I am replaying everything that happened during the 18 hours I spent in Mountain Brook. Arguably, I wasn't feeling like myself, too consumed with the upcoming doom of Jeff's interview which I worried would be my fall from grace.

First, I analyze his mother. Beautiful. Refined. Determined. Dinner with her felt a lot different than it would with my own mother. And then it occurs to me. His mom knew Caroline was there. Lord only knows what Caroline had told her. My presence had to be confusing. No wonder her questions involved who are you, where are you from, and when are you returning?

I doubt that her response had any effect on James. I mean, we made love that afternoon. He took me shopping. He bought me clothes. He bought me this necklace. I remember the look on his face when he told me I was his happy noise. It was the most genuine remark anyone had ever made to me. He adored me. And then I got a text from my lawyer and threw my phone down on the chair and went to the bathroom.

I can see it now. My phone buzzes and James reads my text assuming it's my lawyer again and instead sees this message from Bo and before he gives me a chance to explain he leaves feeling betrayed.

It occurs to me that my actions could have sent him into another episode and that breaks my heart. Why hadn't I thought about that before?

I'm not exactly sure how Caroline found him before me. But when I think harder about the moment I saw them sitting together at the bar I notice two new things. Her body language said she was on the prowl. He was agitated and holding two shot glasses.

Shit. Two shot glasses.

I have to give him grace. Yes, his words were unthinkably hurtful, but he was drinking and probably feeling pretty betrayed himself. And I don't know the context in which they were said. I'm the one who stormed off. I'm the one who got shit faced and went home with another man who I may or may not have slept with.

If James never wants to see me again, I don't blame him. But I at least have to honor the agreement I made with Bo. I get out my laptop and begin to type out a very long list of things to do.

Balzly

I wouldn't have thought the last two weeks of my career in the military would be the hardest, but they have been. Maybe it's because I'm in a fucking miserable mood with nothing to take the edge off all day and being forced to sign my autograph on endless heaps of paperwork while being followed around by the new guy who just got appointed to take over in my place.

Or maybe it's that I have no fucking clue where I'm going next. As in, not sure where my head will be lying tomorrow night when I leave base.

It's not that I don't have options. I could go back home to Mountain Brook. I could get a hotel room until I find something more permanent to rent or buy. Hell, I could go home with the red-headed waitress who has been flirting with me all evening if I wanted to.

Maybe I'd be in a better headspace if I could just decide on my next career move. According to the transition advisor who has been assigned to me from the non-profit group Beyond the Corps, "Someone with my skill set and experience has a ton of options." And she's right.

On my desk is a stack of offer letters from people who think they want me to work for them based on my IQ and my impeccable record in the Corps. Fidelity Life Association in Chicago wants me to take an actuary position with them. Artech Consulting would like for me to come on as a data analyst in Atlanta. Mr. Michael Page (whoever that is) from Sacramento, California needs to fill a senior database administrator position and the salary starts at $129,000. Applied mathematician. Aerospace engineer. Economist. Even the NSA is trying to recruit me as a civilian agent. All these positions require someone who can solve incredibly complex problems related to business, technology, and engineering.

I'm not sure any of them would get what they bargained for. My brain is mush—it has been for nearly two weeks. I can't sleep. I can't eat. I can't think clearly. I'm pissed all day long. Agitated. On the verge of losing it.

I'm sitting alone in a corner booth at the Rusty Pelican, nursing a Black Butte Porter from a frosted glass, waiting for Bo and thinking about how incredibly stupid I am. If I'm being completely honest with myself, I know why I can't make any decisions about my next step. My heart knows exactly where it wants to be, but my mind is constantly reminding it that what I had with Brigid wasn't real. She duped me. She was being paid to connect with me—to try and fix me.

I reach into my pocket and pull out the half sheet of crinkled paper and unfold it. I take another sip of my beer and read it for the hundredth time, trying with every bit of my analytical mind to decipher some hidden meaning.

Thx for taking care of me last night.

You've been a welcomed distraction, but I really need to get back home. I'm sorry if I led you on. Forgive me.

She abbreviated thanks which means she wrote this quickly.

She is thanking me for taking care of her. Hmm. Funny. She was practically oblivious to the world by the time I intervened.

As for me being a welcomed distraction, that part was probably true. I know how upset her predicament at work was making her. The week we spent together was amazing. It was easy. But at the end of the day, her issues were still there, waiting, and I knew she was ready to go home and face the music, even if part of her wanted to hide away with me forever.

Then there's 'I'm sorry if I led you on.' She felt regret—hence the apology. But the regret should have been for lying to me, for hiding her true intentions. The way she says it implies that she never intended for us to be in a relationship moving forward. But she was the one who was upset that Friday morning when we had to check out—feeling hurt that we had no plan to move forward together.

I can't believe she didn't have feelings for me. I can't believe it was all a lie. Not after the time we spent together. I get out my phone and scroll through the pictures I took that week, clicking on every one and zooming in. This has become a daily ritual—pathetic really. I take it all in—her face, her smile, those legs. The way her arms easily wrapped around me. For a smart guy I can't for the life of me figure out how I could have read this so wrong.

Tomorrow is my last official day in the Corps. I look around at the poorly lit hole-in-the-wall bar that's been a hangout for the past several years feeling nostalgic. It's 8:00 p.m. and people who have just finished their dinner elsewhere are pouring in, lured by the Thirsty Thursday sign in the window, promising drink deals. Normally, tonight would be filled with drinking and celebration, but I called off the dogs. My heart isn't in it and frankly I'd be terrible company right now.

Tomorrow I officially close another chapter. Unlike other big endings in my life, the day won't include any type of pomp and circumstance. I just have to report at 9:00 a.m. for some final paperwork and to officially hand over my military-issued gear, which I have cleaned and organized and sat along the wall beside my bed. I don't think I even have to stay all day. The men in my platoon will meet me in the mess hall for lunch and to say goodbye.

I think if it weren't for Brigid, I'd be more focused on enjoying these last few days, but the truth is, I'm so bent out of shape missing that girl that I haven't even wrapped my head around what it will feel like to be gone.

"So we're back to where we started, huh?" Bo says disapprovingly as he suddenly appears sliding in the booth across from me. My senses are shot. I didn't even see him coming.

I'm drunk. So what? It's been a rough week and I've finally gotten the nerve up to meet and confront Bo for his part in this deception.

"I've been wondering when your sorry ass was going to call me back."

"My sorry ass?"

"I know you're pissed." Bo gets straight to the point.

"Now, what would I possibly be pissed about? My buddy, conspiring with my mother behind my back, recruits an imposter who gets me to pour my heart out, so she can report back what everyone already knew to begin with."

"Which is what?" Bo asks.

"That my last trip around the sun has been a complete fuck-up—and now I'm messed up—for good." It comes out louder than I intended and more emotional than it would have two beers ago.

Bo remains calm. It's infuriating.

"You don't like my tactics, I get it. But understand the alternative. Your mother contacted me. She was worried about you and asked how I thought you were doing."

"And?"

"And I told her the truth—that you were scaring the shit out of me. That's when she sent me the money. It was supposed to be for rehab at The Refuge."

"Rehab! Rehab for what?" I start to stand up.

Bo does some crazy maneuver underneath the table and the next thing I know I'm back on my ass in the booth. "For this." He points to his head. "I knew you wouldn't go willingly. The guys and I were trying to get you away from base to relax so we could talk about your next move and maybe convince you to get your head on straight before you take it."

"So the guys were in on this too?" I'm thinking how completely unnecessary it was when suddenly my muscles begin to tense up. Without warning the temperature in the room heats up and I am sweating. I take another swig of my beer but it is sticky in my mouth.

"No man left behind." I hear someone mutter.

Then, everything goes dark and I'm seeing in night vision. My M4 is zeroed in. My finger is on the trigger. The call comes over the radio that the place is clear. My gut tells my brain that something isn't right and in a nanosecond a movie reel races through my mind, replaying every detail of the mission from the moment the intelligence came into the field office. And there it is. My mistake.

"Balzly."

I have time to take a half a breath before the explosion blows me back.

"Balzly."

I can feel the detonation in my bones.

"Balzly. Are you okay son?"

178

It's hard to be in two places at once.

"I'm fine."

"No you're not. You're sweating. You need some water."

Bo flagged down our waitress and ordered two glasses of water and two burgers. By the time the food arrived the ringing in my ear had lessened and Bo was trying to explain how Brigid ended up getting involved.

"So I'm sitting poolside chatting it up with an angel, who just happens to be on an unpaid leave of absence from her job as a psychologist, when the concierge comes out and says our rooms were double booked. Fate. So I asked for her help. Look son. I'm sorry if I crossed the line. I just never thought your mother's plan was going to work."

We eat in silence as seconds stretch into minutes. I think the food helped because the fuzziness in my mind cleared up some.

"I get it. And you're right—I would have never gone along with my mom's plan. But it doesn't matter how well-intentioned you were. I still ended up looking like a jackass. I'm completely humiliated."

"Why do you say that?" Bo asked.

I took another gulp of water and admitted, "I believed the lie, okay? I thought what we had was real."

"Who says it wasn't?" The way he says this matter-of-factly gives me hope. "She called me, you know. She sounded really upset about hurting you."

And suddenly my chest fills up like a balloon.

"When did she call?"

"Yesterday afternoon."

The same day she texted me. *Not sure what happened between us, but I wanted you to know that I hate how it ended.*

"What did she say?"

"She apologized for not responding to the text message I had sent her a few weeks back. Apparently, she had just seen it."

"She never saw that text message because I had her phone when it came through. I read it—that's how I found out about your scheme," I explain.

So she knows that I know.

"Did she say anything else?"

179

"Oh yeah. Went on and on about some new job she's applying for."

"New job? Why would she need a new job?"

"Whatever trouble she was having at work got all sorted out. It sounded more like she just wanted a fresh start."

I wanted to ask him more—pump him for every detail. Did she ask about me? Is her new job in Nashville? Was it a private practice? How did she sound? But instead, I sat and ate my cheeseburger stubbornly.

"I think you still have a shot with this girl."

"What makes you think that?"

"She went out of her way to get to know you and try to help you during her vacation—her free time."

"Because she was being paid." I reminded him.

"For the first 48 hours. She tried to give me the money back, you know. Monday morning she met me in the lobby before I checked out. She said she didn't feel right about taking it. But you know what, she seems like the kind of girl who would have tried to help for free."

And I knew he was right.

"I think you should see this." He laid a large manila envelope down on the table. "It was emailed to me yesterday."

"What is it?"

"It's classified." He smiled and stood up and put his jacket back on. "I need to head out. Thanks for meeting me."

"Yeah, thanks for the burger."

"Good luck tomorrow."

"Thanks, but I don't have much more to do—just return some equipment and sign a few more documents in the morning."

"I meant good luck tomorrow afternoon."

"What's tomorrow afternoon?"

"When you finally decide where in the hell you go from here."

Bo threw a fifty down on the table and I nod to the waitress with a familiar face. I shake Bo's hand and we go our separate ways. I walk the half mile back to base alone, carrying whatever the hell is in this envelope. It's cold out but the fresh air feels good on my skin. I think again about the offers knocking at my doorstep. The east coast. Chicago. California. The south. I could go anywhere, except the one place that I truly want to be.

Two hours later I'm sitting on the end of my bed plucking on guitar strings and sobering up when curiosity gets the best of me. I open the envelope and pull out something unexpected—a formal letter printed on MNPS letterhead. It looks professional.

To Whom It May Concern,

Sgt. James Matthew Balzly (DOB: 04/02/1988) is a 31-year-old male who was seen for outpatient counseling services between October 11 and October 14. James spent a total of 72 hours with psychologist Brigid Taylor, MA, LMHC, NCC.

During his initial assessment, it was observed that he has a remarkable intellect and an eidetic memory. Presenting problems include changes in his physical and emotional reactions. Throughout the course of therapy it was observed that he has difficulty sleeping and has been drinking too much. He experiences overwhelming guilt and suffers from intrusive memories that cause severe emotional distress.

Interventions that were used during treatment included the CBT model (i.e. how thoughts impact our feelings and behaviors). The therapist also assisted James with increasing cognitive coping skills and in identifying triggers that could lead to flashbacks. Sgt. James Balzly is suffering from post-traumatic stress disorder stemming from an event that took place during his deployment to Afghanistan. Recommendations for treatment include continued outpatient cognitive behavioral therapy focusing on changing patterns of behaviors, thoughts and feelings that lead to difficulties in functioning. An increased focus on sleep, healthy eating, and eliminating alcohol along with 12-16 sessions of CBT would be most helpful.

If you have any further questions, please do not hesitate to reach out to me at (502) 546-9690 or btaylor@mnps.edu

Thank you,

Brigid Taylor, MA, LMHC, NCC

I've spent the last six years reading people. It's given me the upper hand in almost every situation. For the first time in my life I am seeing myself from an objective viewpoint and I have to say—it's not wrong. It's pretty spot on actually. Brigid recommends that I continue with cognitive behavior therapy and I know that I will agree. Funny, if Bo and my mom suggested it there would be no way. Just hearing that Brigid thinks this is what I need and I'm all in. I'm willing to do anything for this girl.

I pick my guitar back up and start strumming out a happy tune, one that reminds me of her. That was the moment my decision was made. I will not live without her.

Brigid

The Brain Institute's Nashville location is in the central business district downtown. Four days after I saw the advertisement for an open position and I have already landed an interview! I feel confident. Well, I would if I wasn't currently squatting beside my car on the fourth floor of the parking garage with my skirt around my waist, hiking up my panty hose and slipping into a pair of black slingback heels. The last time I tried to drive in those damn things I got my left heel stuck behind the bar that moves my seat back and forth. It wasn't pretty.

I love being spontaneous. Piper likes to teasingly remind me that actually it is planned spontaneity that I love. She's right. I made the decision last Friday afternoon at The Frothy Monkey that I was going to be spontaneous. For me, that involved making a list of all the spontaneous things I wanted to do. I've spent the last four days marking things off my list.

First, I went home and emailed Sandra from HR (the one who sits at the end of the table and does most of the talking) and put in my resignation. I knew that no matter what happened at the board meeting I'd still feel uninspired with Jeff as our leader. The entire workplace is tainted. I couldn't stand ever seeing Jeff again and even if he was fired (and that's a big if) the memory of that moment lives in my office.

Second, I looked up more information on the Brain Institute position and called just before the office closed to plead my case. I was worried I sounded a bit desperate but apparently they liked my enthusiasm because we set up an interview for today.

Lastly, I called Bo. I apologized for missing his text and went over my thoughts on James's condition asking him if he had any questions. He had one.

"What does James need?"

He needs me.

I referenced my suggestion that he continue with cognitive behavior therapy and that he cut out drinking and focus on exercise and sleep. I got his email address and sent him a formal report.

He asked how everything was at work, and I mentioned that I was pursuing a new position and was hopeful that it would work out. The end of the conversation was sort of awkward because I could tell Bo was fishing for information, but I really didn't want to go into all that had happened between James and me. He told me that if I ever found myself in North Carolina I should stop by the Legion Hall and I promised I would.

I spent the entire weekend updating my resume, which hadn't seen the light of day in nearly a decade. When it was finished I emailed it to the Brain Institute. I caught up on the overdue bills that were littering my kitchen table with the money I was reimbursed.

It's amazing how a little planned spontaneity can send positive energy zipping through my bloodstream. *Nothing can stop me.*

The offices are on the 12th floor, and when I get off the elevator I am absolutely astounded. Instead of your typical boring waiting room I feel like I'm at a Fortune 500 company's California office. The front desk is sleek, the furniture contemporary, and there is a large sign lit from behind that says "The Brain Institute Nashville".

"Have a seat and Dr. Broady will be right with you," the lady behind the desk says. I have a seat in one of the cool chairs and am admiring the design of the office when a man my dad's age wearing an expensive navy suit comes out and introduces himself.

"Richard Broady. Nice to meet you."

"Thank you for taking the time to meet with me, Dr. Broady."

"Not at all. Follow me." We head down the hallway and into an eclectic space filled with color and texture.

"Can I get you anything to drink?" he asks, motioning to a mini fridge built into the cabinets.

"No. Thank you."

"You have an impressive resume, but your enthusiasm on the phone last week is what really got my attention. Tell me a little bit about yourself."

"Well, I'm 31 years old, born and raised in Nashville. I graduated from St. Mary of the Assumption High School where I played on the volleyball team, was in the art club, and wrote the help wanted column for the school newspaper."

"Starting at an early age. I love it." I think he got a kick out of this because he sort of chuckled and shared a genuine smile.

I did my undergrad at Vanderbilt and then got my master's degree at Belmont. I live in 12 South and have been working in the public school system for nine years."

"And why are you leaving that position?"

His question sends me into a Bridget Jones flashback and I almost say, "I've got to leave my current job because I shagged my boss."

Instead I explain to him how I want more time with my clients and less pushing paperwork. I'm tired of having to reject requests to evaluate kids whom I know I can help because of our budget."

"I can relate. I worked for the Atlanta public school district for a time. Tell me, what kind of impact do you think you can make here?"

"I know I can make a positive impact. I believe that better relationships with patients result in better outcomes and you won't find anyone who is better at building rapport. I try to foster collaboration with my patients while being flexible and responsive to their needs. My goal is to give them a safe space to open up and then to use the appropriate diagnostic tools to help them identify struggles."

My first few answers felt a little scripted, but as the interview continued it became more of a discussion about theories and best practices and a vision for the future of psychology. The company's mission aligned with my own and after hearing more about what the position entailed, I wanted it. After an hour or so he thanked me for coming in and said he'd like to officially offer me the position! He would work with his partner to prepare a compensation package based on my degree and years of experience and would email it to me within a few days.

I waited until I got back to the parking garage to scream and do my celebratory dance moves, which may or may not make me look exactly like Elaine from Seinfeld. In hindsight, screaming in a parking garage (even if it was an excited scream) might not have been the best idea because the security officer making his rounds went out of his way to check on me. *How embarrassing!*

As soon as I get in the car, I call Piper, my mom and dad, and then Dave (in that order) —sorry Dave—and tell them my exciting news. Everyone is thrilled, and for the first time today, this week, this month, and even this year I am feeling in control and on top! So basically, my life is no longer the epitome of the I'll Be There For You theme song.

On Friday morning the compensation package arrived in my inbox and I am one hundred percent sold on this new position. I fired up my Stevie Wonder album and danced around the house listening to, "Signed. Sealed. Delivered I'm yours."

When I called to tell Piper the news she insisted that we meet downtown to celebrate my overall awesomeness with a night of drinking and dancing. I couldn't have agreed more.

"What are you going to wear tonight?" I ask.

"The baby-maker." She says matter of factly.

"Oh God." I have to laugh. She's referring to the little black dress she bought when we were shopping at a boutique in Vegas a few years back. When Dave saw it, he famously said, "Don't wear that dress unless you want me to put a baby in you." After a rip-roaring time at the casino we all ended up drunk off our asses in front of the Bellagio fountains. Dave had lost nearly $3,000 that night. I had never seen him so upset. That's when Piper declared that she needed to take her man back to the hotel and comfort him with a little "conjugal prayer". *Dear Lord, help me.* I thought I was going to throw up in my mouth. Ironically, she ended up getting pregnant on that trip.

"What are you wearing?"

"Well, if we're going downtown I'm definitely wearing my lucky boots." I wish I could say they earned their nickname because every time I wear them I get lucky. Instead, it's because I won them in a contest at the Boot Barn outside Gatlinburg during a family trip a few years back. I got to pick any boot in the store and I chose these really expensive Lucchese boots made of full quill ostrich leather. They're hot.

I look at the clothing options spread out all over my bed. "I think I'm going to wear my boot-cut jeans with that black sweater."

"Which black sweater?"

"The one that falls off one shoulder and does that cute bunch when I push my sleeves up a little."

"Ooh! That is cute. Outfit approved. Do you want us to pick you up?"

"No. I'm going to Uber."

"Sounds good."

"Where do you want to go?" I ask, knowing that whatever she suggests will be perfect. She hardly ever gets out anymore without the kids, so I'm confident she already has a plan to assure the night's success.

"So I'm thinking let's meet at Jason Aldean's. Dave said Nate Alligood is playing at the rooftop bar tonight."

"Sounds good. I'll see you around 7:00.

"Love you. Mean it. Bye."

"Love you. Mean it. Bye."

By 7:15 I'm stepping out of an Uber on Broadway looking and feeling like myself again—which, by the way, is amazing. It's a little chilly this time of year and the streets downtown are hopping. A bachelorette party comes roaring down the street on a pedal tavern filled with girls dressed in black and throwing back shots and screaming. Music is pouring out of every bar as I walk two blocks up to one of my favorite places on the strip. Jason Aldean's kitchen has delicious food and I am already planning my appetizer and drink order as I make my way up to the rooftop bar to meet Piper and Dave. Dave was right—Nate Alligood is playing tonight. He's already taken the stage. We've heard him before at The Basement East and he's so good!

Suddenly Piper materializes in front of me and throws her arms around me for a big hug—the kind where we rock back and forth obnoxiously. Before I know it she is leading me through the crowd and up to the second level of the rooftop where it is a little less noisy. Large patio heaters are spread out and people are gathered around them holding drinks.

The back half of this level is a roped-off VIP area with a couple of groups of outdoor seating and pub tables. White Edison bulbs are strung above and there is a small private bar set up in one corner.

"Surprise!" a large group of VIPs scream. That's when I realize they are my people.

Holy shit. This surprise is for me.

"Surprise!" Piper smiles and does her infamous excited clapping. Dave appears pushing a Bud Light aluminum can into my hand and hugging me like a bear.

"Happy for you sis."

Everyone bombards me at once to say hello and congrats on my new adventure. The gang from the neighborhood is all here—Jessica and Liam, Matt & Kate, Adam and June. They are a pretty wild crew and love any excuse to party. A few others from The Frothy Monkey are behind them and I am wondering if they even know about my new job or just followed the sound of a good time.

The girls from work, however, know all too well. Sara, Megan, and Emily all take turns hugging me and telling me how much they are going to miss me. (Work will suck without me. They totally understand and respect my decision. Good luck with my new position. We have to stay in touch.) I wonder if we really will.

Once I had a chance to chat with all of my friends my parents appeared out of nowhere. They were all smiles.

"Wow! You guys are out of the house at 8:00 p.m. What about Jeopardy?" I tease.

"Ha ha! Very funny," Dad says as Mom embraces me.

"We don't want to interrupt your time with friends, but we're just so proud of you." Mom says.

"You've really turned things around kiddo," Dad adds.

"You're not interrupting anything." I insist. "Stay and listen to a few sets with us." My parents agreed and walked off to put in an appetizer order at the bar.

I pulled Piper aside and gave her another hug.

"Thank you for all of this." I pointed to the VIP section. "It's too much."

"It wasn't me." She nodded towards the stage. Across the rooftop Nate Alligood was finishing his song.

"Thank you. Thank you," he said to the crowd. "Most of you are familiar with my latest hit song, 'Drinking Left to Do.'

The crowd cheers and I think about how much I love his southern accent.

"What you might not know is that the song was inspired by a college drinking buddy of mine who joined the Marines after graduation." Everyone quiets back down. "The song is a tribute to all of our guys who didn't make it home," he continues. "Fortunately, my buddy made it back in one piece. And after six years of service and five deployments he has officially retired and is here with us tonight." He raises his drink in the air and shouts, "So help me celebrate Sgt. James Balzly!"

What is happening?

Cheers rise up again as James (my James—well, sort of) walks across the stage with his guitar and stands in front of the microphone.

What are the chances?

I watch in complete shock, frozen in place, except for my eyes which dart around the room searching for Caroline. When they don't find her, they settle back on him. He adjusts the microphone stand, bringing it up higher to his lips.

Something is off about him. He's dressed way differently for one—like a sexy professor. He has on dark wash jeans and a tweed vest and jacket. But it's more than that. He seems insecure, vulnerable somehow. *Weak.*

I want to tell Piper, tell everyone, that my almost James is taking the stage, but I can't take my eyes off of him.

Once the mic is in place he straps his guitar around his neck and licks his lips.

Holy shit.

Suddenly, an obnoxious gaggle of bachelorettes near the front of the stage start screaming like he is a bloody Beatle, but when he looks up, it isn't at them.

It's directly at me.

My heart is thrown from my chest. He looks back down at his guitar.

"This song came out the year I turned seventeen," he mumbles quietly. It doesn't matter. The crowd is hanging onto his every word.

"It's about feeling lost, broken, those times when even your best isn't good enough."

He is so captivating. There are nearly a hundred people standing with drinks under the stars and you can hear a pin drop.

"It's about a guiding light that helps you find your way home."

He looks up at me again and takes a deep breath, "And for me, that's you."

Everyone on the roof turns to look at me as James starts strumming Coldplay's "Fix You." Suddenly, everything is falling into place. *James is here for me.*

Someone takes the beer out of my hand. Someone else pushes me from behind, leading me to the lower level and closer to the stage, but I don't pay attention to who it is. I am completely mesmerized. He told me when we first met that he never played for other people and that's crazy because his hands dance across the strings and he sounds amazing.

When he gets to the bridge of the song, his acoustic guitar gets backed up by Nate Alligood's band, and everyone on the roof is rocking.

"He's hot!" Piper is holding my hand and screaming into my ear.

"How did you get him here?" I ask.

"He got me here."

"Wait, what?" I look at Piper.

"Brigid—he planned all of this!"

I had been so proud of myself this week. Taking charge. Making a decision to change my life for the better. Even after landing an awesome new job, paying off my debts, and making things right with Bo, I still wasn't complete. Now I am.

The entire rooftop is singing the chorus with him and when he begins the epic guitar solo everyone begins jumping up and down. Then just like that, the band stops playing and he walks off the front of the stage strumming the final chords and singing the last line directly to me. He plays the final note and swings his guitar around behind him.

The roar of the crowd erupts around us and the first words out of his mouth are, "Brigid, I'm so sorry."

But he's already forgiven, and all I want to do is be with him. I grab the lapel of his jacket and pull him towards me. His hands are resting now on either side of my face. He is staring down into my eyes and wiping the tears that are streaming down my cheeks. He bends to put his lips on mine and just like that, I am fixed.

"Thank you for all of this." I pointed to the VIP section. "It's too much."

"It wasn't me." She nodded towards the stage. Across the rooftop Nate Alligood was finishing his song.

"Thank you. Thank you," he said to the crowd. "Most of you are familiar with my latest hit song, 'Drinking Left to Do.'

The crowd cheers and I think about how much I love his southern accent.

"What you might not know is that the song was inspired by a college drinking buddy of mine who joined the Marines after graduation." Everyone quiets back down. "The song is a tribute to all of our guys who didn't make it home,' he continues. "Fortunately, my buddy made it back in one piece. And after six years of service and five deployments he has officially retired and is here with us tonight." He raises his drink in the air and shouts, "So help me celebrate Sgt. James Balzly!"

What is happening?

Cheers rise up again as James (my James—well, sort of) walks across the stage with his guitar and stands in front of the microphone.

What are the chances?

I watch in complete shock, frozen in place, except for my eyes which dart around the room searching for Caroline. When they don't find her, they settle back on him. He adjusts the microphone stand, bringing it up higher to his lips.

Something is off about him. He's dressed way differently for one—like a sexy professor. He has on dark wash jeans and a tweed vest and jacket. But it's more than that. He seems insecure, vulnerable somehow. *Weak.*

I want to tell Piper, tell everyone, that my almost James is taking the stage, but I can't take my eyes off of him.

Once the mic is in place he straps his guitar around his neck and licks his lips.

Holy shit.

Suddenly, an obnoxious gaggle of bachelorettes near the front of the stage start screaming like he is a bloody Beatle, but when he looks up, it isn't at them.

It's directly at me.

My heart is thrown from my chest. He looks back down at his guitar.

"This song came out the year I turned seventeen," he mumbles quietly. It doesn't matter. The crowd is hanging onto his every word.

"It's about feeling lost, broken, those times when even your best isn't good enough."

He is so captivating. There are nearly a hundred people standing with drinks under the stars and you can hear a pin drop.

"It's about a guiding light that helps you find your way home."

He looks up at me again and takes a deep breath, "And for me, that's you."

Everyone on the roof turns to look at me as James starts strumming Coldplay's "Fix You." Suddenly, everything is falling into place. *James is here for me.*

Someone takes the beer out of my hand. Someone else pushes me from behind, leading me to the lower level and closer to the stage, but I don't pay attention to who it is. I am completely mesmerized. He told me when we first met that he never played for other people and that's crazy because his hands dance across the strings and he sounds amazing.

When he gets to the bridge of the song, his acoustic guitar gets backed up by Nate Alligood's band, and everyone on the roof is rocking.

"He's hot!" Piper is holding my hand and screaming into my ear.

"How did you get him here?" I ask.

"He got me here."

"Wait, what?" I look at Piper.

"Brigid—he planned all of this!"

I had been so proud of myself this week. Taking charge. Making a decision to change my life for the better. Even after landing an awesome new job, paying off my debts, and making things right with Bo, I still wasn't complete. Now I am.

The entire rooftop is singing the chorus with him and when he begins the epic guitar solo everyone begins jumping up and down. Then just like that, the band stops playing and he walks off the front of the stage strumming the final chords and singing the last line directly to me. He plays the final note and swings his guitar around behind him.

The roar of the crowd erupts around us and the first words out of his mouth are, "Brigid, I'm so sorry."

But he's already forgiven, and all I want to do is be with him. I grab the lapel of his jacket and pull him towards me. His hands are resting now on either side of my face. He is staring down into my eyes and wiping the tears that are streaming down my cheeks. He bends to put his lips on mine and just like that, I am fixed.

Balzly

I've been in situations like this before. I know what it means to lay it all on the line. I was chosen to take the penalty shot in the championship game senior year. I defended my doctoral thesis in front of a dozen faculty members, including two Fields Medal recipients. On the front lines of war, I've interpreted intelligence and called the shots.

The thing is, I've never really thought twice about any of these situations. With the level of confidence I've always had in my own abilities—these things never seemed that risky.

But as I stand on a rooftop stage, preparing to strum the song that was playing the morning Brigid and I first made love, I am completely terrified. I adjust the microphone and try to tell myself I have nothing to lose, but that is the farthest thing from the truth.

If I lose Brigid, I lose it all. And that's why I've spent the last week rearranging my entire world so that it will orbit around hers. She is the strongest force in my universe.

I knew Brigid's brother worked as a car salesman for the infamous Larry Butters, so it was pretty easy for me to track down Dave and Piper. I was grateful they were willing to hear me out and help me get all of Brigid's friends and family to show up tonight.

I knew I was either going to leave here the luckiest man on the planet or be completely destroyed. Either way, I promised myself one thing—I wasn't going to drink.

I didn't have as much trouble as I thought singing in front of a crowd because once I locked eyes on her, my brain went into hyper-focus mode. I saw nothing else—heard nothing else. I completely forgot to stay with the mic stand and ended up walking right off the front of the stage to finish the song, standing two feet in front of her. I guess that wasn't close enough because before I got my apology out she had grabbed my jacket and pulled me in. There were tears streaming down her face and I wasn't sure what they meant, but I took a chance. When my lips met hers I knew I had done the right thing in coming here.

When our kiss ends, applause explodes in my eardrums, and I close my eyes and take a few deep breaths as I hold on tight to Brigid. I don't want to risk having any kind of freak-out in this crowd. I think she can sense all the noise isn't great for me because when Nate takes the stage again, she leads me by the hand back to the VIP area I reserved for us on the other side of the rooftop. I think her friends sense we need some time alone because they stay with the crowd near the stage. I sit down in one of the outdoor seating areas and pull Brigid down beside me.

She is breathtaking tonight. Her hair is loose and wild. The sweater she's wearing makes me want to leave permanent bite marks on her shoulder. Everything about her is taunting me.

"You look incredible."

"I look like I'm in shock," she jokes.

"Was my singing that bad?" I tease.

"It's not that. Honestly, I didn't expect to ever see you again." She says it so flippantly.

"Don't say that."

"Why? It's true." I can see her posture change and some unspoken words threaten to spill out. I nod for her to continue.

"The last time we were together you left me," she is staring at me with pinched eyebrows, expecting an answer. I am clueless.

"At a bar." *Nothing.*

"With no way home." *What is she talking about?*

"To be with Caroline." *Would never happen.*

"Does any of this ring a bell?" *No.*

Brigid is upset about something that never happened. Then it occurs to me. *Maybe she had drunk more than I thought.*

"Sweetheart, I didn't leave you."

"But..."

"I watched you dance and drink all night until you were out of your mind. Some guy was trying to pick you up so I kicked his ass and took you back to my apartment. You were so inebriated—you scared the shit out of me. When I woke up in the morning you were gone, and I was left with this."

"What?" She's so confused.

I pull out my wallet and hand her the note she had scribbled.

Something is happening to Brigid's beautiful face. Her forehead is crinkling and I can see the wheels turning in her brain. "Oh my God, NO!" she screams as she wraps her arms around my neck and buries her head in my shirt.

"What is it?"

"I didn't know you were the bump on the couch!" She is burrowing her head back and forth against the base of my neck.

"What?"

She pulls away so she can look me in the eye but she still is grasping on to me for dear life. "I don't remember any of that. I remember walking away from you upset and when I turned back later you were gone and I never saw you again. When I woke up the next morning, I thought I had gone home with that random guy and I was mortified. I left as quickly as possible. That note was not for you."

Huh. I've spent a lot of time analyzing this note and never considered this option.

"How could you believe I would ever leave you?"

"You did leave me—at the concert. I couldn't find you anywhere and then you turn up down the street, with her." She released her grip on me.

"Okay, true, but I didn't leave you, leave you. I just needed some air. I saw the text from Bo come through on your phone and it seemed like you were only with me for the money. I was hurt, but in my heart I knew there had to be an explanation. I was pretty pissed and I didn't want to do or say anything that would mess things up. So I left to clear my head for a bit."

196

"And what about Caroline?"

"I didn't even know she was still in town. I was at the bar ordering a double-shot and she just appeared. I told her to get lost."

Brigid pulls away from me again and I can feel the distance between us.

"No. You told her that I didn't fuck you like she did."

She's holding back tears and this time they're not the good kind. I reach for her but she pushes me away. I'm in total grovel mode and begin using de-escalation strategies. I'm breathing deeper, talking slower, and have my hands out in front of me, palms up as I try to explain.

"You heard that out of context. I was saying it sarcastically. I was saying that you would never fuck me over like she did."

"But you had just found out that I betrayed your trust."

"That's not even on the same level. And at that point I was really hoping there was an explanation. I knew when my hot head cooled down I would give you a chance to explain everything."

She seems content with this response. After a minute she says, "I would like the chance to explain everything to you."

I look around. For a few minutes I had forgotten we were on a crowded rooftop with live music and laughter filling the air. I can see her friends watching us nonchalantly from the dance floor.

I wrap my arms around her and lean in to whisper in her ear, "I got us a room at the Omni tonight. We have plenty of time to talk about everything. For now, let's enjoy this time celebrating you."

"I like that idea." She gives me a smile that makes me go weak in the knees and then presses her hands on my face. She bites her lower lip in hesitation for a split second before leaning in to kiss me.

We spend the next several hours dancing, laughing, and genuinely enjoying each other's company. As the night progresses she introduces me to everyone. I really like her parents and think we hit it off, which is important to me.

I don't think I realized just how much the situation with Jeff was affecting Brigid until now when I see her out from under the weight of it all. Seeing

197

her with her people and in her element is a turn on. She is radiating joy.

Brigid's parents are the first to leave, then her friends from work. By midnight it's just Brig and I and Piper and Dave. We are lounging in the roped-off area, listening to Dave tell stories about the infamous Larry Butters. Dave is hilarious, authentic, the real deal. I like him instantly. And I can tell that Brigid feels more like herself around Piper than anyone else. I am trying to figure out how I am ever going to pull Brigid away when she speaks up.

"Well guys, I love you, but it's late and every part of me wants to be alone with Hotwheel."

My brows go up, but Piper and Dave seem to understand exactly what she means. They begin to stand up and stretch. Dave reaches out his hand to shake mine.

"Do you guys want a ride home?"

"We're staying at the Omni."

"Gotcha."

"Let us know if you need us to pick you up tomorrow and bring you back to the house."

"Oh, I have my car here. But thank you."

"Alright, you two, have fun." Piper teases. *I like her.*

An hour later, we are in a luxury suite on the eighteenth floor of the Omni Nashville, and Brigid is smitten. It's adorable. She is dancing around in her socks and going on and on about how incredible this room is. I am in love with every inch of her.

"So, you told my brother your car is here," she says.

"Yep. In the parking garage downstairs. Why? Do you want to go somewhere?"

"No. In fact I never want to leave this room." She is looking out the window at the amazing view.

"I just figured you flew here," she adds.

I am behind her now with my arms wrapped around her middle.

"Brigid, I didn't come here to visit you." I kiss her neck. Her perfume is tantalizing. My lips work their way down and land where they've wanted to be all night—on that beautiful shoulder.

I turn her around to face me and look into her eyes. "I came here to be with you."

We spend the rest of the evening lying in bed together, our bodies completely intertwined. Face to face, we begin filling in the empty spaces. Brigid tells me about her trip to Asheville with Paul and how she ended up in Panama City in the first place.

"Bo was in front of me in line to check-in and I had struck up a conversation. When I saw him later, sitting alone at the pool bar, I joined him. He was telling me all about the Legion."

"Of course."

"And about the work he does there to help veterans. He told me he had a buddy who he thought was suffering from PTSD, but he wasn't sure, and that he couldn't get him to open up." She said this slowly, testing the waters.

"He asked about my line of work, and that's how he found out I am a psychologist and was on unpaid leave. When the concierge came out to tell us that our rooms were double-booked, he explained that the room was for his friend that needed help and that the weekend was going to be an intervention of sorts. He asked if I would be willing to share the condo with you just for the weekend. He said that if I got to know you I could give him feedback on how to help. He was convinced it was fate."

Bo has already shared all of this information with me but it is interesting to hear it from her perspective.

"I wasn't going to agree because, well, for all the reasons we both know I shouldn't have agreed. It would be unsafe and probably awkward, plus I really wasn't in a good headspace myself. I really needed a vacation. But then he showed me the picture."

"What picture?" My interest peaks.

"The one of you in your uniform, kneeling on some mountaintop, holding an American flag with a cigar in your mouth."

"And?"

"And I recognized the man in the photograph."

"You did?"

"Yes. As someone I could trust."

"I see. So why did you act so weird around me at first?"

"I was nervous. You were the sexiest man I had ever seen and I had just sworn off men for good."

"How is that working out for you?" I reach out to tickle her, and she bats my hand away.

"The minute I started having feelings for you I knew I couldn't keep the money. I returned it to Bo, but he must have snuck it back in my purse."

"When was that?"

"If I knew that I wouldn't have let him do it."

"No. When did you start having feelings for me?"

"Sunday night. On the patio." She blushes a little and I reach out and scoop her body into mine.

"You called me James," I said simply.

"I saw your name tag before you grabbed it."

"Everyone calls me Sgt. Balzly or just Balzly. When I heard my name leaving your lips, well, I think that is why I ended up telling you everything."

"And now you know how I ended up carrying a big wad of cash around in my purse all week. When I first told Bo I'd help, I never imagined I would end up having feelings for you. I'm sorry if you felt betrayed. That was never my intention. Do you forgive me?" It was a serious question.

"That depends. Do you have romantic feelings for all of your clients?"

"Would any of my other clients covertly find a way to fix all of my trouble with Jeff, even after I ditched them with some half-assed note?"

"I don't know what you're talking about." I've been through interrogation training, so my face reveals nothing.

"I know you are the one who fixed everything with Jeff. How did you do it?"

I didn't flinch until she brought out her fingernails which began lightly dancing across my stomach. *Damn it. She's good.* This act of seduction has me spilling my guts in no time.

"I may have hacked into the admin building's security cameras."

"But I don't have a camera in my office."

"Right, but there is one on your floor. I may have called in a favor with a buddy in the audio/video forensic laboratory. He was able to pick up some audio."

"Wow."

"I knew if I met with him I might end up breaking his neck. Instead, I called him Saturday afternoon. I sent him all the evidence I had dug up and demanded he compensate you for lost wages and legal fees and use his interview to set the record straight or else."

"Or else what?"

"Or else his misconduct would become very public very quickly."

"I can't believe you did all that for me."

"It was the right thing to do. Besides, I'd do anything to protect someone that I love."

She smiled and nuzzled closer to me. "You love me?"

I didn't answer. I just rolled away from her and reached for my jacket, which was thrown across the chair beside the bed. I took a deep breath. When I rolled back over, she was lying on her side with one arm tucked underneath her head and those brilliant emerald eyes peering into my soul. Her question was still in the air, lingering between us.

"There seems to have been quite a few misunderstandings between us lately," I say matter-of-factly.

She let out a quiet scoff. "I'd say."

"Then let me be clear."

I open the palm of my hand, and she lets out a quiet gasp.

"I am in love with you. I want you to be my wife."

Brigid

I didn't think anything could top James' surprise guitar performance. It was the most romantic gesture I could have ever dreamed of. But last night, when he opened his hand and I saw the vintage two-carat halo diamond engagement ring, I was astounded. It was breathtaking. He wanted me to be his wife. I could see the yearning in his eyes.

Happy tears rolled down my cheeks as I said, "I agree. I should be your wife."

James and I spent the entire weekend in that hotel suite ordering room service, listening to music, making love, and talking about everything. He hadn't just shown up on a whim to try to win me back. He chose me.

By Sunday afternoon I can't move. Every part of my body has been ravished and I am perfectly content to never get out of this bed.

"You ready to get moving," he asks as he comes out of the bathroom dressed and begins putting things in his suitcase.

"No." I whine. "How are you even still functioning?"

He laughs. "I am excited to have dinner at your parents house tonight."

"Oh, that. We don't really have to go. They'll understand." I shrug it off and throw myself back down on the luxurious king-size bed.

"Oh, no you don't." He pulls me up. "I want to go. Besides, after dinner I have a surprise for you."

"What is it?" *How could there be more?*

"I know that you adore 12 South and that your lease is almost up on your rental. I've spent some time checking out the neighborhood and the real estate."

"Wait. How long have you been in town?"

"Seven days."

"What? Why didn't you find me sooner," I ask.

"I wanted to get some things figured out first."

"Like what?"

He stands up and walks across the room to fiddle nervously with some items on the dresser.

"I wanted to make sure I could support us here long term."

I have been living alone and supporting myself for eight years, but the way he says this is so sweet I can hardly stand it.

"Okay. Go on." I prompt him.

"I've accepted a position at Vanderbilt University, teaching and researching at the Data Science Institute."

"Oh my God! That's amazing James." That news is enough to get me up and out of bed. "How are you just now telling me this?"

He smiles. "I've been distracted."

"Tell me more about the position."

"I'll be teaching three courses next semester and leading a team in a sort of high-risk, high-payoff research project that will address existing and emerging challenges in information and communication technologies."

I have absolutely no clue what that actually means.

"I have so many great memories from doing my graduate work here. I know Vanderbilt will be a great fit."

"I'm sure it will be." I agree.

He walks over to the desk and pulls out his laptop.

"I found a house on Montrose Avenue that I think you will love. Four bedrooms. Four baths. 3100 square feet. Look at this yard." He is gesturing towards the screen.

I am looking at pictures of a timeless craftsman bungalow that has been completely renovated. It is absolutely gorgeous. I'm not sure how to burst his bubble, but there is no way we could ever afford this rent.

"What do you think?"

"It's amazing. I love everything about it."

"I knew you'd say that." He took a deep breath and seemed relieved. He was flipping through the pictures and pointing out where I could set up my paints and the trundle doggie bed built into the cabinets in the laundry room for Fitz.

At the same time I open my mouth to tell him we can't afford the rent, he says, "I've already put in an offer."

"Oh wow. Um. James. I'm so sorry." I can feel his countenance drop when he hears my tone of voice so I try to let him down easily. "I love it, but I'm not sure we could afford the rent, much less a mortgage."

I can tell he's doing his best not to laugh at me right now. But he can't help it—he starts to chuckle.

"What? Why are you laughing at me?"

"Do you want to double check my math?"

I punch him in the arm playfully. He leads me back over to the bed and sits me down, like what he's about to tell me might come as a bit of a shock.

"I have quite a bit of money saved up between my time in the Corps and, well, some money my grandpa left me in a trust.

A trust. I had completely forgotten about the discovery I'd made in Mountain Brook—the one about his family money.

"We have more than enough to do this, if it's what you really want."

After a delicious celebratory dinner at my parents' place, we drive back across town to 12 South. He never lets go of my hand. I look out the window and think about everything that has transpired between us this past month. I had been completely lost, moving in reverse. James was broken. In that single moment, when he stepped out into the sunlight, and we both laid eyes on each other for the first time, the entire trajectory of our lives changed. Bo called it a God moment. Fate. I call it Providence.

The Jeep turns on to a tree-lined street and pulls up in front of a charming craftsman—every window glowing—and parks.

"All of the lights are on," he says, as he smiles at me.

I squeeze his hand. "We're home."

Epilogue - Brigid

The past two months have been an absolute whirlwind. The kind where every single one of my sexy daydreams ends up coming true. I was a little nervous about James transitioning back into a civilian job, but apparently as long as he has numbers, he's happy because he is loving his work at the Data Science Institute.

And my new position is perfect for me. I love my new office and all of the people I work with. Private practice seems to suit me well and I am able to work with around 30 kids each week. I'm so glad I made the move, especially since the MNPS school board voted to keep Jeff on as superintendent so long as he completed a three-month program on sexual harassment in the workplace.

The morning we found out about the school board's decision, James showed up at my office between sessions with a massive painting by Florent Stosskopf that we had seen earlier that week at the Rymer Gallery. I'm not sure which I loved more—the painting, the sweet gesture, or the smile on his face when he gave it to me.

We ended up getting the house on Montrose Avenue for 1.2 million dollars—a realization that I still can't wrap my head around. The house is big and comfortable and we've been having fun making it our own. Light floods in from the windows in the main room and we have found the coolest eclectic pieces to fill the space. There are built-in bookshelves for all of my novels and a room dedicated to my art, which James encourages me to pursue. Of course our house is smarter than me. James has all these gadgets and gizmos everywhere. He set up an office in the basement and I swear it looks like he is controlling the entire universe from down there. I think his favorite spot in the house is our kitchen. We spend most of our time there in the evenings cooking together or hosting friends from the neighborhood. Dave and Piper are over all the time and James insisted that we make one of the bedrooms a princess room for the girls who love to spend the night. James is amazing with them and it's hard to watch them together without imagining what an incredible father he will someday be.

James' parents drove up to see the house and brought with them a truck full of items from his storage unit. I was a nervous wreck about seeing his mom again and telling her about the engagement but it turns out all she ever really wanted was for James to be happy. Once he told her the truth about Caroline she fired her from Anderson Gardens. And the fact that James is doing so well here in Nashville has made me her absolute favorite person in the world.

Of course it was made clear that she preferred we settle in Mountain Brook. We found the perfect compromise. James wouldn't sign up to teach any courses in the summer and I would save up some leave so that we could get married in Mountain Brook in June. When it comes to event planning his mother is a force to be reckoned with, but I don't mind. All I want are beautiful flowers, beautiful music, beautiful people, and James. Happy noise.

James also proposed that we invest and build a small cottage at Anderson Gardens. It would be an income property that we could stay in whenever we were in town. I told James it was too much and that staying with his parents was fine by me, but he dragged me to the bedroom and reminded me of all of the reasons we needed our own space.

Before James left Marine Corps Base Camp Lejeune, he promised himself he'd follow through with all of the recommendations I made in my report. We both decided that given our current situation he should probably work with a different psychologist. Ironically, when I tried to schedule him an appointment with another practitioner in the office, he was already in our system. His parents had him evaluated by Dr. Broady when he was nine years old at the original location in Charlotte. I pulled his file and brought it home, but lost my nerve and never showed it to James or looked at it myself.

For the last eight weeks he's been seeing Dr. Carney. I think he's finally overcome the sense of helplessness and now has some coping skills to use when he is feeling on edge. We spend a lot of time outdoors. We get bundled up every evening and take Fitz for a long walk around the neighborhood. James has stopped drinking, which you may have guessed was really my number one concern about him from the beginning.

He decided to reach out to Mike's wife. He had the idea to set up a scholarship fund for their daughter and I was the first to contribute. After all, I had an extra $3,000 lying around. That was a rough week, but we got through it together and I think he is finally starting to forgive himself. He says he's sleeping much better now and that making love to me has been the best therapy. I can't disagree.

The holidays are quickly approaching and I'm so blissfully happy that I can't even think of a single thing to ask for. Well, maybe one thing.

Epilogue - Balzly

Perfection. Something I've always strived for and easily obtained. Finding success has never been difficult for me. Making mistakes—that's what's tough. Brigid has shown me the beauty in being vulnerable—in opening your life up completely and letting another walk in.

"I wonder if she'll be more like you or like me," Brigid asks as we stand in front of the fridge staring at a sonogram.

I wrap my arms around her. "She will be extraordinary. Like her mother."

About the Author

Brittany Geswein is a Catholic wife and mother of three who spends her days as an assistant principal in Floyds Knobs, Indiana where she strives to make her corner of the world brighter. Brittany lives for a good love story—especially her own, and finds inspiration for her writing in the everyday chaos of a full life. She writes stories that reflect what she values most: faith, family, and the kind of love that feels like home.

You can connect with me on:

🌐 https://www.brittanygesweinbooks.com

Also by Brittany Geswein

Because the heart always knows—it's just been waiting for you to catch up.
Julia Grace Baker left Autumn Ridge broken, desperate to outrun a grief too heavy to bear. Fifteen years later, she's a successful architect and editor for Blueprint & Beam, a national builder magazine featuring custom home plans. Meticulous, driven, and fiercely in control, Julia has made a career of designing perfect homes—while quietly avoiding the mess of her own. After a broken engagement, she makes an uncharacteristically bold move: buying Leaky Acres, a farm that still holds traces of home. The impulsive purchase feels like a lifeline—a remote remodel project that could make the next farmhouse edition unforgettable, and give her the space to finally breathe. But Leaky Acres holds more than just rustic charm. It holds memories—of childhood laughter, lost dreams, and Griffin Ellis, her first love and the one person who ever truly saw her. Quiet, loyal, and deeply rooted, Griffin never left Autumn Ridge. His steadfast, sacrificial love for Julia has endured in silence—sustained by an unshakable faith in God and a hope he's never fully let go of. As old wounds resurface and the spark between them rekindles, Julia is torn between the carefully curated life she's built and the roots she thought she'd buried. Together, she and Griffin must confront the past they've never truly faced—and Julia must ask the hardest question of all; What if everything she thought she needed was already waiting for her back home?

www.ingramcontent.com/pod-product-compliance
Lightning Source LLC
Chambersburg PA
CBHW020630250626
47154CB00008B/2619